'I won't ever marry.'

Surprised, she stared at him. His statement was matter-of-fact, as if there was no possibility of anything else.

'You don't like women?'

He grinned, and she was amazed at the transformation of his features, softening his rugged look, with creases deepening in his cheeks and a twinkle coming into his eyes.

'I like women, Vivian,' he said in a sensual, warm voice that left no doubt in her mind that he was telling the truth. At the same time, a tingle stirred in her, that sexy awareness that he could zap to life so easily with her.

'Then what makes you so certain you won't ever marry?'

The grin and twinkle vanished. 'I'm not the marrying type,' he said with a shrug.

'Maybe that's for someone else to decide.'

Dear Reader,

Welcome to the wonderful, exciting world of Silhouette Sensation®, the home of the best romantic suspense novels around.

Sara Orwig returns to the line to give us our sexy **HEARTBREAKERS** title, *Galahad in Blue Jeans*: Matt Whitewolf coped brilliantly when he found a little girl wandering alone down a quiet road, and then discovered she'd had her very pregnant mum with her as well!

And we've got three more names you'll recognise as firm reader favourites. Suzanne Brockmann continues her latest **TALL, DARK & DANGEROUS** trilogy (*The Admiral's Bride*) and Marie Ferrarella finishes this set of stories about **CHILDFINDERS, INC.** (*Hero in the Nick of Time*). Maggie Shayne's *Out-of-This-World Marriage* could almost have been called 'The Girl Who Fell To Earth' and is very special—take a look.

Magaret Watson and Ingrid Weaver complete the selection with *The Fugitive Bride* and *True Blue*, both the kind of thrilling, pulse-pounding reading that makes Sensation™ so much fun.

Enjoy!

The Editors

Galahad in
Blue Jeans

SARA ORWIG

SILHOUETTE
SENSATION

First published in Great Britain 2000
Silhouette Books, Eton House, 18-24 Paradise Road,
Richmond, Surrey TW9 1SR

© Sara Orwig 1999

ISBN 0 373 07971 0

18-0007

Printed and bound in Spain
by Litografía Rosés S.A., Barcelona

SARA ORWIG

lives with her husband and children in Oklahoma. She has a patient husband who will take her on research trips anywhere from big cities to old forts. She is an avid collector of Western history books. With a master's degree in English, Sara writes historical romances, mainstream fiction and contemporary romances. Books are beloved treasures that take Sara to magical worlds, and she loves both reading and writing them.

With thanks to Leslie Wainger, Debra Robertson,
Tina Colombo and, always, Maureen Walters.

Chapter 1

Matthew Whitewolf turned the wrench and tightened the lug nut on the tire as thunder rumbled and wind caught locks of his black hair and blew them away from his face. He worked swiftly, wanting to get the flat changed so he could get home before the rain hit. Although the thought of another rainy evening alone at home made him edgy, more aware of his loneliness, the thought of driving down to Taylor's Bar and seeing some of his friends didn't appeal to him, either.

Concentrating, he turned the wrench. As he worked, hairs on the back of his neck rose. He had the feeling he wasn't alone, a notion he shrugged away at first because when he had stopped to change the flat, he had been the only person on the road. He hadn't noticed a car in sight either in front of him or behind him.

His nerves prickled and he couldn't shake the feeling that he was being watched. Telling himself the notion was ridiculous, he glanced over his shoulder and his heart missed a beat.

"Jeez!" he exclaimed under his breath.

A tiny girl with bright blue eyes stood in the road staring at him, a blue blanket clutched in one small hand, a fuzzy, battered bear in the other.

Where the hell had she come from?

He looked beyond her and saw only a tall cottonwood and a couple of cedars three hundred yards down the empty road. He glanced in the other direction to his right and looked at a stand of bois d'arc trees along the wire fence and a clump of golden sunflowers growing in the ditch.

There were no houses except his house a couple of miles away. His wheat fields, now merely golden stubble, stretched away on one side of the road and there was pasture on the other. Where had she come from?

He realized he might be scaring her and mentally swore at himself for being unfriendly. "Hello," he said, smiling.

She stood staring at him in silence, and he rubbed his eyes, wondering if he was having a hallucination. "I'm Matt Whitewolf," he said, trying to gentle his voice and inject as much friendliness as possible while he kept trying to figure out how she got within yards of him without his even seeing her approach.

"Do you have a name?" he asked, and heard another loud roll of thunder. As lightning streaked the sky, the little girl flinched, and his concern escalated. She didn't answer, but continued to stare at him.

"You've been told not to talk to strangers, haven't you?" he asked.

When she nodded, he casually turned back to tighten the last lug nut, hoping he would put her at ease. She had to have come from *somewhere,* and he needed to know where and who she was. He worked without looking at her, trying to keep her in his peripheral vision, half afraid she might vanish as swiftly as she had materialized.

He couldn't drive off and leave her and he didn't know

what to do about her. How had she gotten out here all alone? He was miles from Dakani, the nearest town.

"Do you have a little girl?" she asked in a voice that sounded small and uncertain.

He kept his attention on the wheel, hoping to reassure her. "No, I don't. I'm not married. I have a farm here. I grow wheat and raise cattle, and this land is part of my farm," he said, waving his hand toward the field and smiling at her. "How'd you get here?" he asked, replacing the hubcap.

"My mommy hurts."

His head swung around. "Where is your mommy?"

She turned and pointed down the empty road to the west. All he saw was the cottonwood, the cedars and a long stretch of paving bordered by his empty fields. He finished changing the tire and put his tools away in the back of the pickup.

"Why don't we go find your mommy, and maybe I can help her? Okay?" he asked, wiping dirt from his hands with a rag.

She nodded and another clap of thunder boomed. She jumped and closed her eyes, pulling her blanket up over her face. "I want Mommy," she said, and his heart lurched. He wanted to pick her up and reassure her that she was all right and he wouldn't hurt her, but he knew he shouldn't take the chance of scaring her.

"You show me where your mommy is, okay? Let's go find her before it rains."

Nodding, she turned to walk down the road and he walked beside her.

"You know, we're not strangers anymore because you know who I am and this is where I live and you know what I do. I've lived here a long time, and I promise to try to help your mommy. Now, since we're not strangers, can you tell me your name?"

She shook her head and clamped her tiny rosebud lips together, so he dropped the matter.

"All right, darlin', let's find your mommy," he said, looking at the long stretch of empty road. "We can ride in my pickup. It'll be quicker, and we'll be out of the storm if it starts to rain."

She studied him, and he suspected she was torn between wanting to get away from the storm and refusing to accept a ride with a strange man. When she shook her head, he didn't want to push the matter so he continued walking beside her.

"Are you and your mommy going to visit someone?"

He looked down at the small child beside him as she gave another negative shake of her head. He felt a pang of sympathy because she was obviously terrified.

The first big, cold drops of rain fell. Newton County had had rain on and off for a week now and the ground was saturated. As Matt glanced over his field, he was thankful harvest was over and his wheat sold.

His gaze shifted to the child beside him, and he searched the road ahead again. He still couldn't spot a car and he wondered where the mother was and how far the child had walked. Why hadn't he seen her before he had the flat?

"It's sprinkling. How far do we have to go to get to your mommy?" He knew the question was foolish, but he was so puzzled about the child's sudden appearance, he couldn't keep from asking. She merely pointed ahead.

He tried to shorten his normal stride and slow his steps so he could walk beside her. She was too tiny and too vulnerable, and he wondered how hurt her mommy might be. Had the woman collapsed? Was she unconscious?

"How old are you, darlin'?"

She held up four fingers.

"What's your teddy's name?"

When her mouth clamped shut again, he gave up trying

to converse with her. Another boom of thunder shook the ground and lightning snapped and streaked over the wheat field. The child started crying quietly, great tears brimming in her wide eyes and rolling down her cheeks. "Mommy!"

"We're trying to get to your mommy," he said quietly. "Would you like me to carry you?"

She shook her head no, and he glanced at the darkening Oklahoma sky. The storm was gaining on them, and if rain began to pour, he was going to have to pick up the terrified child.

"Don't cry, baby girl," he said. "Please don't cry. It's only thunder and it makes a lot of noise, but it can't hurt you." He looked at the roiling thunderclouds that were blue-black churning masses. Lightning crackled, streaking across the sky, shedding an eerie yellow-green tint over the native grasses alongside the road.

"Maybe we should go back and get my truck. Will you ride in it?"

She shook her head vigorously. "Mommy."

"All right. We'll find mommy." He prayed that he would soon. As they approached the tall, ancient cottonwood, he saw tire tracks across the damp ground. Following them to the cedars growing beneath the tree, he spotted shiny green metal through their branches. A car was off beyond the bar ditch on the far side of the cottonwood and cedars, almost hidden from his view by the trees.

"Is that your car?"

She put her thumb in her mouth while she clutched the blanket and teddy bear tightly. Knowing it had to be the car, he strode swiftly toward it.

"Let me see about your mommy," he said, worried what he might find. The dark green utility vehicle had rolled to a stop against the massive cottonwood. The shiny hood was smashed, and a wisp of steam rose from the radiator. When he saw someone slumped over the steering wheel, he hurried his steps.

A young woman was sprawled over the wheel. With her longer-than-shoulder-length brown hair and her slender arms, she looked little more than a teenager. He opened the door, leaned across the seat and placed his hand against her throat. Her pulse was strong and relief surged through him. Even as he touched her, she groaned and shifted. When she leaned back, he helped her, sliding his arms around her, grateful that she could move.

She straightened and shock buffeted him. Blood ran from a cut on her forehead, and as he slid his arm around her, he brushed her expanded tummy. The lady was very much pregnant and dazed from the wreck.

As her eyes opened, he stared into the biggest, bluest eyes he had ever seen.

Mesmerized, he momentarily forgot everything around him or the circumstances as he stared at her, and she gazed wide-eyed back at him. All he was aware of was a blue-eyed woman staring at him while some invisible current streaked between them like lightning over his wheat field. Her gaze was unwavering, searching. His gaze lowered for a few seconds to her lips, which were full and looked incredibly soft.

"Mary Catherine—" she whispered, bringing him back to the present with a jolt.

"She's all right," he said at once, assuming the woman was asking about the child. He released the woman instantly, giving her space. "She's right here."

In a glance he saw the vehicle was piled high in the back with suitcases, toys, clothing. A child's car seat was strapped in the back seat.

The cold drops of rain began to come down more often, and he looked out the window. "My pickup is just down the road. In a few minutes we're going to have a downpour.

I'll get my pickup and you two can go home with me, and when the storm is over, I'll see about your car.'' He pulled out his clean handkerchief and dabbed at her temple where she was bleeding. "What happened?''

"I was driving and had a contract— Oh!'' She gasped and clutched her stomach. "It's early,'' she whispered, closing her eyes for a few seconds.

"When's your baby due?'' he asked, alarm fluttering in him like a caged butterfly.

"Not for another two weeks, but I've given birth before. I know I'm in labor.''

"Lord help us,'' he said fervently, meaning every word and calculating the distance to Enid. "Here,'' he said, giving her his handkerchief. "I'll take you to the Enid hospital. I'm Matt Whitewolf. I farm and this is my land.''

She nodded. "I'm Vivian Ashland.''

Matt turned and held open the door. "Mary Catherine, you get in with your mommy. I'm going to get my truck and come back and get both of you. Now, you take care of Mommy.''

The little girl scrambled into the car beside her mother, who hugged her, and he closed the door. Frightened by the woman's labor contractions, he sprinted for his pickup.

As he ran, Matt could see the curtain of gray rain sweeping down the road toward him. He could hear its hiss and knew the heavy rain that had been predicted was arriving.

Vivian Ashland watched the tall, shaggy-haired cowboy run down the road while panic gripped her. He was a total stranger and she had lost all trust in men. Out of habit, she glanced in the rearview mirror, reassuring herself that no one had followed her since she left the interstate.

Heading southwest on back roads this afternoon, she thought they were doing fine. Then without warning a contraction seized her and she had lost control of the car, going off the road and smashing against the big tree.

Another contraction gripped her, tight and low in her body, and she gasped. She ran her hand over her stomach while the pain eased and vanished.

"I don't like thunder," Mary Catherine said, hugging close against Vivian's side.

"It's all right. It's only a rain shower." She slipped her arm around Mary Catherine and held her close. Vivian didn't want to go with a stranger even though he seemed friendly and reliable. She remembered that moment when she had regained consciousness and found him helping her, his arm around her. She had looked into midnight eyes that bore through her, causing a flutter of panic. He was broad-shouldered, powerful-looking, with long black hair that gave him a wild appearance. Disoriented and startled by him, she had started to scramble away from him, but then his dark gaze caught hers and she had been captured, riv-eted by his mesmerizing stare.

Now she wanted to try to get her car started, yet with her contractions, she was going to have to trust him to get them to the hospital. Even so, she couldn't resist turning the key in the ignition. Nothing happened. Vivian bit her lip and hugged Mary Catherine.

She prayed Matt Whitewolf was as trustworthy as he seemed. He said he would take her to Enid to the hospital. She had driven through Enid earlier, only noticing it was built around a shaded square and a large courthouse, but she had paid little attention to the town. When they reached the hospital, who would stay with Mary Catherine while she had her baby?

Vivian patted her temple, looking at his blood-soaked handkerchief. Her head throbbed, but it seemed insignifi-cant next to the possibility of having her baby now. The windows had fogged and she could no longer see the cowboy. As she swiped at the glass, a contraction gripped her, and she forgot everything but her pain.

Cold, hard rain swept over Matt, soaking him in seconds. He jumped inside his pickup, slamming the door while he revved the engine and raced down the road. In seconds he had parked beside Vivian's smashed vehicle.

As he climbed out of his pickup, he yanked on a slicker. When he opened Vivian's car door, mother and daughter were huddled together in the steamy car.

"I'll get Mary Catherine's car seat buckled in first and then I'll get her and come back for you."

"My car won't start."

"I'll check it later."

"Oh!" She bit her lip and placed her hand against her stomach again. It dimly registered with Matt that she wasn't wearing a wedding ring, but his thoughts were primarily on her contractions.

He didn't know anything about babies, but he knew a lot about calves, foals and puppies, and worry chilled him more than the cold rain. It took forty minutes in good weather to get from his place into town. In a storm it would take longer. "How often are you having pains?"

"I haven't timed them."

"Start timing," he ordered bluntly as he unbuckled Mary Catherine's car seat.

"Take her bag and that small blue bag so she'll have some of her things with her," Vivian said. "My hospital case is the gray one, and I'd like the brown suitcase, please. There's a small navy bag of baby things." She glanced at the boxes with her computer and monitor and suffered a pang at leaving her business records behind. "I need to lock up my car," she said, fumbling with her keys as she tried to extract the correct ones.

He placed his hand lightly on her arm. "Lady, stop planning," he ordered. "I'll take care of the bags and car. Let's just get going. Give me your keys."

With a flash of sparks in her eyes, she handed him her key chain, pointing to which keys to take. He pocketed the entire bunch. He picked up the bags and car seat and dashed to fasten it in the back seat of his pickup. He ran back to Vivian's car and shed his slicker.

"Come on, Mary Catherine. Let me carry you to my car."

She turned to cling tightly to Vivian, who gently pried the little girl's arms loose. "Let Mr. Whitewolf carry you. I can't carry you right now."

Mary Catherine was wide-eyed and solemn as Matt picked her up gently. When her thin little arm went around his neck, he turned his head to smile at her as he put the slicker over her head. "You're going to get a little wet, but as sweet as you are, you're not sugar so you won't melt. Let's go."

He dashed to the car and set her down on the front seat. Scrambling away from him swiftly, she climbed into the back and buckled herself into her car seat.

"Good girl. Now I'm going back for Mommy, so I have to leave you alone for just a minute, but you have your teddy bear with you. He'll hold your hand," he said, and she pulled her teddy up close to hug it. She stared at him with huge blue eyes filled with unmistakable fear.

Matt closed the door and ran back to Vivian's car, reaching in to hand his slicker to her. She scooted across the seat toward him.

"It's muddy and wet. I'll carry you."

"I can walk."

"I'll carry you," he said more firmly, and she nodded. Handing her his slicker, he slipped his arms around her. She wrapped one arm around his neck and held the slicker over both of them. He caught the scent of tea roses while soft locks of her straight hair brushed against his cheek. Even though she was pregnant, she was easy to carry, fitting so well into his arms. The slicker wrapped them in a cocoon. Her body was warm, her soft breast pressed against his chest. He placed her gently in the seat and ran around the front of the pickup to slide behind the wheel.

"Oh! There's another," she cried, biting her lip and squeezing her eyes shut, one hand clutching the seat and her other hand rubbing her abdomen. "The contractions are four minutes apart."

"I'll try to get you to the hospital as quickly as I can, but the rain will slow us down."

"I wasn't in labor a long time with Mary Catherine."

"Jeez!" He leaned forward, struggling to see through the blinding downpour and silently cursing the rain that slowed his driving.

Hearing her breath come out in puffs, Matt glanced at his passenger. She sat white-faced and tense. His gaze ran over her swiftly, taking in her simple pink cotton shirt and skirt. Her brown hair was thick and shiny and fell below her shoulders. She was pretty, with a straight nose, prominent cheekbones and smooth, flawless skin. Matt wondered where her husband was. The man was about to become a dad again and he should be with her now.

"Would you like to call your husband?" Matt asked, offering her the cellular phone.

Her eyes widened, and she looked startled before she blinked and shook her head. "No. I'm divorced."

Surprised, Matt glanced at her, wondering how a man could end a marriage to a beautiful woman and an adorable little girl. And another baby on the way. Along with his surprise, Matt felt a swift rush of annoyance with a man he had never met. Vivian shouldn't be here with a stranger when she was in labor. She should have her husband beside her. A protective sense stirred within Matt, and he decided he would stay at the hospital while she had her baby.

"Any other relatives to call? Your parents?"

She shook her head. "Both of my parents are deceased. It's all right. No one was with me when Mary Catherine was born."

"You were divorced then?"

"No, I've been divorced a year now. Back when Mary Catherine was born, my husband was closing a deal. A wife and family always came second to his business," she said.

A foul word directed at her ex-husband ran through Matt's mind as he placed the phone on the seat and hunched over the wheel. "We're really getting it now," he said, trying to see the road through the rain-covered window.

"Oh," she exclaimed softly, and bit her lip. Matt glanced at her and then returned his attention to the road. In minutes he heard her suck in her breath.

"Are you still timing?" he asked, thinking the last contractions were closer than four minutes apart.

"Three minutes almost," she said in a tight voice. "I can't believe this is happening."

"I can't, either," he remarked dryly, praying Rabbit Creek hadn't filled up out of its banks.

He picked up the phone and called 911. As soon as the dispatcher answered, Matt spoke tersely. "This is Matt Whitewolf on the county road about a mile from Rabbit Creek. I have a woman in labor with me and we need an ambulance to get her to the hospital."

He listened as the dispatcher repeated his statement, checked his location and said the ambulance was on its way. Matt switched the phone off.

"Sorry to be trouble," Vivian said quietly.

"Babies aren't trouble," he said, hating that she and her

little girl were alone. "They're very special miracles," he added, glancing at her.

She turned to look at him. "Do you have children?"

"No, I'm not married," he said, suspecting that would not be reassuring news. "I'm not a marrying man," he said, and then wondered what it was about Vivian Ashland that had him telling something so personal. Maybe it was the trust that she and Mary Catherine had been forced by circumstances to place in him.

He returned his attention swiftly to the road, slowing more in the blinding rain and feeling tension knot in him because he knew what this rain might be doing to Rabbit Creek. It might not matter whether there was an ambulance on the way. They rode in silence and he glanced once in the rearview mirror. Mary Catherine stared ahead with frightened eyes, her thumb in her mouth and her blanket and teddy bear against her cheek.

Vivian turned to look at her daughter and twisted in the seat, reaching back to hold Mary Catherine's hand. "We're all right, sweetie," she said. "She doesn't like storms," Vivian remarked to Matt.

He didn't like this one, either. Concentrating on his driving, he didn't bother to answer her. They turned a bend and he swore softly. "Dammit."

"What's wrong?"

As the windshield wipers swished away rain at their top speed, he could see well enough to view the tumbling water that had spread out of the banks of Rabbit Creek. The gray asphalt disappeared from view beneath the surging, muddy water and a road sign stuck up above the surface, looking out of place. He swore again and pumped the brakes, slowing and staring in consternation. Alarm engulfed him. A baby was not a calf or foal. He didn't know anything about delivering a baby.

He glared at the water that he was helpless to fight and

reassured himself that women had been having babies since the beginning of time and this was not Vivian Ashland's first baby.

"I can see the rails of the bridge. Can't you drive through the water?" she asked.

"No. If that water is going fifteen miles an hour—it looks like it's going a lot faster than that—it can be twenty-five thousand pounds of force against the pickup," he said tersely. "It's an old bridge and it's held so far, but it could go at any time. The county was supposed to replace it last spring."

"What do I do?"

He carefully turned the pickup, heading back the way they had come. "The creek is up and over the bridge. I can go around, but the only way open will take a couple of hours, and in this storm, I think the best thing to do is get you back to my house. When you had Mary Catherine, did you have any complications?"

"No," she said in a small voice that made him think of Mary Catherine. "I'm sorry to cause you trouble."

"It's no trouble," he lied. "We'll get out of this storm," he said, heading back as fast as he dared, knowing some of the low-lying areas of the highway could flood if the downpour continued and they could be cut off from his house as well. He picked up the phone and called 911 again. "We can't get through," he told the dispatcher. "Rabbit Creek is out of its banks, and the bridge is under water. We're headed back to my house. I'll keep in contact with Doc Bently in Dakani."

He gave his cellular phone number and his home phone number and listened to the dispatcher talk about an ambulance coming as soon as the water subsided.

Next, Matt called his family physician in the nearby small town of Dakani.

"Doc, Matt here. A woman had a wreck on my place

and she's in labor. I was taking her to Enid, but water is over the bridge on Rabbit Creek and we've had to turn back. We can't even get to Dakani and her contractions are not quite three minutes apart. I'm taking her back to my place.''

"Call me when you get home or if she goes into hard labor. I'll tell you what to do," Dr. Bently replied.

"Can you get here?" Matt asked.

"I'll head down south and avoid Rabbit Creek. I'll be there when I can get there. I'm on my way."

"Thanks. And hurry.''

He switched off the phone and set it on the seat between them, glancing at Vivian. Perspiration beaded her brow and she was still covered with streaks of blood on her cheek and throat and over her pink blouse from bumping her head on the windshield.

"How's your head?"

"Oh, it's fine. A little headache," she answered, sounding distracted. He suspected she was wrapped in her own world of labor contractions. Matt glanced in the rearview mirror at Mary Catherine, who was wide-eyed, rubbing her face with her blanket and looking terrified.

Thunder boomed and the child jumped, squeezing her eyes closed. "Mommy!"

"It's all right. We'll be out of the storm soon," Vivian said gently, twisting in the seat to reach back and hold Mary Catherine's hand again. "Mr. Whitewolf is taking us home with him." She turned slightly to face him. "I'm really sorry."

"It's all right," he answered, glancing at her and wondering what had happened to her marriage.

"How'd Mary Catherine find you?"

"I had a flat and was changing it."

She didn't reply and in seconds groaned softly, and he fought the urge to jam his foot hard on the accelerator.

When he turned the pickup at his gate and rattled across the cattle guard, he lost his concern that he might be unable to get through to his house. From the gate there would be no more deep water to go through.

Driving along the muddy road, he was aware this was the first time he had ever brought a woman home. His home seemed an extension of himself, something he guarded as closely as he guarded his heart. But a woman in labor who was a complete stranger was different from a woman he dated. Even so, he was aware of the first in his life.

Vivian gasped and gripped the door handle, her knuckles white. "How far is your house?"

"Not much farther. Doc said to call when you're in hard labor."

"Not yet."

They lapsed into silence until he slowed as he approached the sprawling ranch house built of weathered timbers with a wraparound porch. Usually the sight of his house gave him a deep sense of satisfaction, but today fear outweighed all else.

Matt pulled into the open three-stall garage of his rambling one-story ranch house. "Here we are."

Vivian Ashland looked paler than before. She frowned and bit her lip.

"Still three minutes apart?"

She shook her head. "No, two minutes."

Sweating, feeling nervous and swearing silently at the rain, Matt climbed out and reached back to get Mary Catherine out of her seat. Before he could, she unbuckled it and climbed over the seat, scooting out beside Vivian. Matt gathered their bags and opened the back door.

As they started to enter his house, he looked into Vivian's wide eyes and he could see her fear.

"I can call Doc Bently again, and he'll give you a character reference about me if it would make you feel better."

''No!'' She blushed a deep pink, the color looking pretty in her pale face. ''I don't need that. I just didn't expect to be with a stranger.''

''I know. Let's go inside.''

''Oh!'' She grasped the door and paused and his concern heightened.

''I think I better get you to bed and call the doctor. I can carry you,'' he offered, following them inside the kitchen and setting down the bags. He switched on a light, barely glancing at the familiar room with its warm oak cabinets and round oak table, the reddish-brown terrazzo floor. Dishes were piled haphazardly on the counter and in the sink. Once again he was aware of the oddity of a stranger in his home.

Vivian shook her head in response to this question. ''I can walk,'' she replied.

His phone rang and he crossed the room to pick up the receiver.

''Matt.'' He heard Walt Bently's deep voice.

''We just got here,'' Matt replied.

''How are the contractions?''

''I think they might be two minutes apart. This is her second baby.''

''I called Meg Preston, and she's on her way to your place now. She should be able to get to your house.''

''Thank God!'' Matt exclaimed, for the first time thinking about the older woman who had been an R.N. in obstetrics before she retired. The Prestons' farm was about twenty miles from his place, but there were no major creeks to cross between them.

''Meg will be there soon. Here's my car phone number,'' Bently said, and Matt reached for paper and pen, jotting down the information. ''Now, put the little mama in bed and get her ready for Meg. She's got her instruments, but just in case, you get yourself all washed up, have a knife sterilized, and if this baby comes before Meg does, you call me and I'll tell you what to do.''

"Thanks. Bye, Doc." Matt replaced the phone and told Vivian that help was on the way.

"If you have television," she said to him, "Mary Catherine can watch the children's programs, or she has a video in her bag."

"Sure," Matt answered, looking at the small child. "Let's go down the hall to the den." Matt watched as Vivian stood and took her daughter's hand. Mary Catherine clutched her small bag tightly to her side along with her teddy bear, as if she needed them for defense.

When they reached the den, Matt switched on lights. As he moved around the room, Vivian handed him a video.

Her knees shook, and she knew it was from nerves, not labor. She was with a total stranger and no one except Mary Catherine knew where she was. She had to trust Matt Whitewolf and she prayed this baby came without complications.

She had thought it would be better to move before the baby came, instead of after, but now it seemed a poor choice. She thought of her friends and her doctor in Denver—everything that was familiar. Too late now.

She watched the tall cowboy as he slipped the cassette into the VCR and turned on the television. In minutes Mary Catherine was curled up on his maroon leather sofa, watching a fuzzy white dog dance across the giant screen.

Vivian leaned close to hug Mary Catherine, knowing her child was frightened, too, and wishing she could give her more comfort. "You be good and watch your show. I'm going to lie down a little while. Okay?"

Mary Catherine hugged and kissed Vivian, and Vivian's heart constricted. "You're a brave little girl," she said, smoothing Mary Catherine's brown hair. "I'll just be down the hall, okay?"

Mary Catherine nodded and settled to look at the television. Vivian headed out of the room, suddenly stopping and clutching the nearest chair as another contraction started.

"Can I help you?" Matt asked.

"I'm all right."

Matt patted her shoulder, feeling inadequate yet relieved now that he knew Meg was on her way. "One thing—the experts will be here soon. Let's get you to a bedroom. Doc said to get you ready and Meg Preston, a nurse, is coming to help," Matt said as he picked up Vivian's things and they stepped into the hall.

His boot heels scraped against the plank floor. They passed three bedrooms that were never used, and without thinking about it, Matt led her to his bedroom and set her suitcases down inside the door.

Vivian stood in the center of the high-ceilinged room that was all wood and glass. Wooden beams crossed the ceiling; wide louvered shutters stood open at the windows. Glass made up two walls while paneling and shelves were along the other walls. His dark oak four-poster bed was king-size, covered in a deep turquoise comforter. She watched him strip down the bed and rummage in his closet and panic assailed her. She was in a stranger's house. This cowboy was going to have to deliver her baby. She closed her eyes, fighting fear that swirled around her like dark floodwaters. A contraction commenced and pain pushed aside worry. Gasping, barely aware of him, she watched as he held out a white shirt.

"Maybe this would be more comfortable for you," he said.

As she accepted the shirt, he motioned toward an open

door. "There's the bathroom. I'll go down the hall and wash up and I'll get some towels for the bed."

Feeling a flush of embarrassment, she shook her head. "This is really embarrassing, and it's more so since you're not married."

"Think about the baby and don't worry about me," he said. "Meg will be here in time. I'll just help you get ready."

She nodded and stepped into the bathroom, closing the door behind her.

Matt let out his breath. "Come on, Meg. Hurry it up," he said under his breath, yanking off his wet shirt and pulling on a dry T-shirt. Picking up clean jeans and socks, he raced down the hall, changed and scrubbed up. When he dried, he pulled out clean towels and sheets and took them back to the bed to spread them. Then he got out one of his seldom-used knives that was razor sharp and took it to the kitchen to sterilize it.

When he returned to the bedroom, Vivian was coming out of the bath. She had washed away the blood from her temple and combed her long brown hair. Over five and a half feet tall, she looked like a fifteen-year-old child in his white shirt that draped over her hands and hung to her knees.

"I feel better now, but the contractions are definitely two minutes apart. And that bed looks good because—" She gasped and grabbed a high-backed rocking chair and a look of shock crossed her face. She yanked a towel off the bed. "My water broke," she whispered, blushing and scrambling up on the bed. "I'm having a contrac—" She broke off. Matt rushed to spread a sheet over her and help her, propping pillows under her head.

"Oh, my gosh, the baby's coming!" she gasped.

Chapter 2

Terror seized Matt and he stared at her. He yanked up the phone and called the cellular number Walt Bently had given him.

"Hello" came the familiar voice.

"It's Matt. Her water broke, and she said the baby is coming."

"Calm down. How many calves have you delivered?"

"Doc, this isn't a calf!" he snapped, and heard a slight chuckle. Surprised, he glanced at Vivian and saw the faintest hint of a smile lift one corner of her mouth, and the sight calmed him like a steadying hand. Once again he gazed into her blue eyes and found warmth and trust, and his fears vanished.

"How many calves, Matt?"

"Too many to count."

"Yep, and I'll wager plenty of them were more complicated births than this is going to be. Besides, a baby is a little thing. You don't have all those long legs to fool with."

"Okay, Walt, you made your point. Now what do I do?"

"Let me talk to the little mother. I'm on my way."

Matt handed over the phone and waited, hearing her pause and watching her close her eyes and knowing she was having another contraction. He reached out and took her hand, wishing he could do something.

She opened her eyes, talked to the doctor and then handed back the receiver. As she did, she gasped and clenched his hand.

"I better see what's happening," he said, moving around the bed. He moved between her legs.

When he shifted the sheet to her knees, Vivian was flooded with embarrassment. They were all but total strangers, yet she was going to have to depend on him and give herself up to him in the most intimate way.

He glanced over her knees as the contraction subsided and his dark gaze met hers. "Good girl," he said. "You're doing great."

"You're not even married," she said.

Amusement flickered in his dark eyes. "I do know a little about females and female anatomy," he said, one corner of his mouth lifting in a crooked grin.

"It's not quite the same," she said, and closed her eyes as another contraction gripped her and she pushed with all her strength.

When it passed, he patted her leg. "You're doing great."

"I'm going to have a girl."

"You know that?"

"Yes, I had an ultrasound, and that's what my doctor in Denver said." Another contraction began, and she clenched her fists and dug her heels into the bed as she pushed.

Matt hurt for her. Where the hell was Meg? He wondered if she had stalled or been flooded out from reaching his house. He tried to give steady encouragement to Vivian, talking to her between contractions.

Again a contraction gripped her and her hips lifted as she pushed while he called encouragement. Then he saw the baby's head. Excitement streaked in him, and his last fears vanished.

"That's it, Vivian! I can see the head! We're going to have a baby, and it's turned right," he said, feeling another surge of exhilaration. "Hang on, push hard! You're doing great! Keep at it!"

Through a blur of pain Vivian heard his deep voice, calm and steady and supportive, sounding as if he had done this dozens of times before.

Two more big contractions and then he was reaching for the baby.

"That's it, Vivian! Here's our baby!" Matt exclaimed exuberantly, suddenly awed and filled with wonder as he grasped the wet baby. He was weak-kneed, overwhelmed by the miracle of birth and this new little person who was so tiny in his hands.

"Vivian, here's your little girl," he said in a husky voice, feeling as if he was holding something infinitely fragile and precious and astounded how they had gotten her here with such ease. Reluctant to give her up, he placed her on Vivian's sheet-draped tummy and put Vivian's hand on the baby, covering her hand with his. "There she is. Isn't she a marvel? Look at all her brown hair. I need to cut and tie the cord now."

Tears stung her eyes, and Matt's fingers tightened on her hand. "She is a marvel," Vivian said, touching her baby. "I almost didn't make it."

Matt heard a voice behind him. Meg strode through the door and opened the bag in her hands. She wore a crisp white shirt and jeans and boots and he could not recall being so relieved to see someone before in his life.

"We have our baby," he said, without realizing what he had told her.

"Well, heavens to Betsy! Good for you! I told Walt Bently you could do this all by yourself." She put down a box, a brown paper sack and a satchel and disappeared into the bathroom, where he heard the water running. In minutes she reappeared, drying her hands and tossing the towel back into the bathroom.

"Now you can step aside and I'll take over here," Meg said briskly, snapping on surgical gloves and moving to the foot of the bed. Her voice softened, and she patted Vivian's leg. "How's Mama?"

"I'm okay."

"Good. You're in good hands. And you have a sweet baby girl. Matt is an old hand at delivering foals and calves. I knew he could do this delivery."

"I'm damned glad you're here," Matt said. He moved around to the side of the bed to look at Vivian while Meg went briskly to work, talking softly to the infant.

"How're you doing?" Matt asked Vivian.

"I'm fine. Thank you," she said, glancing from the baby to him, her shining blue eyes filled with such joy he was awed. "I'm naming her Julia." Vivian squeezed his arm.

Her slender fingers slid around his wrist, and he didn't want her to let go. He knew it was absurd to feel that way, but he was glad they'd had to turn back to his house and he'd been with her. He couldn't resist, and leaned down to brush a kiss on her cheek, catching the scent of roses and feeling her smooth skin beneath his lips.

"You were great," he said softly, covering her slender hand with his.

"Now get, Matt," Meg snapped. "You'll only be in the way and you've done a good job. Go brew me up some iced tea. Get some scales to weigh this little girl and a yardstick so we'll know how long she is. We want all the statistics. What time was she born?"

"About two minutes before you walked in the door," Matt said, glancing at his watch. "About three-forty."

"Very good. Go now."

"Tell me when to bring Mary Catherine to see the baby. I won't tell her yet so you can do that," he said to Vivian.

Reluctantly, he turned and left the room. Now that it was over, his knees shook as much as Vivian's had. He couldn't understand the emotions tumbling in him. He had wanted to gather mother and baby in his arms and hold them close. He felt a part of them—something he had never experienced before in his life with anyone.

In a daze he called 911 to make certain the ambulance was canceled. Then he washed up and went to find Mary Catherine.

"How're you doing?" he asked as he sat near her on a chair. Staring at him with big blue eyes, she still looked alarmed to see him and she didn't answer. He wondered whether she was always so shy or if it was just because he was a stranger. As he glanced around the room, he realized it had already been changed by Mary Catherine. Her bag lay on the Navajo rug on the floor. Her teddy bear was in his leather recliner with a pink blanket spread over it. An alphabet book lay on his sturdy cherry-wood coffee table.

"Mary Catherine, Nurse Preston is with your mommy right now," he said, wanting to let Vivian tell Mary Catherine herself about the new little sister. "Are you hungry?"

She looked at him and he could guess the struggle she was having with her shyness versus wanting something to eat.

"Bring your bear and we'll go into the kitchen and find something you like to eat," he said, wondering what on earth he would have that a little child would like.

He left the room, glancing back to see whether or not she was coming. She stared at him as she scooted off the couch, picked up her bear and followed him.

He brewed a pitcher of tea for Meg and rummaged in the fridge. "Do you want toast? Grilled cheese sandwich?"

She nodded when he asked about the sandwich. She still seemed uncertain.

"Want to come sit down?" he asked gently, pulling out a chair at the kitchen table. She climbed onto it and sat silently watching him as he fixed her a grilled cheese sandwich and poured her a glass of milk.

As he moved around the kitchen, pouring iced tea for Meg, his gaze kept returning to Mary Catherine, eating quietly at his kitchen table, yet watching him with a wary eye. She seemed terrified of him.

He had suffered his own terrors this past hour. The delivery had shaken him to his soul. He had been frightened and then awed, completely stunned by the miracle of birth and the calm, brave manner of Vivian Ashland. The thought of creating another little person, a part of himself, had never entered his mind before and had never been real to him, but suddenly it was the most awesome thing he had ever known. The birth of the baby made him stop and think about the emptiness in his own life.

He remembered when he was a kid, how he used to feel hollow inside when he watched some of his schoolmates with their families. Growing up, the only bright spot in his broken home had been his younger brothers. Now he just thought of himself as the Tin Man who needed a heart.

The brief time Vivian Ashland, her baby and Mary Catherine had been a part of his life had changed him, and he knew he would never, never forget them.

That realization shocked him, too. He shook his head slightly, wondering if he was just caught up in the euphoria of the moment and it would pass and he would forget this day. He didn't think so. Not for a lifetime. Never could he forget Vivian's blue eyes so calm and trusting on him, making him feel strong and capable, as if she thought he could do anything that needed to be done.

He heard someone moving through the hall and glanced around to see Meg. She stood with her hands on her hips and her blue eyes scanning the kitchen. All of five feet tall, she had a commanding voice, and he was deeply grateful she had arrived on the scene.

"You must be Mary Catherine?" Meg said, and Mary Catherine nodded.

"Want to go see your mommy now?"

"Yes," Mary Catherine said promptly. She slid off the chair as Matt handed Meg the scales and the tape measure.

In minutes Meg was back. "Now, where's that iced tea?" she asked.

"Right here," Matt said, handing her a glass. "How big is our baby?"

"She is six pounds and eight ounces, not big but just fine, and she is twenty inches long. Long and skinny."

"She didn't look long and skinny. She looked perfect."

Meg chuckled and turned to his refrigerator. "We have a hungry new mama," Meg said. "I'll cook something for her," she said, looking in his fridge as if it were her home instead of his. "Good. You have a lot of milk. Vivian is going to need it." Meg got out the milk and bread. "Now, where are your pans?"

Matt fixed toast and poured milk while Meg poached an egg.

"Here, take her the milk and toast." She chuckled. "Took an act of God to break down your male resistance and get a woman in this house."

"You know Lita cleans for me," he said, refusing to let Meg ruffle him when she had been an angel to his rescue.

"Ah, that's different. Lita's a kid."

"Not so much a kid. She's pregnant."

"Now you'll know what to do when she has her baby," Meg said cheerfully.

"The hell I will," he replied, wondering how everyone in the county managed to know everyone else's business. The next time he walked into the feed store or Addie's Grill, he knew they would tease him about delivering a baby.

"We can go sit with Vivian while she eats. I'll bring the eggs as soon as they're ready. She's doing real well, and without drugs she's as alert as I am."

"I doubt any of us are as alert as you are," he remarked, and heard Meg chuckle as he left the kitchen.

As he entered his bedroom, he saw all of them—Vivian propped up in his bed, the sleeping baby wrapped in a pink blanket, Mary Catherine beside her new sister—but after a swift glance, his attention was riveted on Vivian, tiny little shocks igniting in his system. He dated, but he wasn't into commitment and he had never taken a woman home to his bed. Vivian in his big four-poster was unique. He was startled and as mesmerized by her as he had been the first moment he looked into her big blue eyes.

She was propped against a mound of pillows in the center of his bed. Her brown hair framed her face, which shone with joy, the pink back in her cheeks. His shirt was partially unbuttoned, and the soft white cotton clung to her lush figure. When her gaze met his, she smiled, her full lips curving and revealing white, even teeth, and he couldn't get his breath. The woman was beautiful. She was a new mother, and he had just helped deliver her baby, but he couldn't stop staring at her, thinking she was a dazzling beauty.

"Okay now?" he asked, unable to resist moving close beside her as he set the glass of milk on a bedside table and handed her the plate with toast.

"We're fine. We're interrupting your life, though."

He shifted his gaze from mother to baby, looking at the tiny infant who seemed such a miracle.

He shook his head. "For a baby, it's worth interrupting. And with the rain, there's not a lot I can do," he said, knowing that wasn't so. There were half a dozen things he ought to check on, but he had an excellent foreman and he knew farm life would move smoothly without him.

"Here's more sustenance," Meg said, entering and carrying a cookie sheet with a plate of poached eggs.

Matt pulled up a chair and sat beside the bed.

As soon as Meg was seated in the rocker, she held up her glass of iced tea. "Here's to Baby Julia."

Vivian lifted her glass of milk, her eyes sparkling as she sipped. Milk was on her upper lip and her tongue flicked out slowly, licking it away. Watching the tip of her pink tongue slide over her lip, Matt stared at her mouth, wondering what it would be like to feel her full, soft lips beneath his.

What was wrong with him? Maybe he should have cut loose and partied a little after wheat harvest instead of coming home to go over his finances and repair tools and see about newborn calves.

This woman was merely passing through his life, he reminded himself. He barely knew her—that argument went up in smoke as he remembered the moment she had given birth and he had held her new baby in his hands. It had been an incredible, breathtaking moment in which he felt a spiritual bond with both of them. Yet she would be gone before he really got to know her.

The doorbell rang, and when Matt left to answer, Vivian watched him stride away. Matt Whitewolf seemed forceful, yet incredibly gentle and encouraging. She was too conscious of him when he was near. And even though she was in a stranger's home, Vivian knew she was as comfortable as she would have been in Denver with Dr. Woodrow and her friends. Today everything had happened so fast, she still was in shock. Even so, here was her precious baby with Mary Catherine beside her and they were safe and well.

Mary Catherine had curled up beside the baby and was asleep, and Vivian knew her child was exhausted by the day's events. She ran her fingers over Mary Catherine's head, twisting straight brown locks around her fingers. She wanted to give her girls the kind of love she had never had. She wished her dad could see his granddaughters! Her mother probably wouldn't have been happy to be a grand-mother because she was never happy being a mother.

The sound of deep voices rose in the hall, and then Matt returned with a shorter man at his side. Her heart did a strange skip as she glanced at Matt, and for just a moment when they looked at each other, she forgot everyone else in the room, feeling a close bond with him. Then Vivian shifted her attention to the stranger.

Half a foot shorter than Matt, the man smiled as he ran his hand over his bushy brown hair and greeted Meg. "Glad you got here, Meg, but probably not half as glad as these folks."

"Our cowboy delivered her just fine."

"Vivian," Matt said, "this is Dr. Walt Bently. Walt, meet Vivian Ashland. That's her daughter Mary Catherine, now sleeping, and the newest addition, Julia Ashland."

"Glad to meet you, ma'am. And glad all of you are doing so well," Walt Bently said, setting his black bag on the table. "Matt will excuse us and I'll check you. With Meg here, I'm sure all is under control."

"Want me to move Mary Catherine to the next bed-room?" Matt asked. When Vivian nodded, he picked up the little girl and left the room while Meg closed the door for the doctor's examination of Vivian and her baby.

As Matt carried Mary Catherine into the next bedroom,

he looked at her nestled in his arms and took stock again of his own solitary life. Whether he was working or at home, he spent most of his time alone. He dated sometimes, but he had never been serious, never could be deeply involved with someone else. He looked down at Mary Catherine's wispy brown hair, and for the first time he wondered if life might be passing him by.

He shrugged away the notion as nonsense, but he rubbed his chin on the top of Mary Catherine's head and held her close, feeling a strange possessiveness toward her that he knew he had no more right to feel than the emotions churning in him when he was around her mama.

He stroked the child's hair lightly and thought about going through life without children. He had never given it a thought before because he intended to go through life without marrying. It stood to reason there would be no children, but now he suspected he might be missing what was really vital.

Yet all he had to do was think of his past and any hope of a future relationship vanished. He was not into commitment, but today he was seeing what it was costing him.

He placed Mary Catherine on the king-size bed in the next bedroom. She still clutched her teddy bear tightly in her arms. He ran his finger along her soft cheek and looked at her long lashes. How could any man have separated from a family like this one? Matt couldn't imagine having such a treasure and not cherishing it. With a shake of his head, he tiptoed out of the bedroom.

Going to the kitchen, he placed a frozen casserole into the oven, called the car dealership and then looked in again on Mary Catherine, who was curled up asleep with her thumb in her mouth. He stood in the door staring at her, remembering those first moments when she had appeared on the road. He wondered how scared she had been to walk so far and accost a stranger. The thought of her walking alone on a country road was unnerving. Yet she was a bright, brave little girl, trying to get help for her mommy.

Meg and Walt appeared, gathering their things. "Vivian is fine and so is the baby. You did a good job," Walt said, picking up his raincoat and umbrella.

"Stay for supper. You, too, Meg."

Both of them shook their heads. "With this storm, I want to get home before the last bit of daylight is gone," Meg said.

"Same for me," Walt Bently added.

"I can't thank both of you enough," Matt said with sincerity. "I don't know what I would have done without you."

Meg laughed. "You'd have done what you do for all those cows and horses, you would have delivered that baby just like you did—like you'd been delivering babies as well as calves."

"It was a damn sight scarier," he remarked, and Walt and Meg laughed.

"Only time I've ever heard you rattled," Walt said. "You were a lot calmer when that bull tossed you and broke your arm and collarbone."

"I knew what to do then—get away from him. I didn't know what to do today."

"Oh, yes, you did," Meg said. "She's a nice lady and you'll have a little four-year-old for company tonight," Meg said, her eyes dancing with mischief. "Time you had your solitary life jolted a little." Chuckling, she yanked on her battered Stetson. "So long, Matt."

"Thanks, Meg," he called after her as she sprinted to her pickup. He turned and offered his hand to Walt. "Thanks again. You were a lifesaver."

"No. You were. She needed help. Good thing you found her and got her home with you. She can stay here until she gets her strength, can't she?"

Startled, Matt hadn't thought beyond the immediate present. "Sure. I've got plenty of room," he said with a strange clash of emotions. He liked his solitude, and the thought of three more people living under his roof with him was unsettling. At the same time, his pulse gave a jump at the thought of having Vivian here longer.

"The lady doesn't have any family except the little girls. She's divorced and she's starting over. You keep her here for a while," Walt Bently said. "She can't start for Houston. With a child and a new baby that's too far and too hard a drive. The usual procedure is another checkup at six weeks, so if you can get her to stay that long, it would be good."

"She'll be here for sure until her car is repaired, and from the looks of the radiator, it was major damage. Anyway, be careful going home."

"It was okay the way I came. Just took a long time. Baby and mama are doing fine, so you can relax. She'll take charge now. I left her some things I brought from the office and instructions. If the baby has any trouble at all, call me. Meg's close and can get right here and she's the best. See you, Matt."

"Thanks a million, Walt."

Matt watched the doctor drive away, and as he closed the door, he heard a baby crying. For a second the sound startled him. It was as foreign to his house as if he had heard a choir break into song. He stopped and stared down the hall and the crying ceased.

Vivian's door was open, so he headed there. Of all the words Walt Bently had said to him, *keep her here* kept dancing in Matt's mind and he knew he wanted Vivian to stay. For the first time in his life he wanted a woman in his house, and the idea surprised him.

Chapter 3

"Come in," Vivian said as Matt knocked on the bedroom door.

Vivian was still propped against a mound of pillows, looking like the satisfied, happy mother, a faint smile on her face and such warmth in her blue eyes that he was drawn across the room. She must have finished eating, washed and changed her clothes because now she wore a blue cotton robe, and a white frilly gown showed above the robe's collar. Blue satin slippers were on the floor beside the bed.

"How are you doing?" he asked in a husky voice, feeling emotions churn in him. He experienced what he knew was a ridiculous joy and pride—as if he were the father of this baby. He knew full well that was absurd, yet he couldn't stop the rush of emotions. He still ached to take them both in his arms and couldn't understand what was the matter with him.

"I'm great," she said quietly, and reached for his hand.

It seemed the most natural thing in the world for his fingers to close around hers. Soft and warm, her hand curled in his.

"Thank you for rescuing us. I don't know what we would have done if you hadn't come along."

"I'm glad I was there," Matt said.

"Would you like to hold her again?"

"Yes," he answered honestly, not understanding his own intense reaction to the baby. He wanted to hold her little Julia again, yet at the same time he felt clumsy and afraid he might not hold her right. He and Vivian still looked at each other, neither moving while silence drew out until she gave a little shake of her head.

"Here," she said. She slipped her hand from his and twisted around to pick up the baby and hold her out to him.

He took her carefully, cradling her head with his hand and looking at her. Wide eyes stared up at him solemnly as if she were assessing him. His heart filled with warmth for this tiny baby. He reminded himself again he had no business feeling that way about her. She was no part of his life. Yet the knowledge couldn't stop the emotions that made him want to keep holding her in his arms. "I never knew a little baby could be so pretty," he said.

"We think so," Vivian replied. "Maybe you're a little prejudiced about her, too, because you have a special interest in her."

Julia's eyes fluttered and closed. "Is she asleep? Is she all right?" he asked, alarmed.

Vivian reached for the baby, and he handed her over. He was conscious of Vivian as he bent down, of brushing their hands, of her face only inches away from his, the scent of roses and talcum assailing him. "She's asleep," Vivian said calmly. "She's had a big day today."

When they looked at each other, he couldn't resist touching Vivian. He lifted silky locks of her brown hair. "Can I get you anything? I have supper cooking."

"You cook? You deliver babies and calves. You're very diverse."

"I'd like to claim credit for all of that, but I have a housekeeper, Lita Hobart. She's in cosmetology school in Enid. Three days a week she comes in and cleans and cooks. Her cooking is very simple, but it's good enough. She fixes casseroles and all I have to do is get them from the freezer to the oven. I think Julia will be my only baby to deliver."

"You don't know what the future will bring," she answered, wondering about his life.

"I hope no more deliveries. That scared the hell out of me."

"You didn't act scared."

"Maybe not once we got into it."

He pulled a chair near the bed and sat down, propping his elbows on his knees.

Vivian looked at the spacious room that was so obviously occupied by a man, with photographs of a bull and of two horses, photographs on a shelf of cowboys at a rodeo, trophies. In some ways it was stark and barren and uncluttered, with no magazines or books in sight.

"This must be your room."

"It is. But I can sleep anywhere tonight."

"Why don't I move? I'll sleep with Mary Catherine. Actually, I do a lot of nights."

"You stay right here," he said firmly.

"I don't want to take your bed."

"I didn't think you'd want to share it," he teased, and she laughed, shaking her head.

"You wouldn't want to share it, either, with a baby."

Something flickered in the depths of his eyes and the moment transformed. Vivian thought about the intimacy they had already shared. Her pulse jumped as tension streaked between them. He was reacting, too. His dark eyes changed, a solemn expression coming to his features and an intensity in the way he looked at her that made her instinctively know this man was going to be unforgettable.

He made her aware of herself as a woman, something she hadn't given particular thought to for months now. The circumstances and her surroundings disappeared. All she was conscious of was the handsome, broad-shouldered cowboy who was staring at her as if he were going to lean forward and kiss her. To her amazement, she wanted him to.

The realization shocked her, and she made an effort to look away, hoping the tension would ease or vanish. She hadn't wanted any man's kisses for too long to remember. She couldn't feel anything like attraction—not at this time in her life. Particularly not with a cowboy whom she barely knew and would never see again after she left his house.

"I really don't want to take your room," she said, staring at the photographs on the opposite wall and trying to avoid looking at him.

"Vivian, you sleep here," he said in a no-nonsense tone that carried finality and replaced awareness with a prickly annoyance.

She turned to look at him. "You must be accustomed to getting your way."

"Maybe so. At least on this place I do. You sound as if that's an accusation."

"Sorry," she said, instantly contrite after all his care and kindness. "I've lived the last few years with a man who had to have his way in everything."

"Well, maybe this time, my having my way means it's better for you, so that might make it a little different."

"It makes it very different," she said, regretting her hasty remark. "You've been so good to us."

"Doc Bentley told me you were headed to Houston when you had the wreck. You're off the beaten path," he remarked dryly, curiosity lighting his dark eyes.

"Yes. I divorced a year ago and now I'm moving my business and family to Houston to start over. My husband didn't want me to leave—our businesses were tied together because he was a client of mine. I'm in the public relations business."

"That must complicate life to have not only your marriage, but your businesses together as well," Matt said.

"It did complicate things terribly. It was one reason he didn't want the divorce."

"I'd think there would be three other reasons he wouldn't want it," Matt said quietly, yet his tone carried a hint of anger, and she knew he was referring to her and the girls.

"He was never interested in Mary Catherine. He wouldn't have any interest in Julia. I got pregnant during a last-ditch attempt at reconciliation last year."

"Are you taking back roads to Houston?" he asked, returning to his earlier remark, and she knew he was curious why she was in his area.

"I left the interstate this morning," she replied, wondering why she was telling Matt so much personal information, yet it was easy to talk to him, and because he had shared childbirth with her, they had a strong bond between them. It was startling to realize that she felt closer to him now than people she had known for years. She smoothed her robe and thought about his last question. He needed to be alerted to any potential problems she might cause him.

"I may have been mistaken, but I thought someone was following us."

"Your husband?" Matt asked, a coldness coming to his voice that chilled her, and she suspected he would be formidable if provoked.

"No, not Baker himself. Probably someone he hired. I never would have noticed except Baker had me followed two years ago, so I've been more cautious and more alert about who's around me. Two years ago I found the bill to the private investigator on the desk and asked Baker about it. My ex-husband is possessive. I have a thriving business and I have male clients. He was jealous and had me followed, so I was watching for someone on this trip. I could have been wrong, but I left I-70 at Hays, Kansas, and drove south to cut across western Oklahoma. I was headed for I-35 and that's how I happened to be in this area."

"We ought to let the sheriff know that you might have been followed. Do you expect trouble?"

"No. I think Baker simply wants to know where I settle and then I think I'll see him again."

"Are you afraid of your ex?"

"No, but I have a restraining order against him."

"Maybe you should get one for the state of Oklahoma."

She thought a moment before she answered. "I don't think I'll be here long enough to need one."

Matt shrugged. "Think it over."

"Our marriage is over, but his ego hasn't adjusted yet. I was part of his image of success, and he doesn't want to let that go. He was into power and control and really didn't care about a family. I think he'll try to get me to come back because his monumental ego was trampled."

"And—will you go back?"

She shook her head. "Never."

"Was he abusive?"

She shrugged. "No, except at the last," she admitted reluctantly. She had said little to anyone about her marriage and it was difficult to talk about it. "He was beginning to be verbally abusive and possessive and then one night he lost his temper and struck me. I packed and left and got the divorce."

"Good enough. Mary Catherine was afraid of him, wasn't she?"

"Yes. How'd you know?" Vivian asked, wondering what he had seen and how he had so easily guessed her child's feelings toward her father.

"She seems terrified of me. I couldn't have caused her fear because I barely know her."

"He did frighten her. He never hit her, but his yelling and his attitude toward me frightened her. His lack of love for her was obvious, even to a child."

Matt's eyes changed, darkening, the slightest shift, yet once again he looked formidable, dangerous. "When you thought you were being followed—did you see the same car? A particular person?" Matt asked, stretching out his long, jeans-clad legs and crossing his feet at the ankles.

"It's difficult to hide a very pregnant woman and a little child. We made lots of stops. I only drove a few hours each day, and along the way we went to parks and museums."

"Then the person following had to stop a lot," Matt remarked.

"Maybe he got tired of our breaks and he got careless. I don't know—maybe I'm wrong and it was just sheer co-incidence that a man happened to be traveling the same place at the same time I was." As she talked, it was a relief to share her worries with him.

"I doubt that," Matt remarked dryly.

"At one rest stop, when I drove through the parking lot, I noticed a Colorado license tag. I spotted the car again on the highway where there had been a wreck and traffic was backed up. When everyone started up again, Mary Catherine began crying about something pinching her, so I had to pull over. In all the traffic, the car had to pass me and I noticed the same tag. Then I paid closer attention to the car. Later, I think I saw it in the rearview mirror. It may have been my imagination or coincidence. Whether it was or was not, I thought I could take a state road from I-70 to I-35 and possibly lose the person if someone was following. I know that my ex will find out where I am eventually, but I was annoyed at the thought of being followed.''

While she talked, she was aware of Matt Whitewolf. His muscles flexed as he shifted in the chair and his white T-shirt pulled tautly across his back and shoulders. He was appealing, filled with vitality. He tugged off his boot and set it on the floor. He leaned forward to pull off the other boot and there was something so casual and intimate in the moment—as if he was starting to undress—that her pulse fluttered.

He leaned back in the rocker and his brown eyes met hers. ''Mind if I put my feet on the bed?''

''Of course not! It's your bed. You can do anything you want.''

''Anything?'' he drawled in a teasing, sensual voice, and she was both startled and more fluttery than before. Was he actually flirting with her?

''What did you have in mind?'' The instant the words were out she couldn't believe she had asked him that in return—and worse, in a teasing drawl. ''Never mind!'' she snapped swiftly, blushing. ''I can't believe I said that to you.''

''Why not?'' he asked, amusement lighting his dark eyes. ''You should be able to joke with me, flirt a little. It's harmless.''

''I don't think anything with you will be harmless,'' she said breathlessly, her cheeks turning pink. ''There I go again,'' she said, waving her hand and wondering what it was about him that brought out this carefree, flirty response in her. Something she couldn't recall doing with any man in too many years to remember.

''Don't stop, Vivian. A little flirting is harmless.''

''I suppose.'' She looked at him intently. ''Is there someone—a woman? Am I keeping you from a date tonight or anything?''

''You're keeping me from sitting home alone on a hot, stormy night.''

''You get lonesome? I figured you like it this way.''

''I do like it this way and I do get lonesome sometimes. Most of the time, I'm happy to be out here by myself.''

''I can't imagine. I can't even remember spending a night home alone since I had Mary Catherine.''

Glancing around his room, Vivian gathered from what Meg Preston had said that Matt was a solitary person, never really opening himself up to others. His room was masculine, looking as if it belonged to a man who liked the outdoors and liked animals.

When his dark gaze studied her, she was acutely conscious of him and aware of herself as a woman. This bond she had with him was ridiculous, yet the tie existed and was strong. Was it because he had been with her through childbirth? She didn't want to have such an intense reaction to a man she would say goodbye to tomorrow or the next day, but for the moment, it was nice to be with him and even the brief flirting was fun.

''I almost forgot to tell you—I called the dealership in Enid and they will be out to tow your car in as soon as they can get through.''

''Thank you, but shouldn't you call a mechanic instead of the dealership?''

''This dealership has the best mechanics around here. You can stay here until it's fixed.''

''I don't want to cause you trouble. We're strangers.''

''You're not strangers now,'' he remarked. ''You stay here. I have plenty of room and help and there's no reason for you not to.''

Once again, she collided with his forceful personality. He spoke with a finality that made her certain he didn't expect to be questioned, yet every time he did so, she bristled because of old battles in her past. Each time, she reminded herself how different this man was from the one she had left behind and how caring Matt had been today.

They talked about horses and his farm and wheat harvest, her future plans and anecdotes about Mary Catherine until exhaustion crept over her. Yet she hated to tell Matt. She liked being with him too much.

Julia stirred and began to cry. Matt stood and leaned over the bed to pick her up. "Hey, sweet baby," he said in a gentle, deep voice, and Vivian's heart lurched at the tenderness and the expression on his face that transformed his rugged features when he smiled at her tiny baby.

"She doesn't seem happy," he said, handing the crying baby to Vivian, who pushed away the sheet and swung her long legs over the side of the bed. "I'll check on Mary Catherine," he said, his gaze sweeping over Vivian's legs as she stood up.

"You feel like getting up?" he asked, taking her arm in a gentle grip.

"I want very much to get up," she said, smiling at him.

Something flickered in the depths of his eyes, and Vivian felt that swift change that happened without warning. His dark eyes seemed to wrap an invisible cloak around her and hold her. Julia was crying and Vivian shifted her closer and patted her back. All the while her pulse was racing wildly and she was too aware of the tall cowboy standing so close to her—she could feel the heat from his body and smell the male scent of aftershave and soap.

"Meg Preston came with diapers and Dr. Bently brought me all sorts of supplies."

"Meg's like the Boy Scouts—always prepared. If you want me, holler," Matt said, and picked up his boots to move them across the room. Then he went down the hall. Vivian jiggled Julia slightly and continued patting the baby's back while she stared after Matt. She was going to hate telling him goodbye.

She changed and fed Julia and was rocking her when Matt returned.

He rapped lightly at the door and pushed it open when she called to him.

Matt crossed the room and flipped the covers up over his bed and sat down, leaning against the headboard and crossing his long legs. "Tell me when you want to trade places."

Vivian watched him, feeling a strange heat ignite inside as she looked at his long frame in the bed. Pillows were propped behind him. He looked sexy, handsome, marvelously fit. As she gazed back at him, his brows arched and his eyes darkened, focusing on her with that intentness that made her feel he could see every thought she had.

"Do you have family around here?" Vivian asked. A shuttered look crossed Matt's features and she regretted her question instantly. "Sorry, that's none of my business."

"It's common knowledge around these parts. My mother's deceased. She abused drugs and alcohol. There were always men. My father was an alcoholic, abusive, a real loser. Thank goodness he didn't last long in our lives. Then I had a string of stepfathers—all common-law husbands. The good thing—I have two younger half brothers— I was the oldest child. I ran away when I was sixteen. My half brothers and my Kiowa grandparents are my family."

"Where do your relatives live?" she asked, hearing the bitter note in his voice and wondering what scars he carried from childhood.

"Jared is a rancher and has a place just outside of Tulsa and Wyatt is a cop in Oklahoma City. My grandparents live south of Oklahoma City, down near Lawton."

"I'm surprised you aren't married and have a family of your own just to make up for what you didn't have," she said, studying him. His dark brows arched, and he shrugged.

"Nope. I've never gotten too close to anyone else. I don't think I know how."

She couldn't keep from smiling. "You got pretty close to us today, I'd say."

One dark brow arched higher. "Yeah, Vivian, you sort of slipped past my defenses."

"You keep defenses against the world?" she asked, teasing him.

"Don't we all?" he asked, watching her, and the lightness left her.

"I suppose so," she said, thinking of the hell she went through over a year ago, watching her marriage dissolve and her dreams shatter.

An alarm began to ping and he glanced at his watch, turning off the alarm and swinging his legs off the bed. "Casserole is done. I'll bring your supper—"

"Oh, no! I can come to the kitchen and Julia is asleep. Mary Catherine must be worn out. She doesn't usually sleep like this."

Placing the baby on the bed, Vivian turned and stood carefully, suddenly blinking. Matt looked afraid she might faint and he instantly stepped to her side to steady her. Her head came up, and she became aware of his hand on her hip. Suddenly, he leaned forward and brushed her cheek lightly with a kiss.

"Careful," he cautioned, and inhaled. He turned away.

Vivian touched her cheek lightly where his lips had brushed against her. Matt Whitewolf. He was completely foreign to her world and men she had known. A cowboy. A rugged, solitary individual. Yet he had been salvation to her today. And maybe that was what tinged her feelings about him and made him seem special. Yet by next week he would be nothing more than a memory. How long would that memory linger with her? she wondered.

Vivian picked up a sleeping Julia and left the room to find Mary Catherine still curled into a ball in the next bedroom. She glanced around the room that held a bed, chest and little else and wondered why he lived in such a large house when he was alone. Had he owned the land a long time? The house didn't appear to be an older farmhouse.

She went down the hall toward the kitchen, hearing him clattering dishes and moving around. Through open doors the hall light spilled partially into the rooms that opened off the hallway. One was empty and one had lights on and a bed with a stack of clean clothes tossed on it and she decided this was the room he had moved into. The house was sprawling, half-empty, and far away from the nearest neighbor. She wondered how he stood the isolation. Wasn't there really a woman in his life? She couldn't imagine there wasn't.

When she entered the kitchen, she looked at a hastily set table and the tall cowboy getting something out of a built-in oven. He glanced over his shoulder at her.

"Have a seat. A big glass of milk—right?"

"Yes," she answered, watching him pour large glasses of milk for both of them. Her gaze ran swiftly over his lean frame and she wondered if he often drank so much milk. He had broad, powerful shoulders that tapered to a narrow waist and slim hips, and Vivian assumed he simply burned the calories away.

He placed the steaming casserole on a hot pad between them, and near the golden casserole, he set down a loaf of dark bread that looked home-baked. With a scrape of his chair he sat across from her. "Now, help yourself. Want me to hold the baby?"

"I'm fine with her. I can't believe I'm hungry again. I haven't been able to eat for so long."

"Because of your pregnancy?"

"Because of my disastrous marriage. I hadn't stopped to think about it, but since being here, I feel safe. I don't have to worry about Baker because there is no way he can find me here."

"I thought you said you weren't afraid—"

"I'm not afraid that he'll become violent, but he upsets me and he worries me when he's around Mary Catherine." She served her plate and passed the spoon to him and their fingers brushed. Every contact with him was noticeable. As he served himself, she watched his large, competent hands. Hands that she knew could be both strong and gentle.

"I guess that I'm just relieved. Maybe it's simpler than that. Maybe it's childbirth, but I don't think so. I didn't have this famished feeling after Mary Catherine was born."

"Well, I have a freezer filled with casseroles, so you can just eat all night."

She smiled at him and saw a flicker in his dark eyes. He was raising his fork to his mouth, but lowered it, placing it on his plate while he reached out with his other hand to touch the corner of her mouth lightly. "That's nice. You have a smile that would light up any darkness."

"Thank you," she said, feeling a rush of warmth. "I think you're giving me more credit there than I deserve. We can't test your statement, because we're not in any darkness," she added playfully, wondering what kind of effect the man was having on her to make her bubbly and trusting and lighthearted. Or—again—was it euphoria from childbirth?

"Vivian, there's a darkness here, and you do light it up," he said solemnly, and her heart turned over.

"Darkness—in you? I don't think so." Her appetite was gone as swiftly as it had come, the supper forgotten as she looked into Matt's brown eyes.

"It's there. I know what I live with. I'm keeping you

from eating," he said, his voice becoming lighter. "Eat your dinner. First thing you know Julia will be calling you or Mary Catherine will need you and you won't have a chance to eat."

"You're right," she answered, dropping the topic yet wondering about him. Was it his past that was the dark shadow in his life? When he had talked about his parents, he had sounded defensive and angry, but he lost that tone when he talked about his half brothers. She took a bite of the casserole, tasting tomatoes and corn and beef beneath the layer of golden cheese. "This is delicious."

He glanced over his shoulder and she looked beyond him and saw Mary Catherine coming with her blanket in tow. She looked tousled, sleepy and worried. She glanced at Matt Whitewolf, put her thumb in her mouth and gave him a wide berth as she passed him to go to Vivian.

Vivian wrapped an arm around Mary Catherine, who snuggled against her.

Matt stood and came around the table. "Let me hold Julia so you can eat."

Vivian handed him the baby, feeling his warm hands brush against her. As he moved away, Vivian looked down at Mary Catherine. "Hungry?"

Mary Catherine gave a negative shake of her head, so Vivian continued eating. "You raise anything besides wheat here?"

"Wheat and cattle. Mostly wheat. We've already had harvest this year. It was a good year."

"Have you lived here long?"

"I bought the place about eight years ago and built the house three years ago."

"You built a big house."

"I'm a big man. I wanted room."

"Then you must be planning on a big family," she said

in spite of his earlier denial of being able to have a close relationship with someone.

He looked startled. "No. I won't ever marry."

Surprised, she stared at him. His statement was given in a matter-of-fact voice as if there was no possibility of him doing anything else.

"You don't like women?"

He grinned and she was amazed at the transformation of his features, softening the rugged look with creases deepening in his cheeks and a twinkle coming to his eyes.

"I like women, Vivian," he said in a sensual, warm voice that left no doubt in her mind that he was telling the truth now. At the same time, a tingle stirred in her, that sexy awareness that he could zap to life so easily with her.

"Then what makes you certain you won't ever marry?"

The grin and twinkle vanished. "I'm not the marrying type," he said with a shrug. "I told you about my background. Who would want to load that on someone else?"

"Maybe that's for the someone else to decide. Did you ever think of that?"

"Not much. I know what I grew up with. At best, marriage is fraught with enough uncertainty. You should agree with that."

"Yes, I'll agree."

"I might be rotten at a deep relationship. I've never experienced one."

"You take your chances. Sometimes it works, and sometimes it doesn't."

Mary Catherine stirred and motioned to the plate of food. Vivian picked up a spoon and fed her a bite.

"I can fix her a plate," Matt offered.

Mary Catherine buried her face against Vivian and clung to her as if he had threatened something dire. Vivian stroked her head, looking at him and shrugging. "She can eat from my plate. Thanks."

They ate in silence for a few moments until Vivian took a sip of milk and then set it down, wiping her mouth with her napkin. "I wish you would take your room and let me stay in one of the other ones."

"You're all settled there and I don't have much I need to get. I lead a simple life. Socks, shirts, jeans, boots—I'm set."

"Sure," she said, smiling at him and he smiled in return. "How many bedrooms do you have?"

"Four."

"That's really large for a man who leads a simple life and intends to live all alone forever."

"I guess the house and farm are security to me. What I never had."

She looked beyond him at the darkened windows. "I think you would be lonesome all the time."

She was surprised by another grin. "No, city lady, most of the time I don't get lonesome. I like the peace and quiet and being off by myself."

"You probably can't wait for us to pack and go!"

"Nope. You're not intrusive, and I'll leave before dawn in the morning. There are some wide-open spaces here where a man can easily get all the solitude he wants."

Julia began to stir and cry, and Matt came to his feet to place the baby in her arms. "I'll give you privacy if you want to feed her. Here's your mommy, little one," he said softly. He leaned closer to Vivian. "Don't you touch any dishes. I'm the speediest kitchen cleaner east of the Pecos. I'm going out to feed my horses," he said, crossing the kitchen and grabbing his hat as he went. He closed the door and was gone.

"Yes, sir!" she replied softly, still half-annoyed and half-amused by his authoritative manner. Yet she was becoming more accustomed to it and knew instinctively that he would never order her to do something that would be hurtful.

Vivian wondered about him and the solitary life he led. As she shifted Julia closer, she thought about all he had told her.

"I won't ever marry. At best, marriage is fraught with enough uncertainty."

In spite of his protests, how much were she and the girls disturbing his solitary life? She suspected a great deal. If not tonight, by this time tomorrow they probably would be. She guessed he was still caught up in the miracle of birth that seemed to awe him today.

I like women, Vivian. She recalled his sensual tone when he answered, a tone that was both sexy and amused and she was certain he not only liked women, but women liked *him.*

And if what she had learned about him today was an indication of his character—and it had to be because he had acted in stress without thinking about it—then it was a shame for him to decide he should never marry.

She laughed at herself. *Stop worrying about the man,* she told herself. He got along fine before she had come along and he would get along fine as soon as she was gone. Probably better than now with her disrupting his life.

"Sweetie, I need to hold Julia for a little while and feed her," she said to Mary Catherine.

"I'm hungry."

"Scoot over on that chair." As Mary Catherine moved, Vivian replenished her plate and set it in front of the child. "I'll butter bread for you in a minute."

"I can do it," Mary Catherine said. "Are we going to sleep here?"

"Yes, we are," Vivian answered, glancing at Mary Catherine and wondering if that worried her and if Matt White-wolf frightened her badly. Until the divorce she had grown increasingly frightened of Baker and had withdrawn into a shell around men, and Vivian knew she was scared of Matt.

"We need to stay while I get the car fixed," Vivian said gently, settling the hungry baby in her arms. "Mr. White-wolf is nice."

Mary Catherine didn't answer but ate quietly, and Vivian hurt for her, hoping she outgrew her fears and the shyness that came over her around others.

By the time Matt returned to the house, dark had fallen. Julia was asleep in the big bed with Mary Catherine curled up asleep beside her. When she heard Matt coming down the hall, Vivian was propped up in bed reading a book she had packed to bring along. She closed the book and placed it on the bed as he knocked at the open door.

"Come in. The girls are asleep."

"I don't want to wake them."

"I don't think there is a remote possibility. Mary Catherine is a sound sleeper, and so far Julia seems to be."

"I need to get my things."

"You know how I feel about that."

He crossed the room to the closet and disappeared inside it, stepping out with an armload of clothing that he dumped on a chair.

"This is absurd," she said, swinging her feet out of bed. He crossed the room to her, placing his hands on her shoulders and leaning down. Her heart skipped a beat at his touch and as she looked into his dark eyes, her pulse accelerated.

"Lady, I thought we had this settled. Let me do the moving. I want to. You stay in here."

"Yes, Captain," she said, finally able to let go of her anger at his imperious manner. Amusement flickered in his eyes, and she became aware of how close he stood, of his hands now lightly massaging her shoulders.

"That's better," he said, his voice changing and becoming husky. "I don't know what you do to me," he said softly, and her heart lurched. Matt leaned closer, his gaze drifting down to her mouth. Everything inside her constricted and she held her breath, wondering if he would kiss her.

Chapter 4

"What I do to you?" she repeated, barely able to whisper the words.

He stared at her a long, tension-fraught time with the air crackling between them; she didn't want it to happen, yet she couldn't move, couldn't look away, couldn't breathe.

Suddenly he turned and jammed his hands into his pockets and strode away from her. She climbed back into bed, pulling the sheet over her legs, and watched him open a drawer and begin pulling out T-shirts and shorts and socks. Why did so much that he did in this room seem intimate? He was merely moving clothes, like gathering laundry, yet each shirt, each item seemed special, personal.

She looked down at the sleeping girls and tried to shift her thoughts. She didn't want to be attracted to any man at this time in her life. Not Matt Whitewolf or anyone else. She didn't want sparks to ignite when she looked into his eyes.

Drawers opened and closed. She stroked the baby's head, rubbing her fingertips over the fine, soft hair.

"Vivian."

Matt stood across the room from her, hands on his hips. "I guess I should tell you the schedule. I get up before dawn and fix a little breakfast and then I'm out of here. I'll be out of your way until tomorrow afternoon. I'll have my pager if you need me. I'll have my cell phone in my truck, too, so I'll call Enid and ask the car repairman if he knows yet when he will come to tow your car. When he does, I'll meet him and take care of everything. Is there anything else you want me to get out of the car and bring to the house?"

He was keeping a distance, physically and emotionally. A shuttered look had come over his features, and he remained standing across the room. "I can call Enid and take care of the car," she said, studying the formidable expression on his face. "I'm glad you didn't look that fierce around Mary Catherine."

"Fierce?" he asked, looking puzzled for an instant, and then the shuttered look vanished and there was no mistaking the desire burning in his dark eyes. He crossed the room, his gaze locking with Vivian's, and her mouth went dry and her heart thudded as she watched him approach the bed.

He came around beside her and sat down so close their hips touched, and she wondered if he could hear the pounding of her heart. He reached out and raked his fingers slowly, sensuously through her hair, barely touching her head in a light stroke.

"Lady, if I look fierce, it's because I'm fighting everything in me that's screaming to stay with you, to talk to you, to look at you, to touch you...."

With every word his voice grew softer until it tapered off altogether as his gaze shifted to her mouth. "I'm trying to do the right thing. You're a new mother. That's sacred, yet when I'm close to you what I feel is damned carnal. It's Fourth of July fireworks. We don't want that, do we?''

''No,'' she whispered, her heart thudding wildly from his words that wrapped her in a golden warmth. ''Oh, no, never,'' she breathed, saying one thing and feeling another. Trying to cling to logic and caution, she knew she should turn away, tell him to go and try to resist any further complication in her life. ''We didn't even know each other yesterday.''

''Vivian, we've seen each other in the depths of crisis— you get to know someone faster and better that way than any other way. All that's true in a person comes out.'' He wound locks of her hair around his fingers and gazed steadily into her eyes.

She should move away, look away. Oh, but what would one kiss hurt? She wanted Matt Whitewolf's kiss. The knowledge that she could want a man's kiss so soon after childbirth shocked her. Why did she suspect even one kiss with him might be earth-shattering?

Baby Julia stirred and began to make mewling sounds, her fists waving in the air.

Matt stood and took a step back. ''You're wanted by someone else,'' he said quietly. ''I'll take my things and go.''

As she watched him walk away from her, Vivian's heart still thudded. She picked up the baby, holding her close and standing while Matt gathered his things in his arms and left the room, closing the door behind him.

You're wanted by someone else. Had he meant that the way it sounded? Someone else. Had he meant *himself?* Why did one look from him set her pulse fluttering crazily? She worked with men constantly and had never had this kind of reaction to one since back to the days she dated Baker.

There had been men who flirted, particularly after they

knew she was getting divorced. Since the divorce there had been a couple of men who had called for dates, and it had been so easy to say no. At no time, not with any of them, did her pulse race. Why now? Of all the unlikely people on earth, this rough cowboy whose world might as well be a planet away from hers, they were so different. Yet with a look he could turn her to quivering jelly. What was happening to her?

As Julia's cries grew louder, Vivian looked down at her baby, shifting her to cradle her in her arms. Love and joy overwhelmed her. What a day they'd had! Now after all the months of waiting, she had Julia.

Vivian held the tiny baby close and stroked her head and kissed her. That first moment of birth, Matt had been as jubilant as she. She smiled and jiggled Julia, who had stopped crying and was smacking her lips.

"You're the sweetest baby," Vivian said softly, moving to the rocking chair to hold Julia close to let her nurse. The wonder and joy of the new baby was exciting. She had to admit, the cowboy who had delivered her was also exciting. She rocked and looked around his room again, wondering about the tall, tough cowboy who could be so tender yet led such a solitary life.

It's the Fourth of July fireworks. He felt that around her? She experienced more than sparks around him, she had to admit. *Neither of us wants it.* Maybe she did a little. She shouldn't and they would part ways soon, but she liked some of the feelings he stirred. The fiery attraction was amazing, and after all she had been through the past two years—divorce, upheaval, pregnancy—it was nice to know she could be attractive. It wasn't going to go any further than that. No dates, no kisses, no relationship, only goodbye as soon as her car was fixed.

Vivian rocked and thought about him, images of him dancing in her mind. Then her thoughts shifted to the baby and she tightened her arms around Julia, saying a prayer of thanks to have her baby safely in her arms.

"My precious baby," she whispered, thankful the baby was here and glad Matt had found them.

The next day Vivian spent most of the day resting and taking care of the girls. Once Matt called from his cellular phone and she answered.

"Whitewolf residence."

"Vivian, it's Matt," he said in a deep voice. "Did I wake you?"

"Not really. I've napped and I was just lying here."

"Sorry to disturb you," he said.

"You didn't. It's nice to talk to someone over four years old."

He chuckled. "Good. I called the car repairman and he's backed up with cars because of the storm. It'll be tomorrow before he can get out to tow your car."

"That's fine, except you'll have houseguests longer. I really can go to a hotel."

"Forget it. The little towns around here don't have hotels and Enid is a distance away. I'll talk to him tomorrow. How's everything?"

"Fine," she said.

"How's Julia?"

"Just great. She's sleeping. Mary Catherine is coloring and I'm resting."

"Good. I've got cows lost, fences down, fields flooded."

She settled in the chair and wondered exactly where he was, enjoying the sound of his voice. They continued talking for a few more minutes until Julia stirred.

"Matt, Julia's crying. I need to get her."

"Yeah. I better get back to work, but this is more fun. See you tonight."

That night Matt called and said he had to keep working

because one of the men's trucks was stuck and he was helping to get it out.

Vivian and Mary Catherine ate early, and Vivian went to bed when Mary Catherine did, without seeing Matt that night.

The next morning Vivian was up before dawn with Julia. She fed and changed her and then pulled on her robe to go to the kitchen. When she opened the bedroom door, lights were on in the hall and she could see light spilling from the kitchen. Just the thought of seeing Matt again made her heart beat more swiftly. She had a mixture of trepidation and eagerness, because she was swiftly piecing together facts about him and believed that she and her girls were a major intrusion in his life.

When she entered the kitchen, he was leaning against the counter drinking a cup of coffee. Dressed in jeans and a blue chambray shirt with the sleeves cut off, he looked alert. His gaze swept over her impassively and he nodded. "'Morning."

"Good morning. Julia got me up. I hope she didn't wake you in the night."

He shook his head. "Takes more than a baby. Sorry I didn't get back yesterday afternoon. It was catch-up day. This afternoon I'll try to go get things out of your car if you'll tell me what you want."

"Sure. I'll make a list, but we're doing fine and there's no rush if you have work to do. I feel we're really imposing on you."

"Nope. If I didn't want you here, I'd send you somewhere else," Matt said as he opened a drawer, retrieved pen and paper and handed it to her, his fingers brushing hers. She both disturbed and fascinated him and he watched her move across the room and pull out a chair, sitting down gracefully.

"I don't believe you'd send us away," she said, smiling.

She sat at the table and her head bent over the list as she began to write. The silky curtain of brown hair fell forward, partially hiding her face, and he remembered its softness sliding through his fingers.

"Want some orange juice, milk?"

"Yes, please, on both. Do you mind getting my computer and do you mind if I hook it up here? That way I can keep in touch with my clients?"

"Do whatever you want. *Mi casa es su casa.*"

"*Mil gracias,*" she answered, and he grinned.

He placed orange juice and a large glass of milk in front of her and stood facing her across the table. "How about toast? Eggs? I'll scramble eggs or poach them if you'd like or I'll fix oatmeal. I'm listing my specialties."

"I can get my own breakfast," she said.

"I'm getting mine, I might as well get yours at the same time. What'll it be?"

"Oatmeal," she answered.

"I'll take everything outside and we can watch the sunrise while we eat. I have an intercom. I'll turn it up so you can hear the girls."

"Fine. Julia just went back to sleep and Mary Catherine won't be up for another couple of hours, so we're not likely to hear from them."

In minutes they were seated outside. As he sipped a cup of steaming black coffee, Matt gazed over his land toward the eastern horizon that was turning silver with the coming of early morning. A faint cool breeze blew across the porch, and he settled back in his chair, too aware of Vivian, yet enjoying the morning and her presence. She sat quietly sipping her juice, and he was glad they could share the moment and glad she enjoyed it in silence just as he did.

A mockingbird's melodic song was the only sound—there was a quiet to the place that Matt always liked. He sipped the coffee and when he glanced at Vivian, her profile was to him, her face raised as she looked across his farmland. She turned to look at him and he gazed into eyes bluer than the morning skies and wondered again if he would ever forget her.

"It's beautiful."

"Very beautiful," he said, thinking about her.

Something flickered in the depths of her eyes, and they were caught in another moment when tension jumped between them and the world faded to oblivion. What was it they did to each other? Neither wanted this electricity sparking between them when they were together, yet there it was, making him intensely aware of her. She held his gaze, giving him a steady look that heated him. She had a frank way of looking at him, a frank way of answering him that he liked.

"Where are you from, Vivian?" he asked casually, yet his voice had dropped a notch.

"I was born in Los Angeles. We lived in L.A. and then in Chicago and then in Denver."

"City lady. You probably hate the quiet here."

"Don't prejudge me. It's a beautiful morning here, and I like the quiet. It's a change that's new to me. At the moment I find it nice."

"Do you have brothers or sisters?"

"No. No family left. Are your half brothers married?"

"Yes."

"So, they're not as concerned about their background as you are," she said with a faint smile.

"Jared sort of rushed into marriage. When his friend was killed, he had to adopt his best friend's baby. He needed a mother for the baby and he got one quickly."

"You make it sound like a business arrangement."

"Nope, but he didn't waste any time. They're happily married and expecting another baby, as a matter of fact."

"So that family background that worries you so much

hasn't hurt him or his marriage—right? Maybe you should rethink your future.''

"Nope. I know what I should do. What are you going to do in Houston?''

"Start over.''

"You think you'll be safe?''

"Yes. Baker is an egomaniac, not a criminal. He yells and when he wouldn't stop yelling at Mary Catherine, I knew I had to end the relationship. I don't think he would ever resort to violence. I can't imagine Baker causing me trouble.''

From what little he knew, Matt thought the man had caused her enough trouble for a lifetime already. He stood. "I better get going. There are horses waiting, and I need to see what damage the rain did. This afternoon I'll take you with me to get the things from your car if you want.''

"I'd like that if the girls are awake. It'll be easier if I go along.''

Matt picked up their empty dishes, carrying them to the kitchen. Vivian sat back, enjoying seeing the eastern sky grow pink with rays that promised a glorious day. She inhaled the fresh, rain-washed air, looking across the green land that ran endlessly to the horizon.

Shortly Matt reappeared, a red bandanna tied around his forehead. He paused at the table and placed a piece of paper in front of her with a number written on it. "That's my pager number. If you need me for any reason, page me. Here are the keys to one of the trucks. I called and the bridge is gone over Rabbit Creek, so page me if you have any kind of emergency. I can get right back to the house.''

"I'm sure we'll be fine,'' she said, standing and pushing in her chair. She picked up the paper and put it in the pocket of her robe.

"Make a grocery list and I'll go get what we need this afternoon.''

"How can you if the bridge is out?"

"I can go to a little town that's west of here. Meanwhile, there's some food in the freezer. Cook what you want for lunch."

"Yes, Captain," she said softly, and he realized he was once again giving orders.

He shook his head. "It comes with the territory. I'm used to running this place."

"And not answering to anyone," she said with a mischievous twinkle in her blue eyes that made him want to wrap his arms around her and try to capture some of that playfulness.

"Vivian, that is so like a woman. Let a woman in your life, and she'll promptly try to change it."

"Only for the better," she said, and this time there was no mistaking the twinkle.

"Well, that's from her standpoint. My life suits me to a T just the way it is, which is why you're the first woman to ever stay all night under this roof."

To his amazement, she laughed out loud, a merry, tinkling laugh that warmed him even though it also half annoyed him because he would have expected any reaction except laughter.

"So a baby's arrival forced you to let a female—three females—into your sacrosanct male domain."

"That's right. Old habits are impossible to break."

"So, cowboy, you think a woman can't change you?" she asked in an exaggerated, sultry drawl that flung a challenge at him.

"Maybe it would be fun to let one try," he rejoined. "What did you have in mind, Vivian?"

"I'll work on it, crusty bachelor, set in your ways," she said teasingly, slanting him another mischievous look. "Go on out to your horses. I'll manage fine here. See, I'm accustomed to giving orders, too."

"That's why mine annoy you," he said quietly, jamming his hands into his pockets to keep from reaching for her. She was flirting, lightly, casually, but the effect on him wasn't casual.

He turned, strode off the porch and crossed the yard in long strides. At the gate he glanced back over his shoulder. She stood watching him and he wondered what ran through her mind. The wind whipped against her, making the blue robe and gown cling to her slender figure, and mentally he whisked them away, remembering her long, shapely legs. Strands of her brown hair blew in the wind and he waved and felt idiotic for doing so.

She waved in return. He let out his breath. "Get a grip, Whitewolf," he told himself, amazed that he had enjoyed having breakfast with her this morning. Never once had he wanted to bring any woman he dated home, and the thought of having anyone else around constantly never appealed to him, but he had been with Vivian almost three days now and had enjoyed sharing the early hour of the morning with her. The flirting had him aroused, wanting to get chores finished and get back to the house to be with her.

He headed toward the garage and one of the pickups. In minutes he was driving across his land, but his thoughts were still back at the house on Vivian, her laughter, her blue eyes, her soft voice. He had to grin when he remembered how she had laughed because there had never been a woman who had stayed at his house before.

As he was checking on a fence along the west boundary, Pete Quincy drove up and climbed out of a truck. Matt glanced over his shoulder at his foreman, who was wiry with skin as dark as Matt's. He was shorter than Matt and had a thick mass of black curls that capped his head. He strode toward Matt in a rolling gait. Despite his size, Pete was one of the strongest men Matt knew and he had never seen Pete back down from a fight. For an instant he thought about Vivian and Mary Catherine and he dreaded telling Pete about them.

"Hey, boss, I got the strays that were lost in the storm rounded up. That thunder spooked them, and they were scattered to hell and gone this morning, but I think we've found all of them."

"Good. We can't afford to lose any."

"Hear you delivered a baby the other day."

"How in hell did you hear that?" Matt asked, always amazed that word got around the county like lightning streaking across the sky. He wiped sweat out of his eyes and stood, rolling up baling wire and jamming wire pliers into his hip pocket.

"Saw Meg Preston whipping up the road. She stuck her head out the car window and yelled that you were delivering a baby and why wasn't I up there helping?"

"I figured you were busy."

"I was. I delivered a calf. How'd it go?"

"Baby's fine." Matt shook his head. "The mother ran off the road—"

"Green sports utility vehicle? I saw it this morning."

"Right." Matt wondered if he might as well stop talking. Pete seemed to already know all there was to know about the situation. "She has a little girl, Pete," Matt said carefully, knowing Pete had never gotten over losing his wife and little girl in a car crash. "The water was up too high at Rabbit Creek to get into town so I brought them home with me, and we hadn't been there any time before the baby came. I'll tell you, I was damned glad to see Meg Preston."

"How old is the little girl?"

"Four," Matt said, knowing it was the age Pete's child would have been. "She's afraid of men. The father wasn't good to them."

Pete shook his head. "I'll never understand life."

"Yeah, well, I hope I don't have to deliver any more babies."

"Boy or girl?"

"Girl—Julia Ashland."

"Good for you, boss! Deliverin' all those calves taught you a thing or two."

"It's not quite the same."

Pete grinned as he turned and strode back to his truck.

At half past two Matt stopped work and returned home to see about Vivian's car and go into town to get groceries. As he drove across a field, he had to admit he wanted to see Vivian. He even wanted to see the baby again and Mary Catherine. Before he took them anywhere, he needed to shower. He was hot, mud-spattered and sweaty. As he climbed out of the pickup, he grabbed his balled-up shirt and went around the garage toward the house.

He swiped the shirt across his brow and pulled off his bandanna to wipe sweat from his neck and forehead. The sound of laughter startled him and as he watched, Vivian got up from the grass and picked up the baby. Mary Catherine was turning somersaults across his lawn and laughing along with her mother. Matt slowed to watch them, realizing they hadn't seen him yet.

Vivian was dressed in a bright red skirt and blouse, her long hair tied behind her head with a red ribbon. He drew a deep breath because she looked beautiful and she filled the yard with sound and laughter and color, and he quickened his step, wanting to be with her.

She glanced up and met his gaze, and even yards away, just mere eye contact with her delivered an impact. His stomach constricted and his pulse jumped. She watched him approach, and he became aware of his disheveled state. He brushed dust off his jeans, but there was no brushing mud off and he was damp with sweat.

Still watching Vivian, he walked through the gate. "Hi," he said, glancing at Mary Catherine, who had become solemn, and as soon as he looked at her, she moved close to Vivian and held to her skirt.

"Hi, Mary Catherine," he said softly, and smiled at her and then looked at Julia. "How's little Julia?"

"She's fine," Vivian said, looking at Matt. She couldn't resist letting her gaze sweep over his bare chest once again. He was thick through the shoulders and all muscle with taut brown skin that had a faint sheen of sweat. There was an earthiness to him, his large-knuckled hands had streaks of mud and he looked like a man who often did hard physical labor.

"They're both awake, so do you want to go with me to get the things from your car?"

"I'd like to," she answered.

"I'll shower first," he said, and she nodded. He moved closer to look at Julia, who was gazing around, her little hands locked together. Vivian was aware of how close Matt stood. She could smell the sweat and dirt and feel the heat from him, yet he still was appealing. Too much so because she was intensely aware of his physical presence. She liked the idea of a man who worked his land; working with his hands seemed direct and honest. Maybe it was a reaction to Baker, who had hired everything done that required physical effort or maintenance.

"Hi, little baby," Matt said softly. Julia gazed around and blew bubbles, and he smiled, looking up at Vivian. "She's beautiful," he said in a deep voice, a silky tone that sent a sizzle of warmth curling in her.

"I think so, too," she said, gazing directly into his eyes. As they looked at each other a long moment, she knew that Matt Whitewolf was attracted to her. It showed in his dark eyes, and she felt it deep down inside each time she was around him.

"I won't be long," he said without moving.

She nodded, yet she couldn't look away. His dark eyes seemed to hold her, desire and curiosity both showing in their depths.

Then he moved away and strode toward the house, and

she couldn't resist turning to watch him. He had a long, purposeful stride that she was beginning to know. Muscles rippled in his back. Her gaze ran across his broad, strong shoulders and down to his narrow waist and trim backside. His jeans rode low on his hips.

"Are we going with him, Mommy?" Mary Catherine asked with a frown.

"He'll take us to the car and you can get some more of your things. He's nice, Mary Catherine. Very nice," she added softly, looking back at the house.

"I'm glad he doesn't yell," Mary Catherine said.

"No, he doesn't yell and that's very nice," Vivian answered. She went inside to change Julia and she saw the door closed to the bedroom he was using.

She changed Julia and then brushed and retied her own hair, looking at her reflection in the mirror and running her hand over her stomach, which bulged slightly but seemed so flat after the past months.

She splashed on a dash of cologne and turned to brush Mary Catherine's hair, humming as she worked. Mary Catherine studied her.

"Are you happy, Mommy?"

"Yes, I'm happy," Vivian said, and realized she was happier than she had been in a long time. A lot of happiness was due to Julia, but she knew that wasn't the only cause of her joy.

"You like staying here, don't you?" Mary Catherine asked.

"Yes, I do," she answered forthrightly, and turned to brush the other side of Marty Catherine's hair as Matt knocked at the open door.

Startled, she looked up and blushed, embarrassed that he might have overheard what she just said to Mary Catherine.

Chapter 5

"I need a different pair of boots. Preferably ones not caked with mud."

She waved her hand. "Come in. It's your room. I still think you should move back into it."

His gaze ran around the room and he shook his head. "Nope." Matt glanced again at the clothes and toys strewn around the room. A sheer nightie was tossed on the bed and the blue robe was lying across it. His gaze lingered an extra second on the nightie as he imagined Vivian in it, and then he realized what he was doing and hastily looked elsewhere.

He crossed the room to the closet, thinking how the entire house had changed. The kitchen and family room had toys and Mary Catherine's little shoes and crayons. How they had gotten so much stuff out of such small bags, he couldn't imagine, but his house had changed. It even smelled different, with the scent of roses and talcum discernible when he stepped into the hall. And now there were scents of food in the kitchen that he hadn't noticed before.

A few minutes ago while shaving in the bathroom, he had heard them come in from the backyard. Mary Catherine's high-pitched voice carried and when she wasn't around strangers, or around him, she sounded carefree and animated, chattering happily to her mother.

He had heard Vivian's soft, low voice in answer, unable to distinguish all her words, yet hearing her talk and finding himself listening intently.

Why was she so damned appealing? He wondered as he now looked through the closet for his boots. There were good-looking women in Dakani and they were ready, willing and able to date. Vivian was not. Nor would she be living within five hundred miles of him before long.

Whatever he was feeling, she was feeling it, too. It was just as unwanted with her as it was with him. Far more so. He could see that she had no place in her life for him. She was a city girl, educated, successful in her own business. No matter what else, their backgrounds were a chasm between them that was unbridgeable. He was a plain country boy, a high school dropout.

He found his black boots and then sat on the chair to pull them on.

"This is taking you away from your work," Vivian said.

"It's a welcome diversion. I called a mechanic to meet us and tow your car. I'm guessing your radiator is smashed, and usually a radiator is a major repair."

"I was driving under the speed limit," Vivian said, watching him. "I'm amazed it did that much damage."

"The ground was wet. You probably slid. You may have stepped on the gas pedal without realizing it." Matt tugged on a boot, his biceps flexing as he pulled.

Mary Catherine watched him intently, and Vivian knew her daughter was afraid of him, yet making her own judgments about him. He was very good with her, too, Vivian realized, always speaking in a quiet, gentle voice, never coming on strong or giving her attention she didn't want. Right now, she suspected he was fully aware of Mary Catherine's study, yet he ignored her.

Grateful to him, Vivian experienced little mental warnings to stop finding him attractive in so many ways. She turned and picked up Julia, who had fallen asleep. "Ready, Mary Catherine?" she asked as she buckled Julia into a baby carrier.

Matt jammed his foot into his other boot, stood up and shook his leg to shake down his jeans and then joined them as they went down the hall to the back door. He locked up, and as they walked to the gate, Pete drove up in his pickup and got out to hand Matt a list.

"Here are things we need if you're going into town."

"Vivian, this is Pete Quincy, my foreman. Pete, this is Mrs. Ashland, her daughter Mary Catherine and her new baby Julia."

They exchanged greetings and Vivian noticed the lingering look he gave Mary Catherine. He stepped forward to look at Julia.

"Let's see this baby the boss delivered."

Vivian smiled at the pleased look that crossed Matt's features for a moment while Pete looked at the baby.

"She's a fine one," he said with a thick voice and a tone that made Vivian wonder what was running through his mind. He stepped back. "Thanks. Nice to meet you," he said abruptly over his shoulder as he climbed back in his truck and swept in a circle, heading back toward the barn.

"Tell you later," Matt said, and she was startled, surprised he realized she had questions in her mind. "I'll get my pickup and come get you."

He jogged toward the garage and she watched him, wondering about Pete Quincy, wondering about Matt, who kept his feelings well hidden most of the time she had been with him. They had known each other not quite forty-eight hours now, yet it seemed a lifetime.

His dark hair flew back as he ran. How much was she turning his life topsy-turvy?

Soon his black pickup swept around the garage and headed toward them.

"Do we get to ride in his truck?" Mary Catherine asked.

"Yes. Would you like that?"

"Yes. Can I ride in the back sometime?"

"Not unless it's from here to the garage. It's not safe out on the highway."

"Can I get in the back later?"

"I'm sure Matt will let you climb into the back. We'll ask when we come home."

"You ask," she said timidly.

Matt pulled up in front of them and stepped out of the pickup.

Vivian lifted the baby carrier into the back seat and started to buckle it in. Matt took her arm gently. "Here, I'll do it."

Amused, she straightened up. "If you want."

He gazed at her, his fingers still holding her arm. They stood close and she could smell his aftershave and saw that he had shaved when he showered.

"Independent lady. You'll have to get used to my ways."

She arched her eyebrow as she looked at him. "You think so? I didn't figure I'd be around long enough."

"We're going to be together, Vivian. It may take a while for them to repair your car."

The conversation was about the car, but beneath it, she had the feeling that he wanted her to stay and it made her pulse race. Her gaze drifted down to his mouth. His lips were chapped; his lower lip was full and she couldn't keep from wondering what it would be like to kiss him.

Startled by her line of thought, she glanced up and saw fires in the depths of his brown eyes, as if he had been able to guess what she had been thinking.

She turned abruptly. "Mary Catherine, are you buckled up?"

"Yes, ma'am."

He strode around the pickup with her. Without thinking she reached for the door the same time he did. His hand splayed out and held it shut and he turned to her, boxing her in.

"I'm accustomed to doing everything for myself," she said, too aware of how close he stood, liking it too much.

"Vivian, I'm an old-fashioned country boy. I open doors for ladies, quaint country custom as it is, so get used to it, lady, because as long as you're here—"

"—you won't be able to change," she concluded with amusement. Something flickered in the depths of his eyes that took all her amusement away, and her heart thudded as his gaze lowered to her mouth. *He was going to kiss her.* The moment became electric, and all her nerves tingled.

Jamming his thumbs into his belt, he stepped aside and opened the door to hold it for her.

With a flicker of disappointment she climbed inside. Tucking her skirt around her bare legs, she caught him looking at her legs. He glanced up. "Pretty shoes."

"Thank you," she said, suspecting he hadn't looked at her shoes at all.

He closed the door and came around to climb inside and glanced back at Mary Catherine.

"All set, Mary Catherine?"

Vivian saw her nod. He started the car and they drove up the road and she remembered the day before yesterday and how terrified she had been of what was happening. She looked back at Julia, who was blissfully sleeping, and gave a prayer of thanks for a healthy baby and for Matt who had come to their rescue.

"You were Sir Galahad to the rescue the other day."

"It worked out. You have a beautiful baby." They rode in silence a few minutes while she looked at the green fields that ran to golden stubble where his wheat had grown. They passed a green meadow with cattle standing around a muddy pond, the water a deep rust color. Hoof prints made indentions along the muddy banks and she wondered about Matt's life, which was so different from her own. He took care of these animals. The land and the life on it had to be at times primitive and basic. And dangerous, because she knew he had to battle the elements constantly.

In the distance to the west she saw cattle grazing in another field of green. Heat waves rose ahead of them, but Matt had turned on the air-conditioning and the pickup was cool and comfortable.

"The mechanic should be there shortly after we get there."

"Do you mind if I set up my computer at your house?"

"No. I'll set up a table and a place for you to work. Maybe when Lita is there she can watch the girls and you can work."

"I don't want to take her away from what you want her to do. I can pay her if she could come on the three days you don't have her."

"Ask her. She'd probably jump at the chance to make some more money."

"What was it back there with your foreman? He looked at us like we were long-lost relatives—actually, he looked at the girls that way, not at me. Did I imagine things?" she asked quietly, hearing Mary Catherine chattering happily to her stuffed bear.

"No, you didn't. He lost his wife and little girl two years

ago in a car crash. Danielle, his little girl, would have been four this year.''

''That's dreadful. No wonder he looked at Mary Catherine the way he did. Does he know she's four?''

''Yes. Everybody knows everything around here. You might as well start getting used to that.''

In minutes Matt slowed and parked on the edge of the road near her stranded sports utility vehicle. Mary Catherine unbuckled her seat belt and scrambled out of the pickup while Vivian got the baby carrier, then they all went to her car. She opened the door, set the baby carrier on the ground beside her and reached inside her car for a box.

Matt gripped her wrist. ''Lady, you direct. I move this stuff. You just sit down somewhere and tell me what to do.''

She straightened up and looked up at him. ''I should have known.''

''Yep, you should have. You're not lifting anything.''

''Look, I lift Julia all day and Mary Catherine occasionally. I really feel good.''

''Maybe so, but you're not moving anything. Mary Catherine can help with the light stuff if she wants to.''

Mary Catherine listened to this exchange, and Vivian wondered if she thought Matt was being mean to her mommy. She smiled and nodded. ''Have it your way again.'' She looked inside her car. ''There's my computer and I want the black suitcases, that large white cardboard box. Mary Catherine can bring her toy box and one box of books.''

''If you want to sit in the pickup and watch, I can turn the air-conditioning on for you. Then both you and Julia will be cool.''

''There's a breeze and it's shady here beneath this tree. She's fine and I'm fine. If I get too hot, I'll go back to the pickup, but this way I can tell you exactly what I want.''

With the door open and the baby carrier beside her feet, Vivian sat on the edge of the front seat of her car and watched Matt and Mary Catherine work. Matt lifted Mary Catherine into the bed of the pickup, directing her where to place the boxes and luggage that he carried over to her.

In minutes she was happily working with him, and Vivian thought it was the first time she had seen her daughter relaxed around any man, conversing with him and seemingly indifferent that she was near an adult male. While he didn't know it, he couldn't have done anything better to win Mary Catherine's acceptance than to let her up into the back of his pickup and let her help him load it with their boxes and bags. Vivian knew how much Mary Catherine loved to help someone and she knew Mary Catherine was fascinated by the pickup.

Vivian continued to direct what to take. "There's a portable crib. I'll set it up for Julia if you'll get it," she said, pointing at the collapsed crib made of canvas and net with folded plastic legs. Matt carried it easily to the pickup and lifted it into the back, helping Mary Catherine place it against a stack of boxes. Muscles rippled beneath his tight T-shirt as he moved boxes and Vivian openly watched him while his back was turned to her.

The dealer from Enid arrived and shook hands with Matt, who made arrangements to get her car towed in and to call back and give him the estimate on repairs. Matt Whitewolf was a take-charge male, more so in some ways even than her ex-husband, yet so different. Every time Baker had tried to take control, it had been to see that things went his way. Each time Matt did, it was to help her, and she could appreciate the difference and really didn't mind except it took some getting used to. Mary Catherine was playing in the pickup and seemed as happy as could be.

The two men turned and headed toward her and Matt

introduced Jake Claiborne, the tall, brown-haired man who would repair her car.

"We'll call with the estimate," he said. "I have Matt's number."

"Thanks," she said, standing and reaching for the carrier. Matt picked it up instead.

"How about sitting in an air-conditioned pickup now?" he asked.

"Fine," she replied.

"Have we gotten everything you want out of the car?" Matt asked.

She glanced at the boxes and suitcases in Matt's pickup. "I think we have more than enough," she said, thinking she had enough to stay with him for a month instead of the next few days.

She moved to the pickup and watched while he stood near her car as Jake Claiborne began to get ready to tow it. Mary Catherine waited in the pickup with her, watching intently. "Can I go stand with Mr. Whitewolf and watch?"

"Yes, you may, I'm sure. Let me ask him." She opened the window. "Matt, Mary Catherine wants to come watch with you."

Turning toward her, he motioned to her to come join him. She was out of the pickup instantly and closed the door behind her. She ran over to stand beside him and he reached down to take her hand.

Surprised that Mary Catherine would let him hold her hand, Vivian looked at the two of them and knew that Mary Catherine was completely enthralled with watching their car get hitched to the tow truck and one end rise off the ground. Her fascination outweighed her fear and shyness.

Finally it was done and Matt and Mary Catherine returned to the pickup as Jake Claiborne drove back up to the road, leaving deep ruts in the soft, wet ground and tracking clumps of thick red clay along the highway.

"I'm amazed he could drive out of here. The ground is so muddy," Vivian said as Mary Catherine and Matt buckled into their seats.

"He has four-wheel drive and there are some rocks along here. Otherwise he couldn't have gotten out." Matt started the pickup and glanced at her. "Are you tired? Want me to take you back home? I can get the groceries."

"I'm fine and I'd like to go into town."

He grinned. "I'll bet you would. You'd like to go into Dallas, probably. Don't get your hopes up. Atwater just has one big store."

"That's fine. I'm enjoying all this," she said, waving her hand. "It's peaceful."

Matt's grin and the wry glance he gave her indicated he thought otherwise, and she knew one of the big reasons she was enjoying the country was the man seated beside her only a few feet away.

Playing one of Mary Catherine's guessing games, they drove to Atwater, a small town with wide streets, tall leafy trees and sturdy frame houses. The main street consisted of three blocks and Matt pulled into a parking spot in front of the grocery store.

Vivian had a list of things to buy and Matt had a list, so they each took a grocery cart. She was astounded when he asked Mary Catherine if she wanted to ride in his grocery cart and help him pick out what she liked to eat and Mary Catherine nodded yes.

"Good. You can change to Mommy's cart whenever you want and we'll be real close to your mommy." He lifted Mary Catherine into the cart and winked at Vivian as he turned away.

Vivian stared in shock, completely amazed that he had won over Mary Catherine so swiftly. "It runs in the family," she said softly under her breath, thinking both she and Mary Catherine were becoming captivated by him. She

knew it had been his quiet manner that had worn down
Mary Catherine's fears and then letting her help him load
their belongings into his pickup.

"Now, what do you like to eat, Mary Catherine?" he
asked as they moved away.

"Peanut butter and macaroni and carrots," she answered,
and Vivian wondered what he would come back with and
how much she should take off her list. She knew if Mary
Catherine lost her shyness around him, she would be her
usual self and that meant she would ask for anything along
the aisles that caught her fancy whether she really wanted
to eat it or not. Yet Vivian wasn't going to tell him to
ignore Mary Catherine's requests. He wouldn't ignore
them, and Vivian was deeply thankful to see Mary Catherine lose her fear of him. The past year she had become
more and more fearful of men because of Baker. Vivian
couldn't think of one time Mary Catherine's father had ever
taken her to the grocery store.

She watched the tall cowboy pushing her daughter down
an aisle, and before they had gone two feet, he stopped and
began gathering boxes off the shelves while Mary Catherine pointed and instructed. Vivian could imagine what his
grocery cart would soon look like. He looked up the aisle
at Vivian, said something to Mary Catherine and turned the
cart so she could see Vivian. They both waved and Vivian
waved back and had to smile.

As she shopped, she was aware of constantly passing an
aisle and looking down it to see Matt and Mary Catherine.
If Mary Catherine spotted her, she waved and she seemed
to be enjoying herself. As Vivian had expected, each time
she saw them Matt's basket was piled higher with groceries.
Vivian hoped they weren't exclusively things that Mary
Catherine wanted.

Soon she noticed every time she spotted Matt, someone

was talking to him. It was always a customer and each time a different one, and most of the time, a female.

When he finally joined her, she looked at his basket, bulging with goods. "Maybe I should get final approval of what Mary Catherine selected."

"Naw, we'll eat it all sooner or later."

"I don't think you can eat all those groceries this year," she remarked dryly, picking up a box of marshmallow-filled cakes that Mary Catherine considered a very special treat.

Matt took the box from Vivian's hands and placed it back in his cart. "There are four men on the place. We'll eat everything."

She leaned over and carefully withdrew a coloring book, a puzzle and a kaleidoscope and looked at Mary Catherine. "Mary Catherine, you have coloring books and your box of toys."

Matt took the things out of Vivian's hands and placed them back in his basket. "She didn't ask for those. I got them for her," he said, with that tone of voice that meant the subject was closed.

Vivian shook her head. "Whatever you want." They began to move toward the checkout. "You know a lot of people here."

His brows arched. "They're here to check you out. Everyone knows everyone, but you're the newcomer and they're curious about you."

"It isn't me they're talking to," she replied with amusement.

"They're looking."

They pushed the carts to the checkout and stopped in line.

"Hey, Matt," said a tall blonde, standing in the next line. Dressed in tight jeans and an even tighter blue T-shirt, she left her grocery cart and came over, moving close to Vivian to look at Julia. "Let me see this little baby that Matt brought into the world. What a sweet baby!"

"Vivian, this is Kitty Brogan," Matt said. "Kitty, meet Vivian Ashland and Julia. You met Mary Catherine a few minutes ago."

Vivian had to bite back a smile at the note of impatience in his voice. The crusty cowboy was back. Kitty leaned forward to look at the baby. "She's beautiful." Her gaze met Vivian's and she laughed. "I would have thought he'd have gotten you to the hospital if he'd had to pick up his truck and carry it across Rabbit Creek himself."

Vivian smiled. "He didn't have much choice in the matter, but he did a fine job as you can see."

"Sure did. And you're staying out at his place! My, oh, my."

The person ahead of Vivian finished and she pushed her cart toward the register. "It was nice to have met you, Kitty," she said.

"Real nice to meet you, too." Kitty placed her hand casually on Matt's arm. "Now, you take her over to the café so everyone can see this precious baby, Matt."

"Sure, Kitty. See you."

"Vivian, don't let him leave town without getting one of Betty's malts."

Vivian merely smiled and nodded.

Kitty laughed and sauntered back to her basket, moving to a clerk who no longer had any customers at his register.

"There isn't some woman in your life I'm interfering with, is there?" Vivian asked as Matt moved his cart close behind hers.

"Nope, there sure isn't," he answered firmly.

They paid for the groceries and Matt asked the clerk to hold them until they could run other errands.

"Sure, Matt," the tall black-haired clerk said, smiling at him. "They'll be right by the door."

"They'll keep the groceries in here and in the freezer while we shop?" she asked with amazement.

"Yep. That's one advantage of a little town." Taking the carrier and Julia from her hands, he turned to her. "I have some things to get at the hardware store and the auto shop." He followed Vivian and Mary Catherine through the door and paused on the walk in front of his pickup.

"Sure you're not getting tired?" he asked.

"I'm sure. I had a nap this morning and one right after lunch. It's nice to get out," she said, gazing up at him, aware of the hot sun and cars passing in the street, but far more aware of Matt.

He took her arm. "Come on. I'll go with you to the café and I'll leave you there while I run my errands."

They entered the high-ceilinged narrow room that had a crowd for the middle of a weekday afternoon. Kitty waved a greeting while Matt led Vivian around the room to introduce her, and Vivian decided Matt hadn't been exaggerating when he said everyone knew everyone else. There was no one in the room he didn't know, and finally Vivian ended up at the fountain with the baby carrier on it while Kitty got crayons and paper for Mary Catherine and people gathered around to look at Julia, who was sleeping through all of the attention. Matt picked up Mary Catherine and Vivian glanced once at her and saw that her daughter looked happy and had her arm around his neck.

"How about a chocolate or strawberry ice cream cone?" Matt asked Mary Catherine after a few minutes.

"Chocolate, please," she replied.

"We'll get something to eat," he said to the crowd, "and then y'all can talk to Vivian some more." Picking up the baby carrier, Matt carried both girls through the circle of people.

Vivian followed him to a booth and a waitress came toward them.

''While you order,'' Matt said, swinging Mary Catherine down from his shoulders to the seat in the booth, ''I'm going to run my errands. I'll get my malt later.'' He set the baby carrier on the table. ''I have to run to the hardware store and the auto shop, then I'm going by to see the sheriff.''

''About—''

''Yes,'' he interrupted, glancing at Mary Catherine, who was happily coloring again. ''I think he should know if you think someone might have been following you.''

''Shouldn't I be the one to see the sheriff?''

''Nope, it isn't necessary. If he wants to talk to you, I'll tell him where to find you.''

''I'm going to be spoiled when I leave here.''

''That's impossible.'' Starting to kiss her goodbye, he leaned down, then blinked as if he realized what he was doing and where they were. He straightened. ''I was about to start wild, wild rumors. You make me forget everything, Vivian,'' he said solemnly. ''See you. Bye, Mary Catherine.''

''Bye,'' the little girl replied without looking up from her coloring.

Vivian watched him stride away and then her gaze shifted and she saw Kitty and several others were watching her. Kitty crossed the room and slid into the booth across from her. ''I'll sit here until Matt gets back.''

''Fine.''

''How did Matt find you? Or how did you find Matt?''

''Actually, Mary Catherine found him.'' Vivian talked about the storm and the car wreck, but she suspected Kitty was far more interested in Matt, and several minutes later Kitty was asking questions about his house until she tilted her head and studied Vivian.

''Want a word of warning?''

"Yes," Vivian said, experiencing a chill because a warning from Kitty could only mean one thing—beware of Matt.

"I probably shouldn't say anything, but the word has it that you're divorced in the last year or so."

"That's right."

"So you might be a little vulnerable. Well, I'll warn you—you're staying with Newton County's number one heartbreaker. Matt knows how to love 'em and leave 'em."

"There's no problem," Vivian said stiffly, hoping she could keep the surprise out of her voice. "I have my life and he has his," she said casually, as two more women walked up to the table to join them.

Vivian answered questions perfunctorily, wondering about Matt, seeing a different view of him than before, realizing she knew little about his past.

Chapter 6

Matt made his purchases in the hardware store and the auto shop and then he crossed the street and headed to the sheriff's office. It was a plain office with a dispatcher's desk near the door. Rita glanced up at him and put away a magazine she was reading. "Hi, Matt."

"Hi, Rita." He looked past her beyond a low partition and saw the sheriff seated behind his desk.

Ty Manning stood. "Hi, Matt. Come on back. I heard you delivered a baby."

"Yep, I did."

"Now I know who to call in an emergency."

"Like hell. I don't want to do it again."

Ty shook hands with Matt and then sat down, motioning toward a wooden chair. "Have a seat. What's up?"

"Mother, daughter and baby are staying at my place. The lady is Vivian Ashland from Denver, Colorado. She has a restraining order out against her ex-husband. She was on her way from Denver to Houston."

"We're not exactly a direct route."

"No. She thought someone was following her on the interstate, so she took state roads through Kansas and Oklahoma to I-35. I wanted you to know and I'd like you to let me know if you get any strangers in town or anyone asking about her."

"Sure. Want me to call Chet Gonzales in Dakani and tell him? You're in his county and he'll have jurisdiction."

"Yes. She says her ex is harmless, but he struck her once and that's when she left him."

"I'll call Chet, and we'll let you know if anyone shows up. Call me if you have any trouble."

"Sure," Matt said, standing. "I want to bring her by on our way out of town. It won't take long to get a restraining order for Oklahoma, will it?"

"No. She can come by here and file for one. Then she'll have to appear before the judge in Garfield County."

"Fine. I wanted to talk to you first before I brought her in. She'll have her little girls with her and it's better not to go into all this in front of Mary Catherine."

"Sure."

"Want to go to the café with me and have a malt? Vivian is there with the baby and her little girl."

"I'd like to go, but I'm expecting a call. If I get my call, I'll be on over. I'll call Chet now."

"Thanks," Matt said, shaking hands with the sheriff again.

"See you, Rita," he said as he left the building and crossed the street. Maybe Vivian had been wrong and no one had been following her. Or maybe the person following had been stranded on the other side of Rabbit Creek. Vivian didn't want to bother with a restraining order, but he thought she should get one. She wouldn't be leaving Oklahoma any time soon if he and Doc Bently could influence her to stay.

As hot sunshine poured over him and rose in shimmering waves from the cracked concrete sidewalk, Matt remembered how shy and frightened Mary Catherine had been the other day. She was warming up to him and he was glad. Thinking about seeing Vivian, he increased his pace. At the same time he looked forward to being with Vivian, he knew he should keep his distance. He shouldn't complicate Vivian's life and he had nothing to offer her. He didn't know the meaning of commitment. He couldn't offer commitment and she wouldn't want it from him. All he had ever known was a broken home and a solitary life.

In the café, Vivian sipped the last of her malt and answered questions about her business and her life in Denver.

"I see we've drawn a crowd." Matt's deep voice was directly behind her and she turned as people moved out of the way.

"You haven't drawn a crowd, the baby has," Kitty remarked dryly. Vivian held Julia, who looked content with all the attention, while Mary Catherine now had a paint-with-water book along with a small glass of water in front of her and was happily smearing water over a page.

Matt greeted people who had come in while he was gone. He shook hands with the men, spoke to the women and finally looked at Vivian.

"I hate to end the festivities, but if you're ready, I think our groceries may be about to melt. I've had them loaded into the pickup."

While people said their goodbyes and moved away, Vivian buckled Julia into her carrier. Matt got his malt to take out and picked up Julia. He held the door open for Vivian and Mary Catherine.

"I parked here in front. I imagine you've had enough questions to last you the next year."

"Actually, everyone was very nice and talked about Julia

and how beautiful she is and speculated on what it was like to have you deliver a baby," Vivian answered, her blue eyes twinkling while he held open the door of the pickup for her.

"Yeah, well, they can keep right on wondering about that. Don't worry, I'm not going into details with the public." He fastened Julia and the carrier into the back seat while Mary Catherine buckled herself in and showed him her paintings.

Matt paused to look, commenting enthusiastically on each one. Mary Catherine beamed with satisfaction and reached for her coloring book to show him more.

"I'll look at the others the minute we get home, Mary Catherine," he promised. "If we don't go right now, our groceries will begin to melt and the ice cream will be soup."

As Mary Catherine giggled, Matt got into the driver's seat.

They drove slowly through town and Vivian marveled at the easier pace, the quiet and the friendliness everywhere she had been.

"There're more than a few people who are curious about me staying at your farm," Vivian said.

He shot her a look that made her feel this was a touchy subject, yet she had already gathered that from comments she had heard from several women.

"I take it all this curiosity about me is because you've never had a woman at your place before except for your housekeeper, Lita. Although I hardly count myself as any change in your status because I was a total stranger—you had no choice in the matter and I will soon be gone forever. Also, I was there for one purpose—to have my baby. That's different from your taking a date home."

"Same way I see it, so I don't know why everyone is so all-fired curious, but it's summer and the weather's hot.

There's nothing much to do except speculate on the only change in the life of the county, meet the new lady and her family and talk about the most eventful thing to happen since the creek washed away the Rabbit Creek bridge. No mystery there, either.''

Vivian laughed and Matt reached over to brush her mouth with his fingertips. "That's good. We're going to make one quick stop at the sheriff's so you can file a restraining order. He'll have it all ready and I'll stay with the girls and keep the motor running and the pickup cool.''

"I should have known," she said, looking exasperated. "Okay, but I don't think it'll be necessary.''

"Might. Doc Bently said for you to stay at my place for a while before you start a long trek with a new baby." Matt turned to look at her as he stopped in front of the sheriff's office. "I want you to stay.''

Vivian drew a deep breath and nodded. She climbed out of the car and crossed the sidewalk while her thoughts were still on Matt. She suspected that it had taken a major effort for him to get out the words that he wanted her to stay. From all she was learning about Matt Whitewolf, he kept his feelings closed away from others. Remarks from Kitty and a couple of others, including Meg Preston, made Vivian suspect he had opened himself up to her more than anyone else in his life. She supposed he could do so for the same reason she found it easy to tell him personal things about herself—they had shared a very intimate crisis where both had bared themselves emotionally. It had forged a bond that was strong, and she was beginning to realize it was also enduring. It had nothing to do with the magic chemistry that continually blazed between them.

Inside the small building she met the sheriff and the dispatcher, and signed the papers to file for the restraining order. In minutes she was back in Matt's pickup.

They drove home and Matt unloaded the truck, looked

at more of Mary Catherine's crayon drawings and then put a casserole on to cook. He hooked Vivian's computer up in an empty bedroom while she fed and changed Julia and then went outside so Mary Catherine could play in the yard.

During supper as they sat and talked, the phone rang. Matt stretched out his arm and picked up the receiver to answer. When his gaze slid to Vivian, she guessed it must be about her car. She had pinned her hair on her head, and she pushed away stray locks that had come loose and fell around her face while she listened to him talk.

"That's the only place you can get the parts?"

Vivian was both mildly amused and annoyed that, once again, the two men were discussing her car as if she didn't exist. Matt held out the receiver.

"It's Jake Claiborne, and he'll tell you about your car. He's the most reliable one around to fix it, so I suggest you go along with what he says. You know you're welcome here. Doc wanted you to stay and so do I."

"That sounds like bad news," she said, taking the phone and listening while Jake Claiborne told her that it would take a week to get the parts and get her car fixed.

Vivian made arrangements and hung up the phone to look at Matt. "I feel like I'm in good ol' boy land."

"Actually, you are," he replied with a crooked grin that melted her annoyance. "That's what happens when you get off the big freeway and out into the country down south."

"Well, you have houseguests for the next week. He said the storm has caused him to have a lot more business and it's going to take several days to get the new parts."

"That suits Doc and me fine."

"We get to stay here?" Mary Catherine asked, her eyes sparkling.

"Yes, we do until next week."

"Or longer," Matt added, and Mary Catherine clapped

her hands. "Doc thinks you ought to stay several weeks before you start the trip to Houston with a new baby."

"A week should be plenty long enough."

"Think about it before you decide." He waved his hand. "I have room here."

"By next week you may change your mind."

He gazed at her solemnly and shook his head. "Nope. I won't change my mind. I'll want you to stay."

A little thrill ran through Vivian with his insistence, and a little voice of reason also cautioned that if she kept staying she might get to liking it too much.

After supper was finished, they sat at the table and talked until Mary Catherine got fidgety. Matt started to pick up his plate and Vivian reached across to touch his wrist lightly.

The moment she did, his gaze flew to hers and he stared at her so intently, she almost forgot what she had been about to say. She moved her hand away quickly.

"Let me clean this kitchen."

"You can do that in a day or two. I'll do the dishes tonight. You three go out in the yard, and when I finish here, Mary Catherine, if you'd like and Mommy says it's all right," he said, turning to Mary Catherine, "you can ride one of the horses while I lead him around the corral. Would you like that?"

"Yes!" Mary Catherine said, her blue eyes sparkling as she looked at Vivian, who nodded.

"I have one that's very gentle," Matt said. "Molasses. You can guess why he's named that."

Mary Catherine jumped down from her chair and ran to the door.

"C'mon, Mommy."

"Sure I can't help?"

"Very sure," he said firmly, gathering plates.

She left to go outside with Mary Catherine, carrying Julia in her carrier.

An hour later Vivian stood watching Matt walk a pinto around the corral while Mary Catherine happily sat in the saddle, her imagination probably galloping away over a field.

Pete appeared and climbed over the rails to drop down inside. "Hi, Mary Catherine. Boss."

Vivian could hear the men talking quietly. Matt handed the reins to Pete and then he turned to join Vivian. Sitting on the top rail, he swung his long legs over the fence and reached down. "Give me Julia and you can climb up here and sit and watch Mary Catherine."

"In this skirt?"

"Sure. Try."

She handed the baby to him and climbed up and found the full skirt was manageable as she tucked it around her legs and sat beside him. "Now I can take her back," she said.

"She likes it where she is," he replied, looking at the contented baby tucked in his arm. "See. She's happy here."

Vivian looked up and met his gaze. "You have a way with children. Or maybe I should say women, children and probably animals."

"I hope so. Out here I need a way with animals."

"What about women and children?" she teased.

His brown eyes focused on her. "Guess I'm going to need a way with them, too."

"Rest assured, cowboy, you have one." She shook her head. "You're bringing out a personality in me I didn't know I possessed."

He smiled. "Out here, you sort of drop the facade and get down to basics."

"My flirting with you isn't basic."

"I think it is," he said in a deep voice, and trailed his fingers over her knuckles. "When sparks fly between a man and woman, flirting is as basic as the sun coming up in the morning."

Vivian's pulse jumped. His voice had gotten husky and desire burned in his dark eyes. She tingled from his slight touch of her hand as well as from his words.

"For a taciturn, solitary cowboy, there are moments you surprise me and say things that take my breath."

His dark gaze impaled her as if he were holding her with his hands. "Good, Vivian," he drawled softly. "Surprises are fun when they're pleasant or sexy."

"It's getting hotter out here." She fanned her face with her hand. "How did this conversation get to sexy surprises?"

"Something you and I bring out in each other, I guess."

"I think Pete has probably done his duty long enough. Want me to walk her?"

"You sit still," he said, handing Julia to her. "I'll relieve Pete." He looked amused, and she wondered if he knew she had deliberately tried to change the subject.

Matt jumped down to cross the corral to Pete. He took the reins and Pete strode over to Vivian, climbing swiftly up beside her. "You have nice girls," he said in a tight voice.

"I'm sorry you lost yours," Vivian said quietly.

"Yeah," he said, wiping his eyes as he looked down at Julia. "She's beautiful."

"Want to hold her? I'd like to talk to Mary Catherine. If you'll just take Julia until I get down off the fence, then I'll take her."

"Sure," he said, and she handed him the baby. He took her with great care and held her, gazing down at her. "I'm sweaty. I hate to get her against me."

"She washes," Vivian said with amusement as she

jumped down from the fence. "You'll be lucky if she doesn't wake and spit up on you."

"I wouldn't care. Go on. I'll hold her until you get back."

Vivian hesitated a second, then she told Pete she would be right back. She caught up with the pinto to look at Mary Catherine. "Having fun?"

"Yes! His name is Molasses and he's nice. I like him best of all the horses."

Vivian smiled as she walked beside them. "Well, it's almost dark and you've ridden long enough that Mr. Whitewolf—"

"Vivian, I told her to just call me Matt. It's easier than Mr. Whitewolf."

"Matt and Mr. Quincy have worked all day, so they're probably tired of walking you around. Besides, it's almost bedtime."

"One more, please, please!"

"That's up to Matt."

"'Course it's okay," he said.

Mary Catherine clapped and Vivian shrugged. "Pushover," she said.

"Big blue eyes will do it every time," he said, looking down at her, his words causing sparks to ignite.

"Matt's told me the horses' names," Mary Catherine said happily.

"Good, you can tell me when you take your bath. I'll go get Julia."

Aware of Matt's gaze on her as she walked away, Vivian went back to take Julia from Pete, who jumped down.

"'Night. See you tomorrow," he said, striding across the pen to talk to Matt a few minutes. He waved to Mary Catherine and she waved back and Vivian heard her childish voice.

"'Night, Pete," Mary Catherine said.

Pete. Matt. These rough, tough cowboys were marsh-mallows with Mary Catherine and they had won her trust swiftly and to a degree that Mary Catherine's own father never had. But then he had never tried to.

Vivian was amazed every time she looked at Mary Catherine with Matt. She was chattering happily to him now. How easily he had vanquished her fear! Just quietness, kindness and attention—why hadn't the little girl's own father learned that? Yet, Vivian knew, Baker's thoughts were wound up in himself and he never cared to try to win Mary Catherine's affections. When they divorced, he had been more than happy to give her full custody of Mary Catherine.

While Matt unsaddled the pinto, Vivian took the girls inside to get Mary Catherine to bed. After her bath Mary Catherine went to the family room where Matt sat with his stocking feet propped up on the coffee table.

Mary Catherine held a book, and Vivian trailed into the room behind her. She had splotches of water on her blouse and skirt from bathing Mary Catherine and more locks of hair were falling down around her face, and she was aware of his quick intense scrutiny.

Mary Catherine stopped shyly beside Matt's chair. "Will you read this to me?" she asked, holding up a colorful book.

Matt stiffened and stared at her without answering.

"Mary Catherine," Vivian said, noticing Matt's silence and wondering what caused it. "Matt's walked you around with the horse. Leave him alone for a few minutes. Come here and I'll read to you."

"I want you to read my book," she said quietly but insistently to Matt. "Please."

"You better let Mommy read it," he said stiffly in a cold, flat voice.

Surprised, even though she could understand why he

would want to relax undisturbed, Vivian noticed beneath his tan his face flushed and that shuttered look had come over his features.

"Mary Catherine, come here and I'll read."

"Sorry, Mary Catherine. I need to do something," he said, getting up and striding out of the room, and Vivian sensed something was wrong, but she couldn't guess what. He had been more than patient with Mary Catherine, pampering her, doing what she wanted, being careful with her and cautious. Suddenly, on the simplest request, he had gruffly refused and left the room. Maybe he had something urgent, but the past few minutes were so unlike him, Vivian was baffled.

With the corners of her mouth turned down, Mary Catherine climbed into Vivian's lap, but in minutes she was laughing at the pictures in the book. As Vivian read to her she heard Matt open the back door. What had disturbed him so badly? Vivian wondered. She couldn't imagine Mary Catherine's request for a few more minutes of his time would set him off, but something had upset him.

The phone rang and she heard Matt come back into the house to answer it.

While thoughts and questions about Matt swirled through her mind, Vivian read perfunctorily and then took Mary Catherine to bed. She tucked her into Matt's big bed and kissed her good-night, singing a lullaby to her. Mary Catherine was asleep almost at once. Vivian crossed the room to look at Julia, in the portable crib, touching her other daughter lightly, feeling a swell of love for both little girls and so thankful again to have Julia.

Vivian straightened. She had had three short naps during the day and she was awake and restless. She decided to read her e-mail and, while the two girls slept, perhaps catch up a little with her work. She went to the kitchen and glanced out, seeing the floodlights on at the barn and corral, wondering about Matt. Were they beginning to bother him?

Beneath the floodlights Matt worked with one of the horses he was training, finally yanking off his sweat-soaked T-shirt and flinging it on the fence. It was almost midnight when he had groomed, watered and fed the horse and headed back to the house.

It was quiet and he wondered whether Vivian was asleep or not. He needed to talk to her when he could about the phone call he had had earlier. He wanted to protect Vivian himself, yet she had a right to know a stranger was making inquiries about her. He yanked off his boots and carried them and his T-shirt to set them in the bedroom he was using. Light spilled from the room down the hall where he had set up Vivian's computer.

In his stocking feet, Matt walked down the hall to that room. Vivian was seated at the table he had put up, her head bent over papers spread before her. She was in a red skirt and blouse, her hair still pinned up with more locks falling down around her face.

He rapped lightly on the door. "Ready for a break?"

She looked startled and then seemed to focus on him, her gaze running swiftly over him, but the look was sensual, like a touch of her hand. "I came in here to look at my mail and then suddenly I got busy. I should have told you—"

"No, you didn't need to tell me. I've been outside with a horse. Vivian, I need to talk to you and I didn't want to talk in front of Mary Catherine."

"What is it?"

"You might as well know," Matt said, "I had a phone call earlier tonight. It was about you."

A knot of anger tightened in Matt. He had debated with

himself whether to tell Vivian or not, but decided she would want to know.

"Chet Gonzales, the sheriff in Dakani, called me. He wanted to tell me that there's a man in town asking about you."

Chapter 7

She stared beyond Matt. "I'm not surprised. I'm not afraid, but I don't like it, either. I expected Baker to send someone to learn where I settle. He's kept up with me through his lawyer and through friends and some of my clients."

"He doesn't have visitation rights?"

"He didn't want visitation rights. Baker and I were together some last year. I told you, there was a last-ditch reconciliation effort and Mary Catherine saw him twice then, but he cares nothing about her."

"Well, damn," Matt muttered, shaking his head.

"I'm certain Baker will try to talk me into going back, so he has to know where I am if he wants to contact me again."

"Will he fight you for custody of Mary Catherine or Julia?"

"He didn't fight me for custody. That's settled. I have full custody."

"He's a fool," Matt said.

"Well, I agree, but I'm surprised to hear a bachelor feel so strongly about little girls."

Matt gave her a level stare. "Families are important. At least the good kind are. If they're bad, they're just something to escape from."

Vivian heard the bitterness creep into his voice and knew he was thinking about his own family. "That was a long time ago," she said. "You can have your own family now and it would wipe away the past."

"Nothing can ever completely wipe away a man's past. It's something he lives with, like his shadow. And I'm not tying someone else up in all my mistakes. I wouldn't know how to be a good family man."

"You could have fooled me," she said, and his dark eyes focused on her, something changing in their depths, and her heartbeat quickened. Each time he let his desire show, she was becoming more ensnared by it. She was acutely aware of him all the time and she responded to the slightest touch or look. Even when she had casually touched him at the table tonight, she had done it without thought, but the moment her fingers had closed on his muscled arm, she had become intensely aware of the physical contact. Now he stood in the doorway, one hip against the jamb, his fingers splayed on his other hip. He was bare-chested, his jeans riding low on his flat stomach, and she couldn't resist letting her gaze roam over him. He was fit, his broad shoulders and chest and arms taut with muscle. His skin was smooth and as dark as chocolate.

"The sheriff said he'll find out more about the man and call us. I'll drive into Dakani tomorrow and see who the man is."

"You don't need to get involved."

He gave her a crooked grin. "Vivian, I'm involved up to my eyeballs. How about a break? Want a cold drink?"

She stretched, her arms going wide and the red blouse pulling tautly over her high, full breasts.

"Yes. If I could figure out this letter, I would have all the e-mail answered. Just a minute, let me save this and close things down."

Matt crossed the room, hooked a folding chair with his toe and sat down beside her. "I thought you'd sleep while Julia sleeps."

"I keep thinking I'll stop in the next five minutes."

Vivian knew he was right and she should sleep while Julia was asleep, but it was the first time in days she had worked on anything for her clients. She closed the e-mail and glanced at the letter she had printed out.

As she studied it, her concentration drifted and focused on Matt, who was sitting close beside her. It was difficult to keep her gaze from roaming over him again. She had her work spread out on the table around her and he picked up a brochure.

"What do you do for your clients?"

"Public relations. I do these brochures, plan ad campaigns, do ads—whatever they need done."

"You did all these? These are your clients?" he asked, leafing through brochures spread near her.

"Yes," she replied without thought because she was still studying an e-mail letter from a Denver client.

"Look at this letter," she said without thinking, trying to get her mind back on her work instead of on Matt. "I can't decide from this man's letter whether he wants me to work on his ad campaign or just do a logo. His instructions aren't clear." She shoved the letter toward Matt.

He gave her a long look, and instantly she regretted asking him. It was past midnight and she knew he would be up by five in the morning. "Sorry. Never mind."

He stared at her and she wondered whether she had offended him or what. He took the letter and bent over it.

"Matt, I'm sorry. I shouldn't have asked you because it's late, and I know you're up early—"

"Vivian, I'm not overworked," he said flatly, with such a strange note in his voice that she stopped talking.

He bent over the letter again and she saw his lips move as he read. Finally he looked up.

"What do you think he wants?"

Matt stared at her for so long she wondered what was wrong. "I don't know what he wants," he answered evenly. "Did I hurt Mary Catherine's feelings tonight?"

The question startled her. He looked so solemn and concerned that she wondered why he was still worrying over Mary Catherine.

"No, of course not. Children get told no all the time, and she forgets."

"She looked hurt."

"She'll forget about it tomorrow. Let's go get that cold drink."

Frowning, he rubbed his temple. "Damn, I hate hurting Mary Catherine. Look, I want to read her little stories to her, but I don't know those stories because I don't recall any stories from my childhood. No one read to me." He looked as if he were debating something and he sounded worried, puzzling her. She waited because he seemed to be groping for the right words to say.

"Why don't you get a few of her little books and tell me what they're about?" Matt asked Vivian.

"Sure. But you can take them and look at them."

He inhaled and rubbed his temple and she knew something was definitely wrong. She glanced down at the letter that lay in front of him. It occurred to her what the problem might be, yet she couldn't imagine that she was right. She tapped the letter with her finger.

"Who's the letter from? If you'll just read his name and

address to me and that first line, I'll start a letter back to him.''

She turned to the computer and waited and then looked back at him. He studied the paper, holding it in his big, dark fingers, and then his gaze met hers.

''You have to be able to read to run this farm,'' she said quietly, unable to imagine that he had difficulty reading, yet that appeared to be the problem. It *couldn't* be reading, but what was it?

''No, I can't read this letter,'' he said gruffly. Beneath the dark tanned skin, she could see he was flushed. He clamped his mouth closed and shrugged. ''I just hate like hell that I hurt Mary Catherine. It's late,'' he said, starting to stand.

She caught his wrist, feeling again that current that jumped between them any time they had physical contact. ''Wait a minute. Matt, what—''

''I don't know how to read,'' he said bluntly.

''You manage this farm, which means you have to do a certain amount of reading,'' Vivian said, unable to believe that his reading was really so poor he couldn't read one of Mary Catherine's little books to her.

''You don't have to read to rope a steer or plant wheat.''

''You have to read to sign invoices and order equipment—''

He waved his hand as if those things required little ability. ''I can read enough to get by in my world. My world isn't your world,'' he said, looking at the brochures spread around her, and she felt as if a huge wall had gone up between them. At the same time, she suspected he hadn't admitted to anyone what he was telling her. She guessed it was taking a major effort for him to open himself up to her like this and that he never would have done so if it hadn't been for Mary Catherine and his fear he had hurt the child's feelings. He might be worrying about Mary Catherine asking him to read to her again.

"That's why you didn't read to Mary Catherine, isn't it?"

"Yes. Vivian, I told you, I'm country. I ran away from home when I was a kid."

"You went all through grade school."

"Yep, but I got by. I knew everyone. Teachers liked me. Probably in grade school some of them passed me because they were afraid my old man—whichever the current one was—would beat them to a pulp if they didn't. Some of them probably passed me because they knew he would beat *me* to a pulp if they didn't. I squeaked through until junior high and then I was playing ball. That was the magic pass through school. It got me out of classes; it got me through classes. By my freshman year in high school I was a quarterback and good at ball playing, so they passed me right on through. My teachers knew I couldn't read."

"So I can't read to Mary Catherine and I know I hurt her feelings tonight," he said with an angry tone. "It's late," he said again, and started to turn away.

Again, Vivian placed her hand on his arm. "Wait a minute. With a little effort, while I'm here, we could change that."

"Change what?" he asked.

Her fingers were still on his arm. She was aware of touching him, aware of him standing so close to her, aware of the intent way he was watching her. "I can teach you to read while I'm here. I've done volunteer teaching of reading and I've worked a little with Mary Catherine on phonics. It shouldn't take much for you to get phonics, and then you can be off on your own."

"I think it's too late," he remarked dryly. "I'm an old dog and you know the saying."

"You're neither old nor a dog. Sit down and let me get one of Mary Catherine's books."

"Aw, Vivian, forget it. If you want to help, tell me some of Mary Catherine's little stories so I won't have to turn her down again. Other than that—"

"I'll be right back. Don't you move."

Amused and embarrassed, Matt watched her rush out of the room. He knew she would be polite, but he had expected a different reaction from her. It hadn't occurred to him that she would want to teach him how to read.

He had never admitted to anyone that he couldn't read. Teachers had known, but since he'd been out of school, he had been able to muddle his way through anything. He picked up the letter that lay on the table and looked at words that he had no idea about. He let it fall back onto the table and looked over the brochures and letters spread on the table. The lady must have a very successful business. These were big companies and big clients. And very impressive ad work. Matt inhaled, wondering if she would be bored out of her mind during the next few days, but then he thought about Julia and Mary Catherine and knew they would keep her busy.

Dropping a slick brochure, he heard Vivian returning. She was barefoot, hurrying, her long hair twisted and pinned loosely on top of her head, long strands tumbling down around her face. The top buttons of her blouse were unfastened and he could see the curves of her breasts, which swung slightly with each step, the red material shifting and pulling as she walked.

"Here are some little books that are basic and one of her alphabet books."

"Look, I get up in not too many hours." He felt ridiculous and he was embarrassed to deal with this and wished she would forget about it.

"Fifteen minutes is all. Fifteen minutes of phonics won't be long and then you can go fall into bed."

Amused by her determination, he took her hand. "Okay, I'll give it fifteen minutes if you'll come to the kitchen and let me get a beer and we can sit in there where I can put my feet up."

"Fine," she said as he released her hand.

She leaned over to turn off her computer and his gaze ran down her backside, his imagination running rampant while he wished she wore jeans or something that fit instead of the full skirt that hid her figure.

In the kitchen he poured a glass of lemonade for her and got a beer and then they sat down beside each other at the kitchen table. He looked at the alphabet book that was meant for preschoolers.

"Damn, Vivian. I do know the alphabet."

"I'm just going to teach you some phonics," she said, like a dog getting a good grip on a new bone.

"Sure." He took a long drink of beer and wondered if he should have gotten something stronger. This could be a long fifteen minutes. "Vivian, I'm no scholar."

"You don't have to be with this," she said, waving the book at him and flashing him a smile. He hitched his chair closer to her to see the book. Her perfume assailed him and he looked at her. She smelled like roses, with a faint smell of baby powder still clinging to her. After a day and most of the night spent with men, hay and sweaty horses, she smelled wonderful. He inhaled deeply again. He was only inches from her, and since he had an excuse, he moved closer. He casually placed his arm across the back of her chair and leaned toward her.

"Pronounce the different sounds of the letter *A*. You know them. That's why this will go so fast and be so simple," she said, looking up at him. "*A*. Say the sounds."

He watched her mouth and forgot what she was asking

him. Her skin was flawless, smoother than porcelain with faint pink in her cheeks, full rosy lips and those enormous blue eyes that were looking at him expectantly. He reached up to remove a pin from her hair.

"Ay—ay—ay," she said. "That's long *A*."

"Ay—ay—ay." He repeated, drawing out the simple sounds while a lock of hair fell to her shoulder.

"Ah—ah—ah," she said.

As he watched her mouth, his blood thickened and his pulse jumped. His fingers brushed her nape.

"Ah—ah—ah," he said, sounding out short *A*, saying sounds he knew full well and not giving a thought to them except that it held her still only inches away. He pulled out more pins and another lock fell.

Vivian forgot the lesson. She was aware of his arm behind her on the back of the chair, his other hand slowly, sensuously pulling pins from her hair. He was inches from her, his dark eyes holding her as if he had placed two hands on her shoulders, his broad, bare chest only inches from her. His gaze drifted over her face and then to her mouth and desire burned blatantly in his dark eyes.

He kept saying sounds and dimly she knew she should be concentrating on what he was saying. Instead she looked down at his chest that tapered to a flat, muscled stomach with jeans that rode low on his hips. She realized how she was studying him and her gaze flew back to the book in her hands. She turned a page of the little book, looking at a big red drawing of the letter *B*.

"*B*," she said. "Buh, buh…"

His gaze was on her mouth, which was where it should be, yet the way he was looking at her mouth had nothing to do with learning to read.

His brown eyes were staring, *memorizing*, her mouth. Her voice faded and then her throat became dry. Every thought fled her mind except one. She wanted his kisses.

She felt an urge that was compelling, *crazy,* to reach out and place her hands on his face, pull his head down and kiss him. He was still taking down her hair, his knuckles brushing her nape lightly, his fingers touching her throat, his hands making little tugs on her scalp. They were all slight touches, but searing nonetheless, building that chemistry and attraction that had flared to life the first moment they had looked into each other's eyes.

Then he shifted closer. His knee touched her thigh. She could smell his aftershave. He was ruggedly handsome, incredibly appealing. Her heart pounded and a hundred arguments and cautions ran through her mind all at once. They were going up in smoke just as swiftly.

He slid his hand behind her head and drew her closer. His arm slid from the back of the chair to her waist, circling her waist. He shifted again, spreading his legs to get even closer.

She placed her hand on his warm chest that felt as solid as granite, his heart beating swiftly. Just to touch his wrist or arm had always sent shock waves through her. Now, touching his bare chest and feeling his heart racing, stirred a quake within her. The impulse to run her hand across his chest was impossible to resist and she let her fingers drift across him. He inhaled, the heated look in his eyes becoming more intense.

"Neither one of us wants this," she whispered.

"Like hell we don't." He leaned forward, his lips brushing hers, and she closed her eyes, her pulse flying as heat flared in her.

"No," she whispered against his mouth, but at the same time she slid her hands over him up to his shoulders, her fingers spreading as she discovered the feel of him. He wrapped his arms around her to pull her close against him. In one swift movement he lifted her to his lap and tightened his embrace as his mouth covered hers firmly, his tongue seeking, thrusting into her mouth in a quest while need and desire intermingled.

Everything inside her seemed to constrict and then unfold, heat and melt. Why was it so good to be in his arms? Was she starved for this? Or was it because this cowboy was very special?

She tightened her arm around his neck, feeling the ends of his thick, coarse hair fall over her arm and wrist. She ran her fingers on his nape, wanting to know the texture and feel of him, the strong column of his neck, the contour of his thick, broad shoulder.

She turned toward him, shifting slightly, feeling his erection hard against her thigh, his thighs beneath her bottom, his arms holding her tightly. It was obvious he wanted her; at the same time, she knew there could never be anything between them. Yet she kissed him back, her tongue playing over his, touching his as his went deep into her mouth, stroking her, stirring a wild need that she wouldn't have thought possible.

His hand wound in her hair, and she heard his deep growl as if he couldn't get enough. Amazed at the fires kindling between them, she kissed him. Desire burned white-hot when she had felt dead to men and desire for so very long. But with this man's kisses and touches, she had come to life instantly. Her hips shifted and an ache began low inside her, a need that she wouldn't have thought she could possibly have. Unwanted, desire raged even though common sense told her she was moving into dangerous territory. It was too soon after childbirth. But how right and good it was to be kissed and held by him! She kissed him as passionately as he was kissing her and she felt as if she had been headed for this moment in his arms since that first meeting.

His hand stroked her head; he ran his fingers through her hair, he stroked her nape lightly, slowly. His kisses were heady, too exciting, more dangerous than she had possibly imagined. More desirable.

He bent over her, tightening his arms, and his kisses deepened, became more intimate. His need was evident in each stroke of his tongue. Beyond the kisses, she could feel a bonding, a burgeoning unity with this man that she couldn't afford to have. They already had a golden chain forged between them by childbirth. Now, with each second that passed, a new one was forming, more links locking around her heart.

She was melting, coming apart in his arms. She moaned, stroked his nape, wound her fingers in his hair while she kissed him as wildly as he kissed her. She had to stop, but she couldn't.

Matt held her tightly as if never wanting to let her go. Like a raging wildfire his body burned with desire for her and her responses to his kisses were blazing him to cinders. She was responsive, sensual, kissing him back, her body curling into his, her hips moving slightly against him. She moaned softly, deep in her throat. She wanted their kisses as passionately as he did.

He leaned over her. He wanted to peel away the red skirt and blouse, yet, on an intellectual level, he didn't want to rush her and have her stop him. On another more primal level, he never wanted to stop and he wanted so much more than kisses.

His roaring pulse drowned out all other noise. His thudding heart threatened to burst through his rib cage. He was hard, hot, shaking with desire. She was so incredibly soft, curvaceous, enticing in his arms. She was wildly responsive and that escalated desire beyond belief. And more than that. She was Vivian, someone already special to him.

He trailed his hand over her breast and heard her gasp, and then she caught his wrist firmly, her fingers locking around him as she pulled away. Her eyes came open languorously, desire burning in their crystal blue depths. Her lips were swollen, deep red now, her cheeks flushed. They looked at each other and he saw desire in her gaze and something more—was it surprise? She was gasping for breath as much as he was. He ran his index finger over the curve of her breast, down to the first button that was fastened. He twisted it free, his fingers brushing her full, soft breasts.

She caught his wrist again. ''No. You have to stop.''

He looked into her eyes and wondered if she knew he didn't want to stop. He wanted her in his arms, in his bed in a way he had never wanted a woman there before.

''I want you, Vivian,'' he whispered, unable to tell her the extent of his feelings or that he had never told a woman even those words before. Yet he had lived his life with his feelings closed up inside him and he couldn't release them now after a few kisses.

''Matt, I can't get too involved,'' she said slowly. ''The past two years I've just been through all kinds of stress and trauma over a broken marriage and then divorce. I'm moving. You and I won't see each other again. We can't do something foolish. I can't do much, anyway,'' she said, her cheeks flushing. ''I just had a baby.''

''It was only a few kisses, Vivian,'' he said, but he knew it was more than that. Never had kisses turned him inside out like hers did. He trailed his fingers along her cheek. ''I know we're going to part, but those kisses didn't hurt anyone.'' She slid off his lap and straightened her blouse while he watched her intently. He stood in front of her and placed his hands on her shoulders because he couldn't resist touching her again. She looked up and the minute they looked into each other's eyes, he was lost.

''Let's keep things the way they were,'' she said breathlessly. He nodded and dropped his hands, turning from her.

''We'll try the reading tomorrow. I'll go over some of

Mary Catherine's books with you then,'' she said, and left the room to hurry down the hall. Vivian was stunned by his kisses, amazed how much she wanted him. This was not the time, not the place and not the man for her to fall in love with.

''It was only kisses,'' she whispered. She glanced into the open door of his room and saw his boots and T-shirt tossed casually inside. A pair of muddy jeans lay on the floor. Why was everything about him special and significant?

She hurried to the big bedroom she shared with the girls. One small lamp burned, shedding a dim yellow glow that threw the corners into dark shadows. Vivian stepped inside and closed the door and leaned against it and felt as if Matt was still close at hand. The whole room shouted his presence. Everywhere she looked there was something of his— his desk, his bed, his closet. It was all his and now every little thing in the room was more important than it had been yesterday.

Had their kisses moved them beyond a point of simple friendship—or had there ever been simple friendship?

She crossed the room to the big rectangular mirror that was above the chest of drawers and gazed at her own reflection, seeing Matt, remembering the past few minutes. She touched the corner of her mouth. Her mouth was red, her hair down, her blouse half-unbuttoned. She had unbuttoned part of it earlier when she was hot, then he had undone another button a few minutes ago. She looked disheveled, but the same reflection stared back that she usually saw, yet she didn't feel the same.

She felt as if something indefinable had changed. His kisses were more than heady or toe-curling—they transformed her world. Since the day before yesterday she had been as close to him as she could be to someone she was not intimate with. Now, with just kisses, she felt even closer.

She moaned softly and turned away, unbuttoning her blouse and pulling it out of her skirt while she began to change into her nightgown. She didn't want to feel this way about him. He was special already, but she didn't want him to become even more special. When she left here, she didn't want to leave her heart behind.

She needed to pack and go, but she couldn't until her car was fixed. As swiftly as that thought came, she looked at Mary Catherine and thought how she was opening up to Matt, trusting him, trusting Pete. That was important, maybe a turning point in Mary Catherine's young life. Vivian knew she had to think of the good changes he was bringing about in her daughter's life. Those two kind, patient men were wearing away Mary Catherine's fears and that was more important than Vivian worrying about sparks flying between Matt and her.

Running her finger along the cool pane, Vivian remembered Matt's confession about reading. She still found it difficult to believe, yet she had heard of people who owned their own businesses and still got by without others realizing they were functionally illiterate.

Vivian rubbed her neck. It should be so easy to help him learn some phonics so he could sound words out himself. "Yeah, Vivian," she said aloud, throwing up her hands. *Easy.* Look what had happened the first five minutes tonight!

Vivian climbed into bed beside Mary Catherine and lay back against the pillows, remembering Matt tonight in the kitchen, his strong arms tightly around her, the look that he gave her that was passionate and made her feel special.

How was she going to keep on resisting him when he was so totally irresistible?

"Don't think about it," she said aloud to herself. She

switched off the light, got out of bed to open some shutters. Now with the lights off in the bedroom, she could see the land spreading away from the house. What was Matt doing? she wondered. Sleeping blissfully down the hall in another big bed?

Chapter 8

Matt had watched Vivian rush out of the kitchen as if a demon were at her heels. It was a good thing she had gone. There was no way he could have stayed around her and not reached for her again.

"Damn," he whispered, knotting his fists. He was on fire with wanting her. He went outside, striding through the darkness, knowing sleep was hopelessly lost.

He saw a light shining behind the barn and headed in that direction, finding Pete under the raised hood of a large flatbed truck Matt kept for hauling.

"That truck busted again?"

"Yep. I'm working on the carburetor," Pete said, straightening and wiping grease off his hands on a rag. He pulled a cigarette out of his pocket and lit it, exhaling a stream of gray smoke. "You can't sleep, either?"

"Nope. It's a hot, sultry night," Matt replied, thinking that was an understatement for what he was suffering.

"I hope that lightning on the horizon is heat lightning."

"Thank heaven I got the wheat harvested before we started getting all the rain. I'm sorry for the people north of us who are getting it."

They stood in silence for a time. "Little girls are cute," Pete said. "Guess that's changed your life. I told Lita about them, and she can't wait to see the baby. She was sorry to miss work, but the workshop she went to was required attendance for everyone in her class."

"That's fine. She shouldn't have been driving with all the roads under water. Vivian is going to ask Lita if she can work for her the days she doesn't work for me during the week."

"Lita will like that. She's saving everything she makes now. Reggie called her last night. She wasn't going to tell me, but I came into the room while they were talking."

"Is he having second thoughts? Does he want to come back, get married?"

"Nope. No mention of marriage. I asked her. Asked her why he called. He misses her, but he doesn't want to marry her. If I catch the bastard coming around her, I'll whip him good. He knows it, too. Can't understand life. I wanted my family and lost them. He can have a family and he throws it away."

"That's what Vivian's husband did. Someone has been following her. Gonzales called me and said a man has been asking around town about her."

"Ex-husband want her back?"

"From what she's said, he wants her. He isn't interested in the babies at all."

"Another bastard. I'll tell the guys and we'll keep watch for any stranger," Pete said, dropping the cigarette to stub it out with his toe. He went back to the truck, and Matt moved closer to look at the engine.

"Vivian doesn't think he'll resort to violence. She said she thinks he just wants to know where she settles."

Pete squinted at him. "She might be wrong about him. People surprise you."

"I feel the same way about the guy that you do about Reggie. I'd like a few minutes with him."

"Look here at this wire," Pete said. Matt bent over the truck and in seconds both of them worked in silence.

It was an hour later when Matt straightened and shook his hair back from his face. "I'm turning in. It's almost time to get up."

"Yeah. Go on. I'll shut things down here and come back to it later. These spark plugs need to be cleaned, too."

"See you, Pete." Matt walked back to the house and tried to enter quietly. His gaze swept the kitchen and he remembered only a little over an hour ago how he had sat here with Vivian on his lap.

With Vivian filling his thoughts, he pulled off his boots and carried them to his room, where he took a cold shower.

Icy water fell over his hot body and as he washed he still thought about holding Vivian. To kiss, she was all he had dreamed about and more. Her responses were intense, instant and fiery. He could never remember a time in his life he had wanted a woman as badly as he wanted her. *What was the matter with him? Why was he so dazzled by her?*

It couldn't be the intimacy they had shared through childbirth. That shouldn't kindle what he was feeling toward her. Most of the time she had been bundled up to her chin in her gown and robe or a blouse and skirt, so it wasn't her body that was setting him on fire. Although that added to it, he had to admit. He had had enough glimpses to know she was a very good-looking woman.

Damn, he hated that he had hurt Mary Catherine tonight. He had seen the look in her eyes when he refused to read to her and he didn't ever want to do that again if he had to make up the wildest story possible. How could he tell a little child that he didn't know much more about reading than she did? She probably wouldn't believe him because all the adults she knew could read.

Damn. It had been a long time now since his inability to read had caused trouble and he had almost stopped worrying about it.

He turned off the shower and began to dry himself. Stepping out of the shower, he moved to the window to gaze into the night, but in his mind he was seeing Vivian, remembering holding her. Teach him to read—he guessed she'd learned her lesson there! That had been an invitation to kisses. How did she expect him to sit inches from her, concentrate on watching her mouth and keep his hands to himself? It had been impossible and it would be impossible if she ever wanted to try teaching him again. The lady was desirable, too sexy, too appealing.

Just thinking about her, he became hot, his body responding to erotic thoughts as he remembered in detail holding her in his arms on his lap. He imagined what he could do if she didn't stop his lovemaking, yet whatever she allowed, he would have to remember to be gentle.

With a groan he secured the towel around his waist, hit the light switch, went into the bedroom and fell across the bed to stare into the darkness. Why was she so special? There were other good-looking women who didn't have two children, an ex-husband trailing after them and a new life to start hundreds of miles away. The county was filled with pretty ladies who were fun to be with.

There was something unique about Vivian. She was self-possessed, sexy, beautiful. He groaned and put his hands behind his head. "It doesn't matter if she's the best-looking, sexiest woman I've ever known—we are worlds apart," he said aloud.

We can't be together five minutes before the differences between us show, he thought, mentally listing those differences. She was educated, classy, sophisticated, citified. He was none of those, just pure country. A dropout who couldn't read well; actually, who could barely read at all. He remembered the brute that had been his blood father and the beatings and how terrified he had been of the man when he was small. The man didn't last long in their family, although the next common-law husband was almost as bad. Matt was from a broken home, unable to know how to really love. He couldn't give Vivian and the girls the love they deserved. *Let her go.*

He needed to drive into Dakani and see who was trying to find her. That was another reason for her to stay a little longer. Let the husband find her here and let them have their showdown here where Matt could protect Vivian. He grinned in the dark. The idea of someone protecting her would get her feathers up. The lady was as independent as a well-fed cat and she wouldn't want anyone's protection, thank you.

"Whoa," Matt said, thinking about how annoyed she got with anyone taking charge for her.

I feel like I'm in good ol' boy land. He remembered the sparks in her blue eyes as she faced him across the table and made that announcement. Well, she was and she might as well get used to it while she was here. Moving to Texas wasn't going to take her out of it, either.

He grinned, thinking about their tiny arguments over whether or not he could help her do something. They were fire and ice together. Some of the time. Some of the time they were just pure fire.

He drew a deep breath and thought about her kisses and how she had melted into his arms and put her whole self into kissing him. In minutes he was aroused, sitting up in bed and knowing that sleep might elude him this entire night, thanks to a lady who was in his bed only a few yards away down the hall.

That thought didn't help any as visions of her in his bed came blazing into his mind.

"Just leave her alone," he said aloud, making resolutions to keep his distance. She didn't want this attraction and he didn't want it. Soon they would part and his world could never under any conditions be part of her world. He wasn't the kind of man for her, and he had never had a serious commitment in his life and he didn't want one now. In the morning—in another hour probably, he would get coffee and then he would get out of the house and not even see Vivian. Lita would be in about eight, but the two of them could get acquainted on their own. Just get out, stay out, stay away and stop getting involved, he thought.

He stretched out again and tried to think about what he had to do tomorrow and what he would do if it turned out to be her husband here looking for her.

The next thing Matt knew he woke and dawn spilled light into the room. He got up, pulled on clean clothes, combed his hair and headed toward the kitchen. He brewed a pot of coffee and poured orange juice.

"Good morning," Vivian said from the doorway.

He turned and his resolutions to avoid her smashed into oblivion. She was barefoot, her hair twisted and looped on top of her head in that casual manner she had with tendrils escaping and trailing down beside her face. She wore a red T-shirt and red shorts, and his first judgment about her legs being long, shapely, fabulous, had been right.

"Wow! You look good," he said, unable to stop staring at her and knowing he better say something or get his wits about him or look away.

His gaze traveled up to amusement dancing in her blue eyes. "Thank you. That's very, very nice to hear after the past nine months. Very nice," Vivian replied.

His gaze drifted down again. Her T-shirt clung as nothing she had worn before did and outlined high, full breasts, and he could imagine their soft weight in his hands. Realizing what he was doing, he looked up. "You like red."

She laughed. "Yes, but the reason I'm wearing so much of it is the way I packed. I didn't pack carefully. I was in a hurry and it seems I have mostly red clothes."

"I like them. Want orange juice?"

"Yes, please. I brought some of Mary Catherine's books and if you'll sit down with me a few minutes, I'll tell you about each story."

His pulse jumped while he fought a small inner war with himself as he thought about all his midnight resolutions to keep his distance from her. If he sat down next to her like he did last night, the same thing would probably result.

"You sit here and I'll sit there," she said as if she could read his thoughts. She pulled out two chairs on opposite sides of the table. She sat down and placed a book in front of the chair she had pulled out for him.

He knew he should walk right out the door, but he wasn't going to disappoint Mary Catherine again, so he sat down where Vivian had indicated he should.

He picked up the little book and looked at pictures of bunnies and then looked over it at Vivian.

"It's the story of Peter Rabbit." She proceeded to tell him the story and he half listened. As she talked, she turned the pages while Matt watched her. He couldn't get enough of looking at her. He was like a fifteen-year-old kid with raging hormones.

She closed the book and picked up another one and started to tell him the story of Little Red Riding Hood. After a moment she stopped. "What is it? I don't have egg on my face because I haven't eaten, but you are staring."

His gaze met hers and he felt knotted inside. He wanted to reach for her even more than he had wanted to last night. "You look gorgeous," he said in a husky voice.

She inhaled, making the T-shirt draw tight across her breasts, outlining them fully. Her blue eyes widened; she licked her lips while her face flushed.

"Matt, we said last night we shouldn't—" she said, her voice changing, lowering a notch and becoming breathless. "Thank you for the compliment. I have to admit, I liked hearing it. Too much. Do you want to hear these stories or should I stop?"

"Don't think about stopping," he said in a thick voice, because she was responding to him with that heated intensity that set him ablaze. "I'll pay attention to the books."

Oh, yeah, a cynical voice within him echoed. Pay attention to *her.* He looked at the book in her long, slender fingers and tried to think about Little Red Riding Hood and the bad wolf, but it was difficult to keep his mind on a child's story. Without looking at her, he was aware of Vivian. He wanted to go around the table and pull her up into his arms and kiss her.

Instead he sat stone-faced through three more stories and then he shoved back his chair and strode to the door. He picked up his pager, and standing in the doorway, he waved it at her. "I have my pager if you need me. Lita will be here soon. Thanks for telling me those stories. Tell Mary Catherine I'll tell her one tonight." He turned and left, striding from the house as swiftly as Vivian had rushed from the kitchen last night.

Vivian got up and crossed the room to the door to watch him climb into his pickup and drive around the barn out of sight. Her pulse was pounding, and even though they hadn't touched this morning, there had been sparks dancing between them and things happening that they didn't have to talk about.

You look gorgeous. His words floated in her mind. How wonderful to hear after nine months of pregnancy! There had been no doubting his sincerity. He looked as if he could have eaten her for his breakfast. For a taciturn, solitary cowboy, he had his moments when he was anything but.

Vivian turned back to the kitchen, looking at the little books on the table. If nothing else, she should try to help Matt with his reading while she was here. He was intelligent, and it shouldn't take much to help him be able to sound out words and figure out words for himself.

Less than two minutes later, she heard a motor and looked out to see him heading back toward the house in his pickup. Her pulse jumped and she dried her hands, going to the door to see why he was returning. When he stopped at the gate, a short, dark-haired, very pregnant woman dressed in jeans and a big, loose T-shirt climbed out of his truck. Matt touched the brim of his hat with his finger in salute to Vivian, then turned around and drove back the way he had come.

"Hi, I'm Vivian Ashland," she said to the young woman approaching the kitchen.

"I'm Lita Hobart."

"Matt told me you would be here today."

Lita stepped inside the kitchen, her dark eyes sparkling. "I can't wait to see your baby. I heard that Matt delivered her and now I'm not so scared in case I can't get back to Enid."

"He was great."

As if Julia knew she was wanted, her cries floated down the hall. "She's awake. Come see Julia and meet Mary Catherine."

In the bedroom Mary Catherine sat in the big bed and was using the remote control to change channels on Matt's large television. Vivian introduced Lita and let her hold Julia until she took the baby back to change her.

"Pete said you're divorced."

"Yes, I am," Vivian replied, leaning over Julia, who was waving her fists and feet in the air and blowing bubbles.

"She's a beautiful baby. I think babies and marriage are wonderful." Lita's smile faded. "I'm not married."

"Did you want to be?" Vivian asked.

"My ex-boyfriend wants to see me again, but he left the state when he found out I was pregnant. He doesn't want a baby. Are you sorry you got a divorce?"

"Not ever."

"Matt told me to page him if any man shows up here looking for you."

Startled, Vivian paused. "Matt told you to page him?"

"Yes. Pete said they're all keeping a watch for any strangers."

Exasperated with decisions Matt had made without mentioning them to her, Vivian stared at Lita. "Well, if my ex-husband shows up here, you don't have to page Matt. The man isn't dangerous. He's an ordinary businessman, for heaven's sake!"

Lita shrugged. "That's what Matt said to do."

Vivian wondered what else Matt had taken it upon himself to do. She picked up Julia to rock and feed her.

Later that day as Vivian combed Mary Catherine's hair and Lita put away towels, Vivian turned to her. "I wanted to see if you could come on the days you don't work for Matt and work for me while I'm here."

"I would like that."

"I need some help with the baby. It'll only be until my car is fixed, but if you're here to watch Mary Catherine and Julia, I can catch up on work."

"I'd like to," Lita said with a broad smile. "I'm saving all my money for the baby. Pete's paying my hospital expenses and Matt said he is getting the doctor's bill."

"That's nice of them."

"It's more than nice. It's a lifesaver for me and a blessing I'll never forget, and I hope I can work and repay them every cent. They're good men."

"Matt is. I barely know Pete," Vivian said, thinking about what Lita just told her. For a solitary, taciturn man, Matt was good to others, so in spite of being a loner, he cared about other people. Her insurance would pay her bills, but Matt had helped in so many other ways.

Vivian knew Matt was kind and generous or he wouldn't have taken her in, but to a certain extent because of the storm, she had been forced upon him. No one was forcing him to help Lita, so helpfulness was just inherent in his nature.

"When's your baby due?"

"About five more weeks, so that's why I'm glad to know Matt delivered your baby and someone here knows what to do. Actually, the doctor suggested I quit this job because of the long drive from town, but I need the work badly. And I like seeing Pete," she added shyly.

Julia's cries summoned Vivian. "I need to bathe and feed Julia."

"May I watch? I know very little about babies. I'll learn soon," Lita said with a broad smile.

"Do you have family here?"

"My mother lives in Alaska with my stepfather. My brother is in Brazil with an oil company, so I don't have any family here. My mother wants me to come to Alaska, but I can't see moving with a new baby. So Matt and Pete are my family."

"How long have you known Matt?" Vivian asked as she filled the tiny tub she had brought for Julia's bath.

"Just two years now. Pete's worked for him since he bought this land."

Vivian listened to Lita talk as she bathed Julia, but her thoughts kept returning to Matt and this facet she had learned about him.

He called three times during the day, but he was late getting in, and Vivian didn't see him again that day or the next until evening. When Mary Catherine was in bed and she had fed Julia, she gave Julia to Matt to hold while she got out the little books and continued the phonics lesson. With Julia in his arms and the table between them, she figured they would keep a distance between them and she knew it was better that way. Yet it was disconcerting to sit only a few feet from him, and as she pronounced letters have him look at her mouth as if the only thoughts in his head were erotic ones.

He was learning to sound out letters and delight filled her when he sounded out a few simple words in one of Mary Catherine's *I Can Read It Myself* books.

The next morning when they ate breakfast outside, she was aware of Matt's constant attention, the approval and desire that burned in his dark eyes when he looked at her. She wore her red shorts and a white cotton shirt and more than once she caught him studying her legs. As they moved around the kitchen, he constantly touched her lightly, his hand on her arm, his fingers brushing hers when he handed her something.

There were no more kisses, but that crackling tension was building, and she was more aware of it each time she was with him.

Jake Claiborne called to tell her that her car was going to take longer to repair than he had expected. Deep down, excitement surged that she would get to stay longer with Matt.

The next week they followed the same routine, and Vivian found she was looking forward more each day to the time for Matt to return home. And she looked forward to his calls, which now were twice a day.

Friday afternoon Matt called Jake Claiborne to check on Vivian's car and learned it would be ready to pick up late Saturday afternoon. He switched off the cellular phone and put it in the seat of the pickup, picking up a chain saw and striding toward the creek. In last week's storm a large cottonwood had been uprooted and had fallen across the creek, damming it up. The creek had gone down and Matt wanted to get the tree out of the creek bed and clear the stream so it could flow into his pond again.

The saw roared, shattering the quiet. As he began to saw, he thought about Vivian. Walt Bently had said to try to get her to stay until her six-week checkup. That was four more weeks.

He wanted her to stay and he was going to try to talk her into it. Four weeks would fly by. How quiet his house would be then! He was becoming adjusted to Mary Catherine's laughter and chatter. He had even adjusted to Julia's crying and he looked forward each day to going home and seeing all three females. They had transformed his house and it no longer was empty, quiet or solitary. Not his house, not his life.

How strong did his feelings run for Vivian? Too damn strong, he knew. Yet there was no future for them. Commitment wasn't his deal, and Vivian would never give up her city life for country living. Four more weeks of her company was all he was asking, yet he suspected he would have to do some convincing to get her to agree to stay that much longer.

Maybe he could tell her he needed the reading lessons to go on longer. He laughed at himself. The damn reading lessons—he was learning to read and it made him feel good, but he was paying a price, sitting across from her and looking at her delectable mouth, having her only a few feet away, yet knowing he shouldn't touch her. It was like putting a kid in a candy store for thirty minutes every night and telling him to look but not touch. Only she was a hell of a lot more tempting than candy.

Matt straightened, put the saw in the bed of the pickup

and went back to wade into the creek and pick up a thick log. He would take the big logs up to the house for firewood this winter.

Winter. This would probably be a damned lonely winter after having the Ashlands fill his house this summer.

"Vivian, I want you to stay," he said aloud. "You've got to be more convincing than that," he told himself. Yet if the lady had decided she wanted to go, he knew he could never convince her otherwise. He knew she would stick to her convictions.

He was late getting home again and decided he would unload the logs from the pickup in the morning. He strode toward the house, his pulse jumping in anticipation of seeing Vivian and her girls. He found them in the yard and looked at Vivian playing with Mary Catherine. Vivian's long brown hair was tied behind her head with a blue ribbon. She wore cutoffs and a T-shirt and she had gotten her figure back swiftly. She looked cool, beautiful, enticing.

"Hi," he said, stepping through the gate.

"Matt!" Mary Catherine exclaimed, spotting him for the first time as his gaze met Vivian's and his pulse jumped.

To his amazement, Mary Catherine ran to him with outstretched arms. Laughing, he dropped the T-shirt he was carrying and scooped her up to swing her high and then set her on her feet. She threw her arms around his legs and hugged him.

"Mary Catherine, you'll get all dusty and muddy," Matt said.

"Don't care," she said, and he bent down to pick her up again.

Holding Julia, Vivian waited under the shade of an oak. He picked up his shirt, then carried Mary Catherine as he crossed the yard to Vivian where he set Mary Catherine on her feet. "Is this where I'm supposed to say 'Hi, honey, I'm home'?"

She smiled. "Lita just left. Supper tonight is cold chicken salad and fruit."

"Anything cold sounds good. I'll go wash up. See you ladies shortly."

Later that night after she had bathed Mary Catherine, Vivian went to the den to find Mary Catherine in Matt's lap, one of her books in his large hands as he slowly read to her. Vivian carried Julia to sit down in the rocker with her. She was gratified that Matt had progressed enough to read to Mary Catherine, knowing what a triumph reading was for him.

Matt had one foot propped on his knee while he held Mary Catherine in the crook of his arm. She was snuggled up against him, and Vivian thought again how grateful she was to him for erasing Mary Catherine's fear of men. She knew Mary Catherine would still be shy around strangers, and that was fine, but she no longer had a fear of all males the way she'd had when they arrived.

Matt glanced up at Vivian and then back to the book, just one of his dark, enigmatic stares that always tripped her pulse. He ran his finger along the words as he read. If Mary Catherine noticed that he read slowly, it made no difference to her. The minute he finished, she pulled up another book. "Read this one."

"It's bedtime," Vivian interrupted. "Since we've been at Matt's, you've been staying up later than usual and tonight's been no exception. Now, off to bed."

Matt stood and swung her to his shoulders and she laughed as she clung to him. When he trotted down the hall, Mary Catherine squealed with pleasure.

Vivian carried Julia with her and trailed behind him, coming into his bedroom to see him dump Mary Catherine on his big bed. She bounced and laughed and bounded to her feet, jumping up and down.

"Mary Catherine, don't jump on the bed."

"It's good-night time, Mary Cat," Matt said, shortening her name and making her giggle. She held out her arms and Matt leaned down to hug her and kiss her cheek, and Vivian's throat knotted. *Don't win your way into all our hearts.* She thought of remarks about him she had heard in town, describing Matt as a loner, solitary, closemouthed, remote, shut off to himself. Yet here he was, opening up to Mary Catherine completely. Opening some to her, too, Vivian knew. She was certain she was the only one to whom he had admitted his inability to read. And he had never let a woman stay at his house before, yet he wanted her to stay until her six-week checkup.

"Tell me one more story," Mary Catherine begged, pulling on his hand. With a nod of approval from Vivian, he sat on the side of the bed, leaning over Mary Catherine, and Vivian's gaze ran the length of his long leg that was stretched out, a scuffed black boot showing beneath the frayed hem of his faded, ripped jeans.

She placed Julia in her crib and went around the bed to sit across from him. Mary Catherine took her hand and still held Matt's with her other hand and Vivian knew that Mary Catherine liked having both of them give her attention. Matt was fast becoming a substitute dad in Mary Catherine's life and Vivian felt another small voice of warning that he was becoming too important to her daughter as well as to her. Maybe it was way too late to try to listen to warnings, she thought as he told Mary Catherine the story of Peter Rabbit.

He kissed Mary Catherine good-night and left the room. Vivian took longer, but finally when Mary Catherine was asleep, she tiptoed out.

She found Matt in the kitchen, getting a cold beer. "Want some lemonade?" he asked.

"Yes, please. I brought Mary Catherine's books. I thought we could go over the reading while Julia sleeps."

"Aren't you getting tired of that?" he asked, amusement lighting his eyes.

"No. You're doing a great job." She went to the table and waited. He crossed the room to her, and she walked around the table to sit down. Matt followed her around the table and pulled a chair beside her.

"Matt, we can concentrate better if you stay on the other side of the table."

"Why? I'll concentrate fine here."

She drew a deep breath. "You know exactly what happened the last time we sat side by side."

"I don't remember."

"Yes, you do," she said, closing a book and standing. "Maybe this wasn't a good idea."

"Hold your horses. I'll just sit here. C'mon and try. I'm ready," he drawled, his voice pouring over her like a thick, sweet syrup.

She was torn between walking out and sitting down. One was the logical, sensible thing to do, the other was exciting and what she had wanted all week. Too aware of him close beside her, she sat down and opened the little book.

They got through the lesson, but by the time thirty minutes had passed, every nerve in her body was quivering; she was conscious of him with a raw need that made her fight her own feelings.

"That's it," she said, closing the book, her frustration outweighing logic.

His hand closed on hers. "One more thing before you turn in. I want to ask you something."

"What's that?" she asked warily, looking into his dark eyes and feeling her pulse jump. He sat only inches away, his legs spread, his chair turned toward her. One arm rested on the back of her chair. The other hand ran lightly back and forth across her knuckles, tickling her slightly, making her too conscious of his touch.

"Will you stay four more weeks until your checkup? I want you to stay."

Chapter 9

With his question Vivian was torn in two directions. How she wanted to say yes and throw caution to the wind. But she was too practical and she had already been with him almost two weeks now, far longer than she had originally intended. He had won her friendship, and the wild attraction between them was something that kept her on a ragged edge.

"Matt, it would—"

"Vivian," he drawled in a honeyed, coaxing voice that vibrated in her like a tuning fork and stopped her reply. "Stay the next four weeks. Mary Catherine is having a wonderful time."

"You've been good to her and good for her. She isn't afraid of you or Pete. I can't tell you how grateful I am to you for that because she was so frightened of men. Baker used to yell at her and send her off in tears."

"Yeah, well, that's over now," Matt replied gruffly. "Hopefully, she can forget. You're working here and you don't have anyone waiting, so staying here isn't keeping you from work or from anyone in your life. It's just four more weeks.''

"That's a month," she said.

"That's not much time out here. Stay." He tucked a tendril of hair behind her ear and let his fingers drift over her ear. Then he placed his hand on her shoulder. She was aware of his touch, more concerned about his tug on her emotions.

"Matt—"

"Vivian, when you go, you'll be gone for the rest of our lives. Give us this little bit of time together. Stay here," he said in a husky voice. "I want you to stay."

She couldn't get her breath, couldn't answer because a firm no wouldn't come and she knew she shouldn't say yes. Trying to think clearly, she stood, pushing back away from him.

He stood at the same time.

"I'll tell you in the morning."

"Why worry through the night about what you'll do?" he said in that deep rumbling tone that was so compelling. "It's not that big a decision. Just say yes." His dark gaze held her immobile and her heart thudded.

"You get your way so easily," she whispered.

"Yeah, let's see if I do," he said, and leaned forward to kiss her, tantalizingly, slowly, rubbing his lips against hers.

She had fought against this moment, dodged it, and yet waited breathlessly for it. His arm slipped around her waist and he pulled her to him. He moved close, tightening his arm around her while his kiss deepened and changed to a breathtaking intimacy that made her heart pound.

Matt leaned over her, holding her tightly against him with his arm wrapped around her waist. She slipped her arms around his neck, kissing him wildly as if a dam had broken inside and all the desire that had been building the past two weeks finally was finding release. She stroked his neck and wound her fingers in his hair while his hand slid down her back and over her bottom, pulling her up tightly against him. She felt his erection, his hardness pressed against her softness. He was solid, warm, strong. His hand slipped lower to the bottom of her cutoffs, stroking her thigh lightly, and then he shifted, his hand going beneath her blouse to her breast.

"Matt—"

His mouth covered hers as he rubbed his hand over her nipple and then cupped her breast. Vivian was fluttery with pleasure that rippled in her. Her breasts were heavy, full, tingly, but the need low in her body made her move closer to him. She moaned softly as her hips thrust against him.

His tongue stroked hers and his kisses were heady. Why did it seem she had spent a lifetime waiting for this moment in his arms? Why this tough cowboy whose world could never be her world, who kept his heart and his feelings to himself? Yet, when he kissed, he gave himself fully. He made her feel as if he wanted her desperately. She couldn't resist, but let her hand slip beneath his T-shirt, and trail across his bare chest.

He growled, deep in his throat, an atavistic male sound of need that made her realize what an effect she could have on him with the slightest touch.

Holding her tightly, Matt bent over her. His body was on fire with wanting her. She was incredibly soft with skin as smooth as vanilla cream. He ached for her, wanted to peel away her clothes, yet it was too soon after childbirth. He knew he had to stop and was amazed she hadn't made him stop yet.

His pulse roared, shutting out all other sounds and his heart thudded violently against his rib cage. Never had a woman's kisses been so devastating. He knew Vivian was special, but he also knew he would have to let her go. Just not yet, not yet.

He cupped her breast, feeling her buttery softness, the weight of her in his hand. He wanted her and before those weeks were up, he hoped she was in his arms in bed with him. He wanted her bare body beneath him; he wanted her passion.

Raising his head, he looked at her. Her eyes were closed, her mouth open from his kisses. "Vivian—" His voice was a thick rasp.

Slowly her lashes rose and the heated fires that burned in her blue eyes were like a blow to his middle. He sucked in his breath as if all air had suddenly been drawn from the room. The lady wanted what he did. He touched the blue vein throbbing in her throat and felt her racing pulse.

"Stay the next weeks. I want you here."

She nodded and he let out his breath, bending his head to kiss her again while joy was rampant, fueling desire. *She would stay! She would stay.* She returned his kiss, her tongue stroking his and thoughts blazed into oblivion.

"Matt," she whispered, catching his hands. "I'll stay, but we can't do this."

"Why not?" he asked, raising his head. Her cheeks flushed and her lips were already red from his kisses. She looked more desirable than ever.

"I don't want to leave here in love," she whispered, and he inhaled, his temperature soaring.

"Given our backgrounds, Vivian, I don't think there's any danger of that," he said solemnly, picking up strands of her long, silky hair and letting them slide through his fingers. "It's early. Don't go to bed yet. Julia is sleeping. Let's go sit outside."

She nodded. He couldn't imagine that she would fall in love with him. There were too many barriers, too many reasons not to. He picked up the drinks and she went with him, letting him hold open the door. She stepped back as he reached for it.

"See, I'm learning," she said.

"You adapt to me amazingly well," he said, making it personal and watching her as something flickered in the depths of her eyes before she walked outside.

He pulled a chair close to hers, turned up the intercom and sat beside her to prop his feet on the porch rail.

"It's beautiful out here," she said.

"I think so."

"Do you sit here at night, too, by yourself?"

"Yes." He laughed and reached for a lock of her hair. "You can't imagine that, can you?"

"Yes, I can imagine you doing that. I heard in town about how solitary you are."

"Well, they're right."

"If you like being here alone all the time, I don't know why you want us to stay."

"I feel like you belong here," he said gruffly, and her pulse jumped. "Logic tells me you don't," he continued, "but it feels that way. How can anyone resist a baby?"

"Most men can resist them easily," she said with a cynical note. "Don't tell me you have always been fascinated by babies."

He chuckled. "You're right. Julia is very special and a very adorable baby."

"You sound like a dad!"

"After helping bring her into the world, I kind of feel like one," he replied quietly, and her amusement faded.

"You were great for both of us. Now all three of us owe you a debt."

"I'll work on that—what you owe me."

"What do you think you'd like," she asked, lowering her voice and flirting with him. "I might not be able to deliver."

"Oh, you'll deliver, Vivian. You're—"

"There I go again!" she exclaimed, interrupting him and throwing up her hands. "What is it about you that brings that out in me? I don't flirt with any other guys I know."

"That's good news," he replied cheerfully.

"There's something about you—" She broke off. "Let's get another subject. I think Lita is in love with Pete," Vivian said, attempting to change the subject. She was aware of how close Matt sat, conscious of his fingers combing through her long hair and surprised she had acquiesced so quickly in agreeing to stay the remaining four weeks. She had rehearsed how she would tell him she had to go when the car was repaired. How she would thank him and then leave. A few kisses, an "I want you to stay," and she was mush.

"I don't know that it'll do her much good. Pete thinks he's too old for her because she's only nineteen," Matt said.

"How old is he?"

"Thirty-six, I think."

"I'm twenty-seven."

"You're a baby. I'm thirty-four," he teased.

"Thirty plus years of doing it your way? No wonder."

"You have twenty plus of doing things your way, so we're a match there."

She smiled at him, knowing he was teasing her. After a few minutes' silence, she returned to their earlier subject.

"Lita talked about Pete all day. She told me that both of you are paying her medical bills."

"She's had a tough time. The guy left her when he found out she was pregnant. She doesn't have family here. She just needed some help."

"That's nice. She loves babies and little children. She's great with Mary Catherine and Julia."

"Good. She'd be good for Pete. I'm glad they're friends

because he needs someone as much as she does, but for vastly different reasons. Whereas, you, independent lady, can take very fine care of yourself.''

"Maybe, Matt.''

He laughed. ''You almost clobber anyone who attempts to do something for you.''

"It's not that bad. I guess it's habit. I grew up that way. My mother was crazy about my dad and neglected everything except him. I ran the household from as far back as I can remember.''

Thinking about her as a little girl, Matt played with strands of her hair while she talked. ''Maybe that's where Mary Catherine gets the gumption to do what needs to be done, like her coming to get me to help,'' he said.

"I don't think that's inherited,'' Vivian remarked dryly.

"I'm sorry you were neglected,'' he said solemnly.

"It wasn't physical. I had what I needed. My parents were so wrapped up in each other, I was an intrusion. When my dad died, I was in my last year of junior high. Mom couldn't manage anything. I worked all through high school. I started with just a file clerk job in a public relations firm, but by the time I was taking college classes, I had moved up in the business.''

"What about your mom?''

"I took care of her until she died two years ago.''

"How'd you meet your ex-husband?''

"While I was in college, I was promoted and had my own clients and that's how I met him. Baker was new in the real estate business and needed some advertising and a logo. I did the PR for his firm and his business grew and mine grew. By the time I finished college, we were married. Three years later, I had Mary Catherine and my own business.''

"You're a very independent, ambitious, successful

lady," he said, drawing his fingers slowly through locks of her hair, letting them fall back on her shoulder.

"I never wanted to be like my mother—totally dependent on a man, totally wrapped up in him. When my father died, my mother's life might as well have ended."

"Well, I think you've succeeded in not being like her."

"You think I'm much too independent, don't you?"

He paused to look into her eyes. "I suppose that's one place where we're alike. I'm independent enough that we clash."

She nodded. "That's nice to hear you admit it. You're used to getting your way in everything. Who's here to oppose you? The cows and horses? I can imagine how many battles with you they win."

He grinned. "Okay, I'm set in my ways." He leaned back in his chair and looked at the sky. "I like living out here. Look at that sky. You won't see that in a city." He reached over and laced his fingers through hers.

"Matt—"

"Shh. I'm only holding your hand. That's nothing."

Vivian knew it was a lot more than *nothing*. Any touch of his set off tremors in her nervous system. She looked at the stars and talked to him quietly, belying the turmoil churning in her. His kisses had her wound up, hot, too aware of him. Even though she wanted him, she was thinking about how swiftly and easily she had capitulated and agreed to stay. In four weeks she might be so hopelessly in love that leaving then would break her heart.

It would hurt now to leave. What would it be like in four weeks?

Amazed how strongly she already felt about him, she listened to the deep rumble of his voice and conversed with him while all time her thoughts were shifting and seething like seas in a storm.

Finally she stood. "Julia is really sleeping. I think I'll go check on her."

He came to his feet at once, resting his hand on her shoulder. "I'm glad you're staying."

"It's against good judgment."

"You'll be fine," he said, "all three of you." He leaned down to brush her lips lightly with a kiss.

"Matt, you can't keep doing that."

He nodded and she left, hurrying inside. Jubilation raged in him along with desire. He burned from her scalding kisses. He wanted her badly and he wanted her in his bed before she left for Houston.

In the meantime, sleep was lost this night. Matt stepped down off the porch and jogged to the road, turning up it and jogging toward the highway, trying to work off the knots her kisses had tied him in.

The next morning after breakfast as Matt was striding across the porch, he glanced at Vivian. "We'll be working up here at the corral this morning, separating some cows and calves. We're selling off some of the calves. If you want to bring Mary Catherine and watch, it'll be fine."

Vivian sat in cutoffs and a T-shirt, with her hair falling loose over her shoulders. Staring into space, she seemed to think over his offer. "Is it dangerous?"

"No, it's not. It's dusty, dirty and noisy."

"We might do that."

"You'll hear us because of the noise. I'm guessing we'll be here in about an hour."

She nodded and watched him stride away. He wore a fresh T-shirt and jeans and his long-legged stride covered the ground swiftly. He climbed into his pickup and drove away.

It was two hours before they were ready, but Mary Catherine was as excited at the prospect as Vivian was. Lita was there to stay with Julia. Vivian took Mary Catherine's hand and they stepped outside into hot sunshine.

Matt had been right. She could hear the bawling of cows, and if Mary Catherine showed the slightest concern or fear, they would come right back to the house. As it was, she could barely hold Mary Catherine back from running off toward the corral. As soon as they rounded the barn, she saw them working in a cloud of dust. It was noisy with the sound of animals moving around, the jingle of harnesses, the yells of cowboys and the slamming of the gates to chutes. She spotted Matt on a large black horse and they moved closer.

As they drew near the rail fence, Mary Catherine became quiet and Vivian thought she might be afraid. The horses were big, the men were yelling, and animals were moving constantly. Matt was bare-chested, with a red bandanna tied around his head. He looked wild, as foreign to men she had known as if he had come from another planet. She thought of his Native American ancestors because now he looked like one of them.

"Want to go back to the house?"

"No." Mary Catherine shook her head vigorously. "Can we sit on the fence like you do when I ride Molasses?"

Vivian watched a few minutes and decided it would be safe to sit and watch, so she helped Mary Catherine to the top rail where she clung tightly. Vivian perched beside her with an arm around Mary Catherine's waist. Matt was busy, and if he knew they were there, he didn't acknowledge them. She suspected he hadn't seen them because he was working his horse with a cow and a calf that were trying to avoid him.

Vivian watched him wheel the horse around, heard him yell as he got the calf separated and drove it into a chute. He turned his horse, saw them and rode over to them. Riv-

ulets of sweat had cut through dust covering his shoulders
and chest.

"Been here long?"

"No. A few minutes."

A cowboy's deep yell caused Matt to turn. Vivian followed his gaze and saw a cowboy in a battle of wills with
a balky horse. The horse reared, pawing the air, but in
seconds the cowboy brought the animal under control and
was working, trying to cut a calf from a cow.

"Like this, Mary Cat?" Matt asked Mary Catherine, and
she nodded her head. Her blue eyes were enormous as she
watched all the milling animals.

"The language may not be great," Matt said to Vivian.

"It's so noisy and so much is going on, I don't think it
will matter. It's too hot and dusty to stay here long."

"I wouldn't stay if I didn't have to," he said with a flash
of white teeth, which were an even sharper contrast than
usual because of the dust on his face. "I better get back,"
he said, and turned away.

As Vivian watched him work, she realized that while this
didn't seem so dangerous, a lot of his work must be. He
dealt with animals and elements of nature and she knew a
lot of the time he must encounter hazards.

In half an hour Mary Catherine was ready to go. Vivian
helped her climb down and took her hand to return to the
house, where she showered and changed after bathing Mary
Catherine. This afternoon they were going to Dakani with
Matt to get her car, and Vivian was looking forward to it.

After lunch Matt told Lita she could take the afternoon
off. Vivian and the girls left to ride with him into Dakani
to get groceries and supplies. When they walked to the
pickup, she saw one of the men waiting.

"Royce's going to ride in with us and drive your car
back."

Vivian laughed. "I can drive my car back, Matt."

"I want you and the girls with me and he wants to go into town, anyway. C'mon, you'll like meeting him."

"I know I'll like meeting him," Vivian said. "Why wasn't I consulted about this? Why do I bother to ask?"

Matt grinned. "You'll get used to my high-handed ways in a few more weeks."

She shook her head and smiled, wondering if she was going to get too used to his ways.

When they drove into Dakani, Vivian looked at a town that was larger than Atwater, but had similar wide streets, cars angled in front of the stores and a center strip for parking in the middle of the main street. There were more shops, more early-1900s brick buildings.

Matt turned off Main along a side street to a large car dealership, where Vivian paid for her car and gave the keys to Royce to drive it home. When she climbed into the car, Matt drove back to Main Street.

"You'll have more choices here because Dakani is bigger than Atwater, but not like Enid," he said as they drove along Main Street and he turned into a parking place. "I'll take y'all to get ice cream this afternoon, and it'll be the same as Atwater. Everyone in town will want to meet you and see Mary Catherine and Julia."

"That's fine. Everyone was nice in Atwater," Vivian said, wondering how many ex-girlfriends Matt had in these parts.

They parted, agreeing to meet at Addie's Grill. Matt stood on the hot sidewalk and watched Vivian walk away, his gaze lingering on the sway of her hips. She wore the red skirt and blouse again and had her hair in a long braid that hung down her back. She was bare-legged and wore sandals, and he wished she were in her cutoffs. She twisted to look over her shoulder, her gaze meeting his, and then she turned and went down the street. Wondering if she was checking to see if he was watching her, he was amused.

She was something to look at, all right. And she would be here four more weeks. Just the thought of having her around the next month made his pulse race.

He bought his supplies, including a new sandbox for Mary Catherine, met them at Addie's Grill and waited patiently while people met Vivian and Mary Catherine and looked at Julia. They kidded him about the delivery, but he didn't mind. Then he took Vivian and the girls to the grocery store, where Mary Catherine once again rode in his cart.

When they were back in the pickup, he drove to the hardware store, running in to purchase one thing. He got back in the pickup and drove down Main Street.

"That was fun today," Vivian said. "There are several ladies here, too, who had endless questions about you and your house and how I like staying there."

"Probably Caitlyn and Becky."

"You guessed right," she said, noticing he was barely listening and kept watching the rearview mirror. And then she realized they were doubling back where they had already driven along Main. "Did you forget something?"

"Just a minute, Vivian," he said, suddenly stopping. Before she could reply, he was out of the pickup. She turned to watch him run to the black car several yards behind them. Traffic moved slowly and the car turned to go around Matt, but he blocked its path and the driver stopped. Matt dashed to the door, jerked it open and yanked the driver out of the car.

Stunned, Vivian glanced at Mary Catherine, who was happily buckled up and playing with a new sticker book in her lap, oblivious of their stop.

She looked back as Matt confronted the stranger. Matt stood with his feet apart, his fists doubled, and he looked ready for a fight. Had Baker found her? Vivian wondered.

Chapter 10

Fury burned as hot as the sun beating down on him as Matt faced a square-jawed, thick-shouldered man who was several inches taller and at least sixty pounds heavier than he was. "Why are you following me?"

"Hey, mister, I wasn't following—"

Matt took a step closer. "We're going to settle this here and now," he said quietly.

"Okay. You can find out easy enough. I'm following the woman in your car."

"Why? Are you Baker Ashland?" he asked, eyeing the man who looked like a linebacker for a pro team.

"No. I was hired by Ashland to follow his wife."

"Ex-wife—right?"

"Yeah, ex."

"Why?" Oblivious to cars creeping past them on the wide street or the stares of people, Matt knew there would be a thousand questions from the locals later, but at the moment he didn't care.

"Look, get outta here. I can charge you with assault."

"There will be assault if you don't answer my question. I'll get the sheriff. He can think of ten reasons to lock you up and lose the key and you'll be buried here in Dakani. You're not in Denver now—you're in a little town where we protect our own."

"Hey! I'm just doing a job."

"What's the job? I want to know if she's going to be abducted, harmed in any way—"

"Hell, no. You know we're blocking traffic."

"My patience is going," Matt said, raising his fist slightly.

"I'm hired to see where she is and where she's going. That's it. No abduction, no harm. Damn, her ex is a suit. He just wants information."

"Yeah, so do I."

"That's it. I'm legit and I was just hired to follow her and report back. Simple."

"You get out of Dakani."

"While you can't tell me what to do, I'll be damn glad to get out of this two-bit flea trap that doesn't even have a movie theater."

"What's your name?"

"Rocky Thornton and I've never met the woman."

"Look," Matt said, leaning close, his voice dropping and becoming deadly quiet, "stay off my place. It's within my rights to shoot trespassers."

"Hey, buddy," the man said, throwing up his hands. "I don't want on your place. What the hell would I do there except watch cows chew grass? I'm outta here."

Matt walked away, half wishing it had been Baker Ashland, yet surprised at how angry he had been to discover they were being followed. He usually didn't have cause to lose his temper except on occasion when he'd had too many beers and someone wanted a brawl at Taylor's Bar. Even then, he had never burned with rage like he had just now.

The thought of anyone threatening Vivian, Mary Catherine and Julia pushed him over the edge. The guy had known who Matt was, and from his reply to Matt about staying away from his farm, Rocky Thornton must have already checked out his house.

The black car passed Matt, and Thornton didn't glance around. At the next corner, he turned and disappeared. He'd been either careless or stupid about following them. Matt had been aware of him for some time, but he wanted to be certain he was being followed before he confronted the guy.

Matt climbed into the pickup, glancing at Mary Catherine, who was happily pulling stickers out and didn't seem aware that he was back or that he had been gone. He looked at Vivian, whose face was white, her eyes wide and filled with worry.

"Should I ask when we get home?"

"Probably. There's no need to talk about it right now," he said, wanting to avoid alarming Mary Catherine.

He picked up the cellular phone, punched in a number and in seconds had Sheriff Gonzales on the line. "I just met Rocky Thornton."

While Vivian listened to Matt's phone conversation, her curiosity was rampant. She had been shocked by Matt's actions. The man had been larger than Matt, but that hadn't seemed to make any difference to either one of them. She looked at Matt, who sat listening quietly, a muscle working in his jaw, and she realized he was still angry. She remembered her own anger when she thought she was being followed, but it was nothing compared to Matt's. For once, he had made his feelings plain.

Would the private detective quit now? Vivian wouldn't be surprised if he did. Unless Baker was paying an exorbitant amount, which he might be doing. When Baker wanted something, he put himself totally into achieving it.

"He was right behind us," Matt continued telling Gonzales. "I just wanted to ask him what he was doing."

That was putting it mildly, Vivian thought, yet the sheriff might know Matt well enough to guess what had just transpired.

"I don't know where he is now. I think he'll stay away from my place. Okay. Thanks." He switched off the phone and dropped it beside him.

Questions swirled in Vivian's mind, but it wasn't until Vivian had tucked Mary Catherine into bed at nine o'clock that night that she and Matt were able to discuss what had happened that afternoon in Dakani. Vivian had changed to cutoffs and a T-shirt. She found Matt sitting in the dark on the back porch and she came out to join him. He had shed his T-shirt and boots and sat with his feet propped on the porch rail. His hair was combed back from his face and tied with a strip of rawhide.

"Finally, I can hear what that was all about."

"It was the guy you thought you saw following you down here."

"I never really got a good look at him, but today I saw it was the same black car with Colorado tags."

"He's Rocky Thornton. Said Baker Ashland hired him to follow you and find out where you settle. He's as dim as a burned-out bulb to follow us like he did and drive a car here with Colorado tags."

"Wasn't that a little drastic today?" she asked, studying Matt.

His head swung around and he looked at her. He lowered his feet from the porch rail and turned to her, making her pulse jump. He picked up the thick braid and untied the ribbon around the end of it, beginning to loosen her hair. "I don't think it was drastic. He's lucky I didn't flatten him. I'm not one of your suits, Vivian. People out here live close to the earth and they're forthright and plain about their feelings. He's scum to follow a woman and two little babies.''

"I don't want you to fight someone over me."

Matt unbraided Vivian's hair, combing his fingers through it. Placing one arm across the back of her chair, he drifted his hand over her nape as he leaned closer. "You don't, huh?"

"No, I don't," she answered, aware of Matt watching her and conscious how close he sat. "You could get hurt and you could hurt someone needlessly. He hasn't harmed me."

"I'm not worried about getting hurt."

"I'm sure you're not," she said, thinking how fierce he had looked today.

"So just let him follow you?"

"Well, I don't like that, either, but you might just talk to him."

He grinned and she could see his white teeth in the darkness. "That's all I did today. Just a question or two."

"After you yanked him out of the car."

Julia's cries came over the intercom and Vivian started to stand, but Matt squeezed her shoulder. "Stay where you are," he said. "I'll change her and bring her to you. I'll turn my back so you have privacy while you feed her."

"You don't—"

"I know I don't need to. Stay put."

"Yes, sir."

He grinned and was gone and she shook her head. He was going to do what he was going to do. She would like to see him changing a diaper. What would the P.I. think if he could see Matt now?

Vivian waited to hear a call for help from him, but in a surprisingly short time he reappeared holding Julia, with a thin cotton baby sheet spread between her and his shoulder. He lowered her carefully, holding her head, to hand her to Vivian.

She took the baby and he moved his chair, pulling it closer to the porch rail and turning away from her. "You don't need to leave, Vivian. I'll turn around and give you privacy. Just stay here where we can talk."

She shifted Julia, who was hungry and began to suck greedily. Matt's voice was quiet and deep as they talked.

"Think the P.I. will quit now?" she asked.

"Why would he quit? He gets paid for dealing with situations far worse than today. I didn't scare him off. I think he'll hang around and try to see where you go when you leave. I imagine he's keeping tabs on your car."

"Have you asked Jake Claiborne if he's contacted him?" Vivian asked.

"Thornton hasn't contacted Jake, but he contacted one of Jake's mechanics. He knows your car was repaired. He'll inform Baker and probably hang around and keep watch on the farm."

"Watch us here?"

"Sure. He can park on a section line with some high-powered binoculars and see us come and go. Or he can risk trespassing, but Pete's told the other farm hands to watch for any stranger. I don't think Thornton will set foot on my farm."

"No, I don't think so," she said, unable to imagine the man trespassing after the encounter today. "You weren't afraid of him at all, were you?"

"No, I wasn't. Fear is the last thing I would feel with someone like that."

She gazed into the darkness beyond the yard and goose bumps broke out on her arms in spite of the summer night. "I don't like to think about someone out there watching us."

"Forget it, Vivian. You're safe here and all Thornton can do is watch. He won't do that if I catch him."

"Matt, please don't resort to violence."

He laughed. "That guy only understands violence. A punch in the nose isn't violent."

"It is!"

"Is this another difference between us? Sheriff Gonzales promised to keep watch. He and his deputies are going to drive by the farm fairly often, so he will handle it if he catches Thornton. I won't promise no violence if I catch him on my land. He's not going to trespass on my property and spy on you and Mary Catherine and Julia. No way."

"I give up."

"You might as well."

They sat in silence for a time. When she had finished nursing Julia, she put the baby against her shoulder and heard a tiny burp. She smoothed the thin batiste shirt Julia wore and cradled her in her arms.

"Want to hold her?" Vivian asked Matt.

He twisted around and stood, moving his chair back beside her, and then he leaned down to take Julia in his arms. "What a sweetie," he said softly to her, and Vivian again was amazed at the gentle streak in him.

He sat down, cradling Julia. She seemed content and lay in the crook of his arm, gazing up at him. He talked to her a few minutes and then Vivian asked him a question and soon they were talking, avoiding further conversation about Rocky Thornton.

They talked for a while longer and then when Julia stirred, Vivian picked her up to take her to bed.

As she leaned over Matt he stood and handed Julia carefully to her, then he leaned down and brushed Vivian's mouth with a light kiss. "Good night, Vivian," he said in a husky voice.

"'Night, Matt."

She went inside, her mouth tingling from the faint brush of his lips. Was she making an incredible mistake by staying for four more weeks? They were thrown together morning and night and the sparks flew any time they were together. She thought about the private detective. She didn't like the thought of being followed, even though that was all the man was doing.

Three nights later as Vivian sat on the porch with Matt, they could see lightning on the horizon and she kept remembering that first night with him and wondered if the lightning made him think about it, too. They had developed a routine in the evenings, and after Mary Catherine went to bed, they sat on the porch and talked. Vivian kept Julia with her and Matt gave her the privacy to nurse the baby, so Vivian should have been satisfied with the arrangement. With Julia in her arms or his arms, Matt had to keep his distance. But instead of finding such an arrangement less disturbing, she was more disturbed by it. Being together day after day was tying her in knots.

Now as she sat beside him in the dark and watched lightning flashes on the horizon, she was prickly with awareness of him.

When Julia cried and she rose to go, Matt brushed her lips lightly with a kiss. He did this when he left for work in the morning, too, and each of those little light kisses that might be so casual to him were far less than casual to her. They were building a fire within her that threatened to blaze out of control.

After she had gone, Matt sat in the darkness, his body hot, tied in knots over Vivian while he planned Saturday night. He had asked Lita to stay with the girls so he could take Vivian to dinner and to a honky-tonk for a little two-step.

Today he had talked to Sheriff Gonzales who said he

hadn't seen anything of the P.I. and maybe he had left town. Matt didn't think so. From what Vivian had told him about her ex, he didn't sound like the kind of man to give up easily. That was why Matt had driven Vivian to Enid two days ago to appear in court to get a restraining order against Baker.

Matt watched the lightning and the mass of clouds boiling on the horizon. Before long he realized it was all moving closer and he suspected they would get rain tonight.

He sat quietly, knowing he wouldn't sleep if he went to bed. Vivian had wrecked his peaceful nights as no other woman ever had.

Why had she picked Houston? Was there a particular reason? Could she work as well in Oklahoma City, which was a lot closer to the farm?

Let her go. How many times had he told himself that, yet instead, he touched her every chance he got.

In the distance thunder rumbled, and Matt thought about stock, the barn and the pickup, mentally checking off livestock and equipment to make certain things were ready if they caught another big storm. The stars were gone now and clouds covered the sky. Gusts of hot wind whipped across the porch. Matt got up and walked down to the barn, checking doors and gates before returning to the house and locking up. He showered and threw himself across the bed, trying to think about rain instead of the woman in his bed at the end of the hall.

In the night a loud cry wakened Matt. He came to his feet instantly, yanking on jeans. "What the hell?" he said as he tried to fasten buttons.

Mary Catherine's screams mingled with Julia's crying. As he yanked open the door and hit the light switch, his heart pounded. No lights came on, and his fear escalated.

"Vivian!" he called.

Chapter 11

"Matt," Vivian cried from not too far away. "The lights are out."

"What's the matter with Mary Catherine?" he asked as he groped his way toward Vivian. His eyes adjusted to the darkness, and when lightning flashed he could see Vivian standing in front of one of the open doors to a bedroom. She was holding Julia, who was crying.

"I was taking Julia to the kitchen when Mary Catherine woke up. She's terrified of storms and I was just on my way to her."

He reached Vivian. "Come on. I'll help you to the bedroom and then I can take Julia while you quiet Mary Cat. Is Julia hungry?"

"No. I don't know what's wrong. She's been fed and she's just unhappy."

He slid his arm around Vivian's waist. She was wearing her gown and robe, but both were thin and he could feel her slender, warm body and he had an instant reaction.

Without hesitation he led her along the hall and into the bedroom. He crossed the room to Mary Catherine, and when lightning flashed he saw her sobbing in the middle of his big bed.

He picked her up and she clung to him, wrapping her arms around his neck. "I'm scared!"

"You're safe, Mary Cat. We're in the house and not one raindrop can touch you." She buried her face against his neck and he turned to Vivian, who was patting Julia and trying to calm her.

"Want a little glass of milk?" he asked Mary Catherine. "I can put chocolate in it."

"Yes," she said without raising her face. "Turn on the lights."

"We can't turn them on right now because of the storm, but the house is just the same in the dark as it is in the light."

"I'm scared."

"I'm holding you and nothing can harm you. When we get your milk, I'll let you hold a flashlight. Do you know what a flashlight is?"

"No."

"I'll show you, and you'll like it."

Vivian listened to Matt's voice fade as he walked down the hall. She patted Julia as she walked and then rocked the baby. Gradually Julia grew quiet and then fell asleep. Vivian put her down in her crib and turned to go find Matt and Mary Catherine, but he came through the door with Mary Catherine in his arms.

"I told her stories until she fell asleep." He placed Mary Catherine gently in bed and pulled a sheet over her, placing her teddy bear beside her.

"Thanks for your help. She's terrified of storms."

"Want something to drink? I won't sleep now."

"Yes."

Thunder rattled the panes and rain drummed on the windows as he reached out. "I left the flashlight in the kitchen. Give me your hand. I know where we are and where the furniture is."

She held out her hand and he took it, his warm fingers closing over hers. As she moved beside him, he shifted his arm around her waist. "This is better."

She could see a faint glow from the kitchen where he had left the flashlight. He walked down the dark hall with the sureness of a cat. As soon as they stepped into the kitchen, he turned to her. When thunder boomed and a flash of lightning streaked outside with the bang of a rifle shot, Vivian jumped.

"Hey, not you, too," Matt said quietly, rubbing her nape. "Scared of storms?"

"No. Well, I don't like them, but I know that's ridiculous. It just was scary to have Mary Catherine screaming and Julia crying and the lights out in a house I'm not that familiar with, although I should be by now."

He was rubbing her nape, looking down at her, and as she talked, she forgot about the storm raging around them. He was bare-chested, his jeans lower than ever and partially unbuttoned. He stood only inches away in front of her and she became acutely aware of him, forgetting conversation. Her gaze ran across his broad chest and strong muscles and then she looked up to find him watching her. He tipped her chin up and her pulse drummed. She wanted him to kiss her and her pulse was racing madly.

Heat flashed in Matt and he slid his arm beneath her robe, his hand trailing over the thin cotton gown she wore. He pulled her against him, feeling her hands brush across his chest, slide over his shoulders and then her arms wrap around him. She was soft in his arms, pliant, warm and eager.

She had all but reached for him first, and Matt's heart

pounded. Every day he thought about her constantly and he had erotic dreams and wild fantasies about her.

Now she was standing in his embrace, clad in only her gown and robe. He wanted to tear them both away, but he knew it was still too soon for her, yet how passionate she was! Her tongue stroked his, going into his mouth as he kissed her. He felt her tremble, heard her moan softly, and he slid his hand down her back.

Each caress of his hands was fuel to the blaze kindling in her. He pushed away her robe and then he slid the strap of her gown off her shoulder. With a lingering caress, he pushed the other strap. He leaned back, releasing her slightly to look down at her. She was bare to the waist for him and she drew a deep breath, her breasts tingling before he touched her.

"You're beautiful, Vivian," he whispered, stroking her breasts, and then he cupped them in his large hands, his skin dark against her pale skin.

She closed her eyes, winding her fingers in his hair as he bent to kiss her, his tongue flicking over her nipple. She ached with desire, wanting him, knowing she couldn't— she shouldn't think about anything more. Physically, it was too soon; emotionally—she wasn't ready at all. Yet caress by caress, moment by moment, she was losing her heart to him. Being so good with both girls won her over. Being so kind to her won her over. His kisses and caresses were golden shackles that made her a prisoner of her heart and readied her body for seduction.

He pushed up the hem of the gown, his hand trailing along her thigh.

She caught his wrist to stop him. "Matt, it's too soon. We shouldn't. There are a thousand reasons," she whispered.

"I'm just barely touching you," he said against her lips,

and then kissed her, bending over her and trailing his hand around to run his fingers lightly across her bottom.

She moaned, her hips thrusting against him while she clung to him, and kissed him passionately. In minutes he knew he had to stop or he would be doing things he shouldn't.

"Matt," she whispered.

He moved his hands up, to cup her breasts again, to kiss and fondle her and keep her from telling him no. And finally he wrapped his arms around her, holding her close against his heart as he bent over her and kissed her hard and long, feeling her heartbeat drum wildly with his. He said more with his kisses than he ever could with words. With hungry, passionate kisses, he hoped she realized how much he wanted her and what she could do to him so easily.

Vivian clung to him, her hips thrust against him while she kissed him. She slid one hand over him, touching his shoulder, his arm, his back, down over his hip, and he groaned as she stroked his thigh, a faint touch through his thick jeans, yet it was a fiery brand.

He wanted to feel her hands all over him, to touch her all over, to drive her to the height of passion.

Instead, he held her and kissed her until she finally pushed against him. "Matt, we have to stop."

He looked down into her wide blue eyes, which in the dimly lit room still showed desire burning in their depths. His heart pounded and he wanted her with all his being and had to struggle against impulses that made him want to keep right on kissing her. She wriggled out of his grasp and stepped back.

"We can't. I can't. I have to stop."

"I know it, Vivian. It's kisses. Nothing more."

Only it was a whole lot more to her. Her gaze raked over him and she saw his arousal, knew how he wanted her. Oh, it was so much more than just kisses! His touch was wakening desire again, turning her back into a woman who felt alluring and strengthening a bond that already ran deep. She knew he felt inadequate sometimes because of his limited reading ability and his country ways. Yet his country ways were direct, honest and strong. She liked them, too. He said what he meant and meant what he said which was important. She could trust him completely—*had* trusted him totally with not only herself, but with Mary Catherine and Julia. He hadn't let her down.

Was she already falling in love with this tall cowboy who had come into her life like the storm they had both been caught in?

The realization shook her and she pushed it out of her thoughts, yet he was watching her closely and his eyes narrowed as if he could follow the train of her thoughts.

"Maybe I should just go back to bed—"

She started to turn away, but he touched her arm. "C'mon, Vivian. We'll get something to drink. You're not going to sleep right now, are you?"

"No," she answered, aware of his fingers so lightly brushing her arm.

"C'mon," he coaxed, and moved away from her to get cold drinks. They sat and talked for more than an hour. The lights flickered several times and then came back on. Finally Julia's cries interrupted them and when Vivian stood, Matt did, too.

"Call me if you need me," he said.

"Sure."

Because of the storm Matt was busier than ever the next few days. Creeks had flooded and ponds were overflowing. Vivian saw him at breakfast and late at night, but not in between. He still called to talk to her most days at least once, sometimes more often.

By the fourth week her body was mending swiftly and

her strength was returning. With Lita around six days a week to help, Vivian had more freedom and she was beginning to walk early in the morning, following the hard-packed dirt road from the house to the road. When Matt found out what she was doing, he took all of them out one evening to show her another road that led away from the barn across his farm.

"I'll feel better if you walk here," he told her as he carried Julia and Mary Catherine skipped along beside Vivian. "You'll be in the middle of the farm, not up by the highway."

"Since we haven't seen any more of the P.I., maybe he went back to Denver."

"Maybe, but there's no need to take chances."

"Even if I walk up by the highway, I don't think I'm in danger."

"I'll say it again—there's no need to take chances. I'll worry less."

She smiled at him. "You don't need to worry about me."

"Right."

They strolled in silence and she looked at leaves twisting in the evening breeze on a tall cottonwood ahead of them. Shadows were lengthening and a mockingbird's melodic cry could be heard. "It's so peaceful out here, you forget the turmoil elsewhere."

"That's right," he said, turning to study her. She became aware that he was watching her and wondered what was running through his mind.

"You fit in here better than I thought you would," he said, and she laughed.

"You sound as if I'm in a prison."

"That's how some city folk would view it."

"It's a nice change at this time in my life. This is a good place to bring a baby into the world."

"Yeah, sure," he said, smiling at her. "Next time, Vivian, pick a big city hospital that has facilities. Thank heaven Julia didn't have complications."

"There won't be a next time, thank you," she said. "I have my family."

"You might marry again."

"No. That hurt too badly, too much."

"Life's full of risk."

"I don't notice you taking any where marriage is concerned."

He shrugged. "I have better reasons than you do."

"Not from my viewpoint. From what I see, you're selling yourself short. And when we go into town, my goodness, there are some ladies who would love to go out with you."

"No one told you that!" he said with disgust.

"They don't have to. They hang on every word I say about you."

"Baloney, Vivian. Up ahead where the fence is, you need to stop and turn around and head back to the house unless you want to come face-to-face with my bull, and I'll tell you now, you don't want to."

They strolled leisurely back to the corral, where Matt gave Mary Catherine a ride on Molasses. After her bath, Mary Catherine found Matt on the porch and asked him to read to her before she had to go to bed. She climbed into his lap and Vivian sat nearby, rocking Julia while she listened to Matt read one of Mary Catherine's books.

He had become familiar with the book and his reading skills were increasing, so he read at a faster pace, no longer moving slowly over the words and having to point at each one. Vivian knew he was sensitive about his reading and that he didn't care to even receive compliments. She also knew he was quietly pleased with his progress, and a couple of times when she had to leave him to take care of Julia, she had come back to find him reading.

Now she looked at the cowboy and her daughter. Matt was in his jeans and T-shirt, one booted foot propped on his knee, holding Mary Catherine in her frilly pink pajamas. She had her arm around his neck, her skin so pale next to his dark brown skin. She looked fragile in his arms, yet she looked as if she belonged there, something she had never had with her own father.

With a pang Vivian realized how sentimental she was getting and looked away.

When Matt closed the book, she stood, shifting Julia in her arms. "All right, Mary Catherine, it's bedtime."

Mary Catherine tightened her arms around Matt's neck. "Please, please, one story in bed."

"Mary Catherine, he's read two stories to you."

He glanced at Vivian and she knew he was going to do exactly what Mary Catherine wanted. He stood, holding her and her books easily. "One story in bed and then night-night."

Mary Catherine grinned as he shifted her to his shoulders and she clung to him, wrapping her fingers in his hair.

"What a pushover," Vivian mumbled as she walked beside him.

"How could I say no to two pleases?"

Vivian smiled and then wanted to throw up her hands in exasperation when they reached the bedroom and Matt turned to dump Mary Catherine on the bed, making her shriek with laughter and bounce right up.

"Now she's good and awake again," Vivian said.

"She'll go to sleep," he said good-naturedly, and sat down to pull off his boots, stretching his long legs out before him. Mary Catherine promptly climbed into his lap again and he picked up another book to read.

Vivian put Julia down in her crib, gathered the girls' clothes and carried them to the laundry room to wash.

Matt watched her go and then looked down at the book. Mary Catherine was a warm, soft bundle in his arms, trusting and sweet, and he had only loathing for any man who would yell at her.

He turned a page and wished he could put his feelings into words to at least halfway thank Vivian for the phonics lessons. She had opened a new world to him, and already he could see endless possibilities.

Vivian had changed his life forever in so many ways, yet it was impossible to tell her.

When she returned, Matt was finishing the story.

"Now, tell Matt good-night. It's bedtime," Vivian said to her daughter.

He stood and leaned down to kiss Mary Catherine.

"Goodnight," she said. "I love you."

Vivian saw Matt's chest expand as he drew in a deep breath. He brushed Mary Catherine's hair from her face. "I love you, too, Mary Cat."

Satisfied with his answer, she smiled as she snuggled down in bed. He turned and looked into Vivian's eyes and she experienced a sweeping sense of devastation. Mary Catherine already loved him. Vivian stared into his brown eyes. How much did *she* feel for him?

He looked as shaken as she was by Mary Catherine's declaration, staring at Vivian solemnly until she realized how the silence was stretching between them.

"I'll come out when she's asleep," she said quietly, moving around him to Mary Catherine.

He left the room without a word and she sat on the side of the bed to take Mary Catherine's hand.

"Do you love Matt, too?" Mary Catherine asked solemnly, gazing up at Vivian.

Vivian looked down into anxious blue eyes. "He's very

good to us,'' she answered, mulling over Mary Catherine's question and knowing that more and more, in spite of all caution, she was falling in love with him.

Midmorning the next day when the phone rang, Vivian answered, ''Whitewolf's.''

''Hi.'' The voice was deep and familiar.

Pleasantly surprised because she hadn't expected Matt to call this morning, she smiled. ''Hi. I thought you were working up here by the barn this morning. I didn't think you'd call.''

There was a moment's silence. ''Is this Lita?''

Startled, she realized she wasn't talking to Matt. ''Sorry. I thought it was Matt. No, this is Vivian Ashland,'' she said cautiously, thinking of the P.I. ''You sounded like Matt.''

''I reckon so. I'm his brother Jared. I wanted to leave a message for him.''

''He said he would be at the barn. If you'd like, I can take the phone to him.''

''Sure.''

''Just a minute, let me tell Lita.''

Vivian went to the den to tell Lita, who sat on the floor with Mary Catherine while Julia slept nearby.

''Now I'm on my way. You live just outside Tulsa, right?'' Vivian asked Jared while she walked outside to find Matt.

''Yes, ma'am. You know about me, but I don't know about you.''

''Well, I'm Vivian Ashland and a friend of Matt's.''

''You live around there?''

''As a matter of fact, no I don't, except right now I'm staying here. I'm from Colorado. I hear you and your wife are expecting a baby.''

''That's right. In three more months.''

"That's really wonderful," Vivian said. "You have a little girl, too."

"Right. Merry. You know a lot about me."

"Matt has told me about you and his family."

"Has he now?" Jared drawled.

"Your voices are very much alike," she said, looking in the open barn. She heard a clang and went around the barn to find Matt behind it with his head beneath the hood of a large, battered truck.

"Here's Matt. It was nice to talk to you, Jared."

"Thanks, Vivian. Nice to talk to you."

She held out the phone. Matt had shed his shirt and had his hair tied behind his head. He wiped grease off his hands and took the phone.

"It's Jared." She started to turn away.

"Wait," Matt said as he raised the phone to his ear. She paused and looked around. The truck was beneath the shade of a tall cottonwood and it was still relatively cool for a summer morning. She moved a few yards away and stood beside the truck in the shade.

"Vivian Ashland," she heard Matt say. "She's living here."

She gave Matt a look with arched brows, wondering what his brother must think with that kind of answer. She felt as if she was intruding and started to go, but Matt held up his finger to indicate he wouldn't be long.

"Yep. No, we just met a few weeks ago. She went into labor when she wrecked her car on my place and she had her baby here, so she's staying awhile." He winked at Vivian.

How simple he made it sound. She could imagine his brother's questions.

"That's right, born in my house." There was another pause.

Matt had one hand splayed on his hip, his booted foot

propped on the bumper of the truck while he talked. He looked handsome, too appealing in spite of sweat and splotches of grease. She turned her back so she wouldn't stare at him, touching the rough wood of the flatbed of the truck.

"I did. Sure did. Want to ask Vivian?"

She turned around, wondering what they were discussing.

"Yeah, I still need it. Good. Thanks, Jared. How's Faith? And Merry? Give them my love. Sure, Jared."

He punched the off button and set the phone on the truck and pulled on his T-shirt. "That'll cover some of the grease," he said, wiping his hands more thoroughly. "Well, you may meet brother Jared soon. That call has his curiosity running wild."

"Because I'm here?"

"That's right."

"This is what you get for never bringing a woman home before. That makes my staying here—which is perfectly logical and harmless—an event to stir everyone's curiosity."

He approached her and put his hands on either side of her, leaning against the truck and hemming her in. As he leaned closer, her pulse jumped. She could feel the heat of his body, smell the mixture of aftershave and grease, and his dark eyes made her pulse race.

"There," he drawled, "you just admitted that your staying here is perfectly logical and harmless. I'm glad to hear you say what I've been telling you all along. You know, I don't get to see you much during the day. This is a treat," he said, his gaze traveling over her features as if he were memorizing them.

"You just saw me a few hours ago at breakfast," she said, and her words were breathless.

He was looking at her mouth with that gleam of intention

in his eyes that told her he would kiss her. "Matt, we said we'd not let things get out of hand," she said, yet there wasn't a note of firmness in her protest.

"I'm not letting anything get out of hand," he replied, sounding amused. His gaze met hers. "Think I'm going to throw you down here in the grass and take you?"

"There's a wildness in you that makes me uncertain what you'll do." Now her pulse raced wildly.

"Scared?" he teased in a low, husky voice that would have never stirred fright in her.

"I'm not scared of you. I couldn't ever be," she said with complete honesty.

"That's good, because you shouldn't be."

"I'm scared of me," she admitted quietly, and he inhaled, making his chest expand.

"When you say things like that, do you expect me just to turn and walk away?"

"I know I shouldn't say things like that, but there's something about you that causes me to flirt and confess and share and do things I don't usually do."

"That's good, Vivian," he whispered solemnly. "I want the part of you that's the deepest, innermost part. I don't want you to hold back anything."

He leaned down to brush her throat with his lips, but it was his words that made her tremble. He kept his feelings all bottled up ninety percent of the time, but every once in a while he let them surface, and when he did, the effect on her was devastating.

"Aah, Matt," she said, sliding her arms around his neck. "You're irresistible."

He wrapped his arms around her to kiss her, turning both of them so he could lean back against the truck and spread his legs, his hand going down to her bottom to pull her up against him. He kissed her hard and she returned his kisses, making his pulse pound. Her kisses heated him more than the hot sun climbing high above them, and Matt hoped desire was building in her just as it was in him.

He raised his head because he knew she had to get back to the house. Her eyes held blue flames of desire. "You're going to be mine, Vivian."

She put her fingers lightly on his lips. "I can't be. I just can't be. I'm not ready for that and you've told me over and over how you never wanted a serious relationship. Matt," she said solemnly, taking her fingers from his mouth and trailing them along his jaw. Her gaze was as direct as his. "Any relationship I have will be more than serious. It'll be forever. At this point in my life, I can't and won't enter into any relationship lightly. I rushed into marriage when I was young and what a mistake I made! I don't ever want to make that mistake again. You've convinced me you don't want anything serious."

"That's a real pretty speech," he drawled in that honeyed, rasping voice that was seductive all by itself. "But I'm telling you, Vivian, you'll be mine." He kissed her throat lightly, his breath and mouth warm against her, making her tingle while his words swirled and caused a clash of emotions.

She framed his face with her hands, feeling a faint stubble and knowing that often now he shaved when he came in and cleaned up in the evening. He watched her while she stared back at him.

"If that's true—that I'll be yours, then you better get ready for commitment, Matthew Whitewolf," she said in earnest. "Because it won't be any other way."

She turned and yanked up the phone and left him, striding away and knowing he was standing behind her, watching her. Her emotions were a roller coaster, riding high with his emphatic declaration that took her breath away and then sliding to the depths because she didn't want to fall in love with him and leave here and have one more sorrow to pack along with her.

She threw up her hands. *You'll be mine.* "Do you know what that means, Mr. Whitewolf?" she snapped, talking to herself. "It means you'll be involved, too. Did you ever stop to think that you might fall in love even if you didn't plan to? That we should be careful because we're wading into dangerous depths? The man has me talking to myself," she muttered, glancing over her shoulder. He had come around the barn and was standing with his hands on his hips, immobile, watching her. Had he seen her throw up her hands? Could he possibly hear her? She reassured herself that he could not. She headed toward the house again.

What were the depths of her feelings for Matt? Should she pack and go now, get out before she got more deeply involved with him? The question that haunted her at night now floated into her mind. Was it too late? Was she already in love with him?

She knew that with each day, he was becoming more important to her. Desire and friendship were interwoven to such an extent there was no thinking of one without the other. Yet, love? She wasn't in love. She would know if she were in love. She turned around to look at him again and they stood staring at each other across a hundred yards from the house to the barn. What ran through his mind? When she thought of his kisses, excitement streaked like lightning in her.

As she stared at him, he touched his forehead with his finger and waved at her in a salute, and then turned to disappear around the barn.

She rushed back to the house and took Julia from Lita, knowing the baby would get her mind off Matt.

It was after three when Lita had nothing to do and said she would take Julia and Mary Catherine outside for a while. Vivian went in to work at her computer.

First she retrieved her e-mail, looking at the screen and then glancing out the window, her thoughts on Matt.

What do I feel for him? she wondered. He was very special to her. He had become her best friend so swiftly, so easily. She could tell him anything, yet again, she knew that was because of the shared intimacy of childbirth.

She was mending, gaining back strength and energy—and along with it the desire Matt had awakened was becoming something to reckon with in her life. Each kiss now was more fiery and made her want so much more of him.

She stared at the computer screen and tried to concentrate. Four new messages. She watched as the numbers counted down as each one was placed in the in-box. She scrolled through them to take them in order of importance, but the name on the second letter jumped out at her and her fingers froze on the keyboard. She stared at the name Douglas Sayles.

Baker's attorney had sent her a message. She pulled it up, read through it and knew that Baker Ashland was far from out of her life.

Chapter 12

Through supper that night Matt noticed that Vivian was quieter than usual and he wondered if it was because of their conversation by the barn this morning.

He gave Mary Catherine her customary evening ride on Molasses and perched on the fence beside Vivian while Pete led Molasses around the corral. Matt held Julia in the crook of his arm, but with his other hand he rubbed Vivian's shoulder.

"This is the first chance we've had to be alone since this morning. What's wrong?"

She turned to look at him. "What makes you think anything is wrong?"

"Tell me everything is fine."

"You're right. I was going to tell you after I put the girls down. I got an e-mail letter from Baker's lawyer today."

"The restraining order doesn't apply to intermediaries?"

"No. And he knows how to find me. I still have the same e-mail address. Even if I didn't, Baker knows two of my clients, so he could have gotten a new address from them, anyway."

"Does he want you to come back?"

"Yes. Baker is offering to put a quarter of a million dollars in my account if I'll come back to Denver. He'll do a huge ad campaign with my company and, in addition, get me two big clients. In other words, he would guarantee me and the girls a good future."

Startled by the offer, Matt stared at her. "Baker's worth that much?" he asked, thinking once again how different her world was from his. *A quarter of a million dollars*— that was so far beyond his scope. The farm was mortgaged, and he had some major equipment to pay for. He had bought a combine three years ago and it would take another two years to finish paying for it if he had good crops and the weather didn't play havoc with the farm.

A lead weight smashed his heart. The offer had to be tempting no matter what a bastard Baker Ashland was. She had two little girls to raise, and any single parent had double duty and a tough job. For the first time, Matt wondered how big Vivian's business was. It might be far more successful than he had imagined.

"You said he made you this offer if you would go back to Denver. Was it back to Denver or back to him?"

"It was back to Denver. That would help him save face, soothe his ego, and if I went back, I'm sure he would claim that I was coming back for a reconciliation. I would be there in town, doing his business, seeing him constantly, and it would look like a reconciliation."

Matt dropped his hand from her shoulder and knew she was slipping away from him. She was so solemn, she must be giving thought to going back. How could she? A voice inside him screamed protests, but common sense told him that no one would easily turn down such an offer if she had two little girls to think about.

Matt looked down at Julia, who was peacefully sleeping, snuggled up against him. He didn't want Vivian to return to Denver where Baker was or to take Mary Catherine and Julia back there. Yet what right did he have to argue with her and try to talk her out of it if she wanted to go? It was a fabulous offer, he had to admit, but that didn't make him like it. His cold loathing and contempt for Baker Ashland escalated a notch.

Every impulse in him wanted to urge her to turn down the proposition, but he knew he had nothing to give her in place of going. He couldn't provide commitment; he couldn't do one thing to increase her business or her income. He didn't have one damned thing to offer her.

Watching Mary Catherine happily riding Molasses and laughing with Pete, Matt thought about how terrified the little girl had been of him when she had first arrived. Did Vivian want to take her child back into that situation for any amount of business or money?

"Don't go," he said harshly, knowing he should keep his mouth shut but unable to keep silent.

Watching her, he caught the surprise on her face.

"Matt, I wouldn't think of going back," she said.

Relief was thick and overpowering, as if a rock had lifted off him. But then he thought about how solemn she had been, so something about Baker was worrying her. "If you're not even considering going back, why are you so down?"

She inhaled and his gaze drifted down over her profile. The late-evening sun slanted across the land and she was caught in its rays, highlighting the sheen of her hair, emphasizing her crystal-blue eyes. "Because if he wants me badly enough to give me that much money and make a giant offer, he isn't going to give up easily when I tell him no."

"Oh, hell, is that what's bothering you? You have a restraining order, and while you're here I'll keep him away."

"That's only the next two weeks. I'm thinking about the rest of my life. He'll come after me in Houston. If he wants me back this badly, he's not going to give up when I say no. And for a man with the money and influence Baker has, a restraining order is a mere slap on the wrist."

"His money won't do any good in Newton County. Sheriff Gonzales can cause him grief if he tries to come see you."

"I don't think he'll come until I'm settled in Houston. He's gotten a full report from the P.I. about you. I imagine he'd just as soon avoid you as not."

"He must love you."

"No, he doesn't love me. You can't imagine his ego because you don't have that kind of ego. Everything he does has to be the biggest and the best. Eventually, I'm sure he'll marry again, but the divorce is a failure and Baker can't admit to any failure in his life. This is for show. If I go back, he can make it look good to others, and eventually he can lead people to believe he decided to dump me. Baker has no love for me or for the girls. Absolutely none for them. I wouldn't take them back to him for triple what he offered."

"You're casual about money."

"Some things aren't worth money. You saw how frightened Mary Catherine was of you when you met her. She's that frightened all the time of her own father."

Matt tightened his fist and silently called Baker Ashland some foul names as he watched Mary Catherine and Pete laugh about something. "Pete told me he's taking Lita to a movie later tonight. She's in one of her classes until nine o'clock."

"She talks about him constantly and he stops by sometimes to talk to her."

Matt couldn't think about Lita and Pete. His thoughts had gone back to Vivian. Matt wondered what kind of house Vivian had left behind. Once again, he felt out of her league, knowing she may be accustomed to luxury and life in the fast lane. His farm was a quiet place where one led a simple life.

"Saturday night I asked Lita to stay. I'll take you to El Reno to eat ribs," he said, wondering about her former lifestyle.

"Sounds like fun," she said, giving him a full-fledged smile that made him draw a deep breath as if all the air had been punched out of his lungs. When she smiled, she was irresistible, so beautiful, he didn't want to stop looking at her.

"You don't do that enough," he said in a husky voice.

"What? I'm not doing anything."

"You're smiling."

"You'll have to admit, there's been a lot to keep me from smiling—smashing my car, having a baby in a storm, trusting a total stranger, being followed, hearing from Baker."

"Maybe we can tip the scales the other way," he said quietly, wanting to reach for her but not wanting to stir up a storm of questions with Mary Catherine. "A beautiful new baby, Mary Catherine less fearful, a friend who finds you absolutely irresistible, a quiet place to rest after childbirth, a repaired car."

She laughed. "Okay, you win. I'll remember all that and try to smile more."

"If we weren't out here where Mary Catherine can see and I weren't holding Julia, I would show you some other reasons to smile," he said in a husky voice.

"For a quiet, introverted man, you have your moments when you say things that just take my breath away."

"Do I, now?" he asked. "Does anything else I do take your breath away?"

"You know the answer to that one," she said, knowing he was flirting and liking it too much.

He took her hand in his, spreading his fingers and looking at her slender ones, pale against his brown skin. "The introvert and the extrovert. You like being with people, don't you?"

"Yes, I do. That's why I like my business. I work with people daily and it's fun."

He placed his hand on her knee, still holding her hand in his. "Mary Catherine is good for Pete. I think he's getting over some of his grief."

"Good."

"I better go relieve him so he can get into town and pick up Lita."

Matt jumped down and headed toward Pete while Vivian held Julia and watched him walk away, her gaze drifting down over his long legs, remembering the feel of his body pressed against hers. He hadn't wanted her to go back to Denver, but he hadn't offered anything more than what he had already talked her into, two more weeks with him. Yet had she wanted or expected him to? Not at all, she told herself.

The concern she experienced earlier returned. Baker wasn't giving her up easily. He would never have made that size of an offer if it wasn't enormously important to him to get her back to Denver.

It was a week from Saturday night before she and Matt got to go out, because the following Saturday Mary Catherine didn't feel well and Vivian didn't want to leave.

When the Saturday night came, Vivian dressed in jeans and a blue cotton blouse. Her hair was tied behind her head with a blue ribbon. Matt was in a long-sleeved white shirt and jeans and when she walked into the den where he was waiting, she had to struggle to keep from staring at him because he looked incredibly handsome.

After instructions to Lita and Pete, they left the house. Vivian sat in the air-conditioned pickup, watching the land flash past.

"I like you in jeans. You look great."

"Thank you," she answered cheerfully. "So do you."

He gave her a warm look. "We'll get back to that one later."

She watched him drive for a moment until he glanced at her and then she turned away. The first of next week was her checkup. Then it would be time for her to leave. Why was she going out with him tonight when she would tell him goodbye in days? Tonight would just make the goodbye more difficult. "I've never had this much trouble resisting something I should avoid before. I stopped drinking cola. I stopped drinking coffee because of the caffeine. I've never smoked and don't drink alcohol except for an occasional glass of wine. I've been able to stop eating chocolates except on rare occasions."

Slowing at the turn to the highway, he looked both ways. They swung up onto the highway and he glanced at her. "What can't you resist?"

"You," she said simply, receiving a quick, probing glance from him. "We shouldn't be going out together. This is going to make it more difficult next week."

"You know you don't have to leave just the minute six weeks are up. You can stay a little longer."

"Like how much longer, cowboy?" she asked him playfully, half-annoyed and half-pleased with his wanting her to stay a little longer.

He grinned. "Until we get tired of each other."

"Is this some kind of proposition?"

"No. When I proposition you, lady, you'll know it."

She laughed. "I think I better pack and go and get on with my life. You'll have to agree, though, tonight isn't the smartest thing either of us has done."

"I don't agree. You won't, either, when you sink your teeth into those ribs."

"I answered Baker's lawyer," she said, changing the subject.

"Good. Have you heard back from him?"

"Yes," she said, wishing now she hadn't brought it up because she didn't want to think about Baker tonight. "He's telling me all the advantages of accepting Baker's offer—and of course, there are plenty. He's promising he'll only see me at work when I want to see him."

"Would he keep a promise like that?"

"Of course not. Baker will make lots of empty promises to get his own way. I e-mailed another refusal back to him, but I'll hear from him again. And again. And then the lawyer will come see me to try to persuade me in person. I know, restraining order or not, I will eventually have to face Baker."

"I sort of hope that happens while you're here. That's a good reason to stay longer."

"I can deal with Baker. I've had plenty of practice."

"So let's not talk about him again tonight."

They chatted as they made the long drive to El Reno and ate in a rustic restaurant with a sawdust floor and a tantalizing smell of barbecue hovering in the air. The ribs were as good as Matt had promised, and afterward, they drove back to Dakani and beyond its town limits. Halfway between Dakani and the farm, Matt turned off the road at a long, low building built of concrete blocks. Guitar music blared from a loudspeaker and doors and windows were open wide.

"Here's the local honky-tonk. It's noisy, jumping and

smoky, but the music is pretty good and the beer is cold. Okay?''

"Are there going to be fights?'' she asked, seeing a pool table inside the door.

"Probably, being Saturday night, but if it becomes a brawl, I'll get you out of here.''

"Deal.''

"Okay, lady, we'll go in and start enough rumors to run all the way to my brother in Tulsa.''

As they got out of the pickup and walked toward the door, Matt put his arm around her waist possessively. "Now, don't get independent on me. This is no place for your liberated-woman side. Country boys love pretty women and they're not politically correct about showing it. I have to claim you or I won't see you again tonight because every single guy here will want to dance with you.''

"I wasn't complaining,'' she said, and he looked down at her sharply. She smiled as they went up the steps and entered the smoke-filled room.

The noise was deafening. Couples circled the floor doing the two-step while a guitarist played and sang accompanied by a drummer. In minutes Matt had a table, a beer and a ginger ale ordered and he was leading Vivian to the dance floor.

They moved together in a fast two-step and she realized she hadn't danced a two-step in too long to remember. Matt was light on his feet, and she could follow him easily, swiftly circling the floor and enjoying getting out. He watched her while they danced and she was caught up in his dark gaze, forgetting the noise and crowd and smoke, knowing this was another night she would remember for a long time to come.

Three dances later was a slow waltz and Matt pulled her into his arms. They danced easily together, moving in unison while he still watched her with a hungry look that all but set the air between them on fire.

"You're a good dancer. You haven't been sitting out there on the farm by yourself every Saturday night," she said lightly.

"Nope, but there's never been a Saturday night I liked dancing like this one."

The next piece was even slower and Matt pulled her closer, resting his head against hers as they barely moved while they danced. She was pressed tightly against him, their thighs touching, their bodies together and her desire escalated. It had been building and growing all these weeks, the nights spent together sitting on the porch or out on the fence rail, the breakfasts, the moments together with the girls, the long phone conversations with him during the day. She was torn between wanting to be in his arms and wanting his loving and knowing if she gave herself fully to him, she would give her love right along with her body. She couldn't treat love casually or lightly.

She danced slowly with him, wondering about him. What was the depth of his feelings? The depth of her own? Was she in love with him? Was it circumstances? She didn't think so. They were together constantly, but she had worked closely with some of her male clients and never had any reaction to them.

When the piece ended, he didn't release her until she stepped back. "The song's over," Vivian commented.

"I didn't know," he said in a husky voice, running his finger along her cheek.

Matt wanted her more than ever and he had waited patiently while she had recovered and gained her strength and gotten to know him. He hadn't rushed her, but he was through waiting. He wanted her to be his lady, his woman. He couldn't think about tomorrow or next week or her going out of his life.

"How about going home?"

"Fine with me. The smoke is getting to me, anyway."

He draped his arm across her shoulders, and they threaded their way through the crowd toward the door. Several yards from the door, Vivian looked up as a beefy giant of a man dressed in a T-shirt and jeans entered. Shocked, she stopped, knowing she was facing Rocky Thornton, Baker's private detective.

Chapter 13

Vivian was shaken, disturbed, to look up and find the private detective facing her. She had known a confrontation with him would come sooner or later. She glanced at Matt and noticed the look of fury on his face when he spotted Rocky Thornton.

"Hey," Thornton said, putting up his hands instantly and looking at Matt. "I just wanted to say a few words to Mrs. Ashland."

"Get the hell out of here," Matt said tersely.

"Your husband asked me to speak to you. May I just talk to you for two minutes?"

Matt stepped forward and people around them moved away, but Vivian's hand closed on his arm. She felt the knot of muscle and knew in just a minute there would be a fight.

"Matt. Wait. I'll talk to him outside."

She turned to Rocky Thornton. "Two minutes is all," she said forcefully. "I'll be right back, Matt," she said, walking outside ahead of the detective. Thornton's request to talk was not unreasonable and she would just as soon have it now and get it over and done.

"I got the lawyer's e-mail and answered it. My answer was no and I will not change my mind. You can tell Baker, whatever he offers, I'm not going back to Denver," Vivian said to Thornton.

"He asked me to tell you to think about the girls and what he will provide for them," Thornton said in a flat, gravelly voice.

"I am thinking about them," she said, furious that he would try to use the girls as leverage. "Mary Catherine has been terrified of men because of him—frightened of her own father. I won't take her back. Has he thought about what it's like for a child to grow up afraid of her father? I'll send his lawyer another answer. The two minutes are up," she snapped, and turned to walk away. She saw Matt waiting by the step, and then he came striding toward her.

"Okay?" he asked, putting his hands on her shoulders.

"I was shocked to see him standing there only a few feet in front of me."

"When we get in the car, I'm calling the sheriff."

"Why? I talked to the detective willingly."

"Sheriff Gonzales needs to know."

"Thornton's still here," she said, feeling dazed now that the encounter was over.

"So am I," Matt said, hugging her close. "Don't let him spoil a fun evening."

"I won't, but the surprise is still sending little shock waves through me." She looked around the lot. "He's gone."

"Yeah, he hightailed it out of here the minute you walked away. I saw him drive off."

She put her arm around Matt's waist and he looked down at her, tightening his arm around her. As soon as they climbed into the pickup, Matt picked up the phone to call the sheriff. He started the motor and switched on the air-conditioning while he told Chet Gonzales about Rocky Thornton. Matt switched off the phone and put it down.

"Chet said he'll find out where Thornton's staying. He may talk to him, give him a warning to leave you alone."

"Thanks, Matt. There aren't many things in life that Baker has wanted and been unable to get. It's difficult for him to accept this."

"He's going to have to."

They rode in silence and Matt knew she was adjusting to what had happened. The whole incident had happened in less than five minutes, yet he had seen the color drain from Vivian's face and he knew she was shaken.

When he turned off onto his own road, he decided enough time had passed for her nerves to begin to calm. He slowed and parked, leaving the motor running as he reached over to unbuckle her seat belt.

"What are you doing?"

"Getting your mind on something else," he said as he wrapped her in his embrace and leaned over to kiss her. There was a delay of about one second before she responded and then the tension went out of her as she melted into his arms and returned his kiss. He kissed her long and thoroughly, satisfied that he had driven Rocky Thornton out of her mind.

"I'm not ending this evening out here smooching in the dark, but I wanted you to get back on track. We've had a fun night."

"Yes, we have."

He put the pickup in gear to head home.

"Wyatt called today. That's my brother, well, half brother actually, in Oklahoma City. He's talked to Jared. I think they're all coming over next weekend to meet you."

"I'm leaving."

"You can't. They're coming to see you and I want them to meet you."

"Matt, that's—"

"Hey, Vivian, please."

There was a pause and she nodded. "Talk about someone wanting to get his way."

"Mine is for a good cause. You'll like my brothers."

"Do they know we're not dating?"

"What did we do tonight?"

She stared at him. "It was two friends out together."

"What's dating? Not two enemies out together."

"They'll expect to come over and meet someone you're going to marry."

"They know better than that. Believe me, they do. They just want to see the first woman to stay at my house. Now that that record is broken, my life should be peaceful once again."

"Oh, sure, until you bring the next woman home to stay."

He chuckled. "You know I'm not going to do that. You're it, lady. The one and only."

Vivian listened to those words that meant so little the way he was using them, yet could mean so much. They'd had a regular date tonight, and he had described it as such. Was she breaking through this cowboy's wall that he kept around his heart? Did she want to? She better find her answer to that question fast. She had to decide her own feelings before she took a long look at his.

She was staying another week longer. How easily he had talked her into staying to meet his family. They were dating, she was meeting his family, she lived at his house, they kissed—wild, fiery kisses that melted her, kisses like she had never known before. What *did* he feel for her? Did his feelings run deep and was he refusing to acknowledge them? Or was he unable to put his feelings into words?

They were beginning to have all the characteristics of a couple falling in love, except from remarks he continually made, he wasn't in love. He wasn't talking about it, at any rate. Was she in love with him? She never could answer her own question. She knew he was important to her. More so every day. She was wildly attracted to him. He was her best friend now. Maybe the best friend she had ever had.

She stared into the black night and thought about moving to Houston. Was she going to a life that in some ways might be as solitary as Matt's and never know what it was like to be loved completely by him? Never know fulfillment with him?

That first afternoon her relationship with Matt had leapt beyond casual because everything about childbirth was intimate. Whether they made love or not, she would always remember him, but did she want to go out of his life without ever experiencing passion with him?

Matt drove up to the back gate. As they walked to the house, he put his arm across her shoulders. "Lita's got a long drive back to town. I told her to stay here tonight," he said, "but Pete's going to drive her home."

"Good. I'm amazed she drives out here every day to work. Her baby is due Wednesday."

"Are babies ever on time?"

"Sure. Julia was early, but a lot of them are on time."

They went inside to talk to Pete and Lita. After Vivian paid Lita, she and Matt followed them to the back door to tell them good-night.

"If they don't date, it'll be a shame," Vivian said softly. "Pete needs someone."

"That's your womanly need to match-make and see that every single male finds a mate."

"Look at them. She needs someone and I think she loves him. He is one of the loneliest people I've ever met. He still gets tears in his eyes sometimes when he looks at Mary Catherine. A new baby in his life would be grand.''

"I'll have to admit, new babies are special."

"Only to certain types of men. It's amazing people in two counties that you're one of them. When you picked up Julia in Addie's Grill and held her, I think half the women there fell back in love with you."

"No one there was in love with me. Believe me. I haven't had a date until tonight in so long, I can't tell you when."

"Oh, sure."

Matt locked up and switched off the light. He put his arm across her shoulders and they walked down the hall to his door. One small light burned in his bedroom. He turned to face her, placing his hands on her shoulders. Vivian's pulse jumped because he would tell her good-night and she was sure he would kiss her and she wanted him to so badly, she wasn't sure she would wait.

"Julia has slept through the night now three nights this week. Maybe she's going to again tonight."

"I hope she does so her mom can." His dark eyes had that intense, blatantly hungry look that made her feel he wanted her desperately and made her even more eager for his kiss. "It was fun tonight, Vivian."

"I had a great time and the ribs were delicious. I haven't been out like that in too long to remember. Thank you," she said without thinking about what she was saying. "Matt, it was the most fun I've had."

"I doubt that," he said softly in a husky voice as his hands unfastened the ribbon that held her hair behind her head. He dropped the ribbon to the floor. "I think we can have a lot more fun now," he added, his gaze lowering to her mouth. He leaned down and his mouth covered hers and she was lost.

She stepped into his arms, was dimly aware when he moved them both into his room and shoved the door closed.

"Matt, I have to hear—"

"The intercom," he whispered, framing her face with his large hands, his gaze searching her face. "Vivian, I've waited."

His words took her breath because she could guess the unspoken words he was telling her. Now was the time to love him or to walk away from him, and all the debates she had held with herself on long sleepless nights had to be decided in this moment. As black as midnight, his eyes had darkened with desire, and there was no mistaking their message.

She knew what she wanted and at this moment in time, it seemed right to tighten her arms around him and shift closer against him. Something flickered in the depths of his eyes, a certainty, a satisfaction.

He leaned down to kiss her throat, his breath warm against her while he trailed tantalizing kisses to her mouth. Kissing her hungrily, he placed his hands at her belt, tugging her blouse out of her jeans. He pulled her blouse free and unbuttoned it, pushing it away. Her heart pounded, her reserves falling away with her clothing. From that first stormy afternoon he had given so much to her; now she was going to give back to him.

His head rose and he looked at her.

"You're gorgeous," he said in a husky voice that made her tremble. He reached out to unclasp her practical cotton bra and push it away.

"Matt, I'm nursing now."

"I know. You're beautiful, Vivian." He cupped her breasts in his hands, his thumbs circling her nipples. Sensation streaked from his touch, building fires low within her that heated and fueled needs he had awakened weeks ago. Vivian clung to his arms, the muscles taut beneath her fingers.

"Matt," she whispered, his caresses as intoxicating as wine. All evening—no, much longer than all evening—she had wanted his hands and mouth on her, and wanted her hands on him. How right this seemed. Nothing about it could be casual. She framed his face with her hands, pulling his head up to stand on tiptoe and kiss him passionately, thoroughly, conveying her feelings to him the same way he was imparting his to her.

He groaned and pushed her away. "Let me love you, Vivian," he said, stroking her breasts. "You're beautiful. How many nights have I dreamed of you! I can't tell you. I can't work for thinking about you—" He broke off as he bent to take her breast in his mouth. Trembling, she closed her eyes. He made her whole again. She felt like a woman, desirable, needed, complete in his loving. Never once in her life had it been like this. Matt was doing everything he could to pleasure her, to heighten her passion. And he was succeeding. If only he knew, he was succeeding beyond measure.

His shirt had too many buttons and her hands shook. While he caressed her, she tried to undress him, yet his hands were a distraction that made her falter and hesitate. Finally she pulled the shirt free of his jeans and pushed it away, feeling his warm chest and broad shoulders.

When her hands slid to his belt, he groaned. She unbuckled it, sliding it through the loops and dropping it to the bare floor, the buckle making a clatter. She twisted the buttons of his jeans and he uttered a primitive growl. Watching her, he stepped back to tug off a boot. He balanced on one foot, pulling his boot free and tossing it aside, yanking away his sock. With his gaze riveted on her, he pulled away the other boot and sock. The moment he straightened she stepped forward, pushing his hands away as she finished unbuttoning his jeans.

He reached into his jeans to retrieve a packet that he tossed behind her on the bed. "I have protection."

"I thought you might," she whispered.

While his fingers trailed over her breasts, she pushed down his jeans. She hooked her fingers in his briefs and pushed them down, freeing him. He stepped out and she tingled, burning with need as she looked at his magnificent male body, his shaft hard, ready for her. She ran her hands across his chest, feeling his heart thud, trailing her fingers down across his flat stomach, down lower.

He inhaled, his fingers knotted in her hair as she stroked him and slid her hands over him, discovering the textures and shape of him.

"I bared myself to you weeks ago; now, finally, you will for me," she whispered, kissing his jaw, his ear, caressing his neck.

His hands were everywhere and then her jeans fell to the floor and his hand slid over her bare hips. He stepped back to look at her again. Every slow, consuming look was a searing blaze that made her all but melt into a boneless heap.

He knelt, his fingers caressing her thighs, moving her legs apart. She gasped and clutched his shoulders.

He picked her up easily, holding her warmth against him, carrying her to his bed to lay her down. He climbed into bed beside her and moved between her thighs. They looked at each other. Her long hair spilled over the pillow and over her shoulders. She was naked, beautiful. All woman with all of a woman's mysteries, yet she was also part of his heart in a way no one else had ever been. She had changed his life, brought companionship and children into it, given him a new world with his reading. Now he wanted to pleasure and give and do anything he could for her.

As he bent to kiss her, he continued to watch her, trailing his tongue along her inner thigh, hearing her gasps of pleasure, and feeling her fingers winding and clutching his hair.

All her attention was focused on his caresses, his hands between her legs. As he stroked her, she gasped and arched against him and he leaned down to kiss her while his hand caressed and rubbed and deepened desire.

She cried out with pleasure, her cries muffled. Beneath his touch she moved in a frenzy while she ran her hands over him. This was Matt making love to her, sharing with her another intimacy, and in that moment she knew without a doubt that she was in love.

There wasn't opportunity to wonder about her discovery, to dwell on it. Thought had spiraled away on passion's wild ride as she thrust her hips against his hand and moved, clinging to him and crying out while he took her to a brink.

She clung to his strong shoulders and then she pushed him back, her fingers closing around his hard shaft. He gasped and wound his fingers in her hair tightly.

She stroked him, moving down to take him in her mouth and kiss him, her tongue slowly curling over his thick shaft. Vivian wanted to explore every inch of his marvelous, virile body that she had looked at so many times.

Matt was on fire, his fingers locked in her hair. He wanted to pleasure her, but momentarily, he was lost in what she was doing to him. Deep down, he knew this was a once-in-a-lifetime moment. He had never wanted a woman the way he wanted Vivian now. Her touch was feather light, yet it burned to his soul. This woman was everything desirable. He felt a kinship with her that was unbreakable and he knew her better than any other person on earth because of what he had been through with her.

With a savage groan he came up and pulled her to him, crushing her in his arms as he kissed her.

He leaned over her, feeling their hearts beat together,

kissing her while time vanished until she moved away, lying down and pulling at his hips to move him between her legs.

Trailing slowly over her, his gaze drank in her beauty. This night she was his woman. Her lush body was beautiful, pink and white and pale with the thick brown triangle of hair at the juncture of her thighs and her long, flowing brown hair spilling on her shoulders.

"Oh, Matt, come here," she cried, locking her long legs around him. His heart pounded and he struggled to keep control of his own needs, wanting to give her more. He touched her between her thighs. Her eyes closed and she inhaled, her fingers clutching his thighs.

Matt stroked her soft flesh, feeling her moist and ready for him, listening to her cry out while she arched against him.

"Matt!"

He thought he would burst with the need that burned through him. He had dreamed of this, thought about it, imagined it for too long. He would take her to bliss and she would take him there, too.

Tonight was special; he knew that without stopping to think about it. Vivian was special. His lady, in his arms, beneath him, giving herself to him.

"Matt!" Her insistent cry fueled his blazing passion, yet he held back and stroked her and kissed her.

"Vivian, you'll never know how much I've wanted you," he said in a voice that was only a rasp. He picked up the small packet and removed the contents. She reached out to help him, taking over the task and putting the thin sheath in place while his dark eyes devoured her.

Vivian held his hips, her legs locked around him while she tugged him closer. He lowered himself between her legs and came down over her, a weight that she relished.

The tip of his shaft probed against her. She reached down

to hold him and guide him, moving her hand away as her hips arched and she cupped his bottom and tried to draw him deeper. He slid slowly into her, filling her, driving her wild.

"Oh, please," she cried, her hips thrusting against him.

Sweat broke out as he thrust slowly. She was tight, which surprised him. He slid into her, heard her cries, and he withdrew partially, then slid into her again in a long, slow stroke that made her gasp and arch against him and cling to him.

"Vivian, you're mine now," he whispered in her ear as he moved, knowing he was building the tension in her.

Vivian thought she would burn to ashes from ecstasy as she moved against him. She stroked his smooth back, her hands sliding over his bare, firm bottom down to his muscled thighs, which were rough with hairs curling against her hand. "Matt, Matt," she whispered, relishing knowing it was him who was loving her, his body joined with hers.

Had they been rushing headlong to this moment all evening? How long had she wanted it before tonight? Why did it seem like forever that she had known him and wanted him?

She clung to him, holding him, stroking him, loving him while her body moved in a frenzy that grew more intense. He was holding back for her and she knew it was costing him. Yet she knew he was doing what he wanted and doing it for her, putting her first even in this when all else burned away except passion.

The climax burst in her, sensations blasting her, their union rapture. She heard him cry her name, felt him shudder as he pumped into her.

As they moved together, she was caught on the spiral again, tension racing in her, building to burst in another climax that he seemed as aware of as she was. They moved together and then slowed.

Matt gasped for breath, sliding his arms beneath her, trying to hold her as close as possible. "You're my lady now, Vivian. Part of you is mine." He showered kisses across her temple and stroked her hair away from her damp forehead. She was gasping for breath as much as he was and he could feel her heart thudding as violently as his own.

"It works both ways, Matt," she answered solemnly. "Part of you is now part of me."

"We're as close as two people can get and it's damned good," he said with satisfaction. He looked at her and then leaned down to kiss her long and thoroughly.

He rolled over, taking her with him to hold her in his arms. "Aah, lady, you're marvelous."

His words thrilled her, yet even in the euphoria from their lovemaking, she knew what was missing. There were no words of love or commitment or anything beyond this moment. She closed her mind to that. She hadn't expected promises or a proposal or vows tonight when he pulled her into his arms; she knew better than to expect such words from him now.

But she was in love with him. Her own questions about her feelings had been answered. Their union was more than physical as far as she was concerned, whether he viewed it that way or not.

She slid her hand over his shoulder, feeling the hard, solid muscle, touching his thick hair. Wise or hopeless, she was in love with this self-sufficient cowboy whose world was the opposite of the one she had always known. Since he didn't feel the same as she did, she had some big decisions to make.

"Matt, I need to think things through—"

He touched her lips. "Shh. Not now. No intrusions on this night. Tomorrow will come, Vivian. We can't stop it, but right now, take this moment. You're my woman, in my arms. That's enough. Right here in this bed, there are no barriers between us. They're out there," he said roughly, his voice becoming harsh while he looked at her solemnly. "They'll fall into place when we get out of bed, but they don't exist here. Take what we have and hold it tight right now."

A knot closed her throat. He was everything she could love in a man. His words hurt because they clearly said he intended to continue his solitary life. If she tried to be practical, she knew he was right. There were so many differences between them—and she hadn't thought that through—her heart hadn't taken into consideration the differences. Matt spoke the truth—the barriers were out there, but not here in his arms. She would do what he was doing, seize the moment and shut out tomorrow. She tightened her arms around his neck and held him. "Come here, cowboy," she whispered seductively.

He kissed her again and she held him tightly, relishing being locked in his strong arms, his body and hers together, legs intertwined.

When they stopped kissing, he shifted and propped his head on his hand to look down at her.

"Ah, Vivian, Mary Catherine was like a little angel dropping into my life that afternoon. She brought you to me."

Vivian stroked his thick black hair from his face, trailing her fingers over his cheekbone, down to his jaw. "Well, you were Galahad dropping into my life that day. That's for certain."

"I've been called some things in my life, but I've never been called Galahad," he remarked with amusement in his voice. "Some knight—a dusty cowpoke. You would have managed, someway."

"I don't think so," she answered lightly. She stroked his shoulder, holding back words she wanted to say, knowing if she told him her feelings, it would be a wedge between them.

"I think you melted every bone in my body."

"Let me check that out," she said, squeezing his thigh, and he chuckled. "I can't find anything soft."

"You keep that up and I'll be far from soft."

Withdrawing, he shifted over her and scooped her into his arms. "Come here. If my tottering legs can carry us, we'll shower."

She laughed. "You don't feel as if you're tottering."

After they finished washing, Matt switched off the water, toweled Vivian dry slowly, his hands sliding the towel over every inch of her with deliberate strokes until she was quivering with desire.

She took the towel to dry him, and all the while, his hands still roamed over her. His body was magnificent and she wanted to look and to touch him forever. Excitement coursed in her as he took the towel from her hands to toss it aside. He carried her to bed and moved over her, getting another packet. As soon as the sheath was in place, he slid into her.

Matt held her, moving slowly, feeling her hips thrust against him, each movement a searing taunt. He was like a starving man at a feast. He had wanted to love her, but in his imaginings it would stop there. Now, in reality, he didn't want to stop, and so soon after they had loved, she did something, gave him a look or touched him, and he was consumed by an even larger need for her.

"I can't get enough of you, Vivian," he said harshly, his voice a rasp.

"I hope not," she replied, and then they kissed and words were gone, but he wondered about her answer. What had she meant? Thoughts ceased, and he loved her until both of them lay gasping in each other's embrace.

"Are we going to sleep tonight?" she asked languidly.

"I don't know. I haven't for the past month, so why

should I tonight when I can do what I've been wanting to do every night for over a month now?''

She tightened her arms around him and moved closer against him, her face tucked against his throat. "I didn't know loving could ever be like this."

"Nope," he answered gruffly while his hand stroked her shoulder and played with her hair. "Neither did I, Vivian."

They lay quietly in each other's arms, and Vivian thought only of the past few hours. She would do what he suggested—keep tomorrow out of thought. When she heard his steady breathing, she shifted to look at him. She loved him completely and forever.

Why did love come like this, so unexpected, even unwanted? Slipping up on a person like seasons changing or days lengthening—something that was happening around you, but you never noticed until it was a fact.

She knew he hadn't changed. He didn't see her as part of his future. Reality intruded painfully. She blanked out her worries and held him close, kissing him lightly.

She dozed to wake to his kisses. They loved again and then slept until she heard Julia's cries.

Extricating herself, she slipped out of bed, trying to find her clothes, pulling on his shirt, which would cover her to mid-thigh.

"Want me to get her?" Matt's deep voice was a lazy rumble in the stillness.

"No. I have to feed her."

He came out of bed and crossed the room to her to take her into his arms and kiss her, a kiss that contradicted all his words about barriers and differences.

"I have to go." She turned away, regretful that their idyllic interlude was over.

Chapter 14

While Vivian fed and rocked the baby, her thoughts drifted to Matt. She was in love with him. The night had been magical, something already moving into memory, yet a memory that would last forever.

Her feelings for him both surprised her and seemed inevitable. Maybe she had started falling in love with him that first day. She knew his toughness, his charm, his vulnerabilities. Yet in the depth of his heart, was love still locked away?

He wasn't going to change or propose or make a commitment. If he had been ready to establish something lasting, last night would have been the time. Everything he had done had conveyed love except the spoken words.

Was there love in his heart? Was it because of old inadequacies that he couldn't declare his love? He had told her about his past—that he had never known love before, never known what it meant to be a family. She knew he was sensitive about his country ways, too, and he viewed her as far more educated and sophisticated. Did he still feel their differences were so great, and was he misjudging the depth of her feelings?

There were moments he could be very articulate, but he still kept his deepest feelings to himself. She was certain she would never have known about his reading inability if it hadn't been that he thought he would hurt Mary Catherine. That and the close bond from Julia's birth.

Vivian knew Matt had opened himself up to her more than anyone else in his life, but he had to open his heart completely if he wanted her to stay.

To stay. She hadn't thought about it before because it hadn't been a consideration. She couldn't stay now, of course, because he hadn't asked her to. But did she want to take off for Houston next week? She could stay a little longer. He had asked her to do that. Yet more nights like last night and it would tear her to pieces to leave him.

Here she had done exactly what she had cautioned herself against when she first came—fallen in love with him. The special magic chemistry between them was irresistible and Matt had so many wonderful qualities. But his self-sufficiency and worries over his past and over what he perceived as his inability to have a lasting relationship were a barrier between them.

Should she pack and go right away and put distance between them and then see if she still was in love with him? Logic said yes. How could she reason anything out when she'd spent a night like last night in his arms? Impossible.

Last night. Thoughts and memories heated her and tormented her because she wanted to be with him again right now. Already, it seemed she had been away from him far too long when actually it had been less than an hour.

But she knew the barriers were up now, keeping a distance between himself and everyone else. What had last night meant to him? There had been no indication by his words that he wanted more from her than that one night.

At the same time, he acted like a man in love. The words he had said to her hadn't been casual or lighthearted.

Vivian rocked the baby and let memories tumble in her mind until she heard the phone ring.

She held Julia against her shoulder and went to find Matt.

She heard him in the kitchen and her pulse jumped at the prospect of seeing him. When she stepped into the room, he looked around and then his gaze slowly trailed down over her and she remembered she was wearing only his shirt.

"My shirt never looked so good," he drawled, sauntering across the room. He was bare-chested, dressed in jeans. He glanced at Julia. "How's little baby?"

"She's fine," Vivian said perfunctorily, too aware of Matt closing the distance between them. He didn't stop, but walked up to her and kissed her lightly. He put his arm around her waist, yet stood back because of the baby, then his hand slid down and back up, pushing up the shirt and running his hand across her bottom. The touch was light, yet it awakened desire.

"Matt," she whispered.

"I didn't want you to forget."

"I'll never forget," she replied solemnly, and he drew in a long breath. She moved away from him. "I heard the phone ring."

"It was Sheriff Gonzales. He wanted us to know he found the motel where Rocky Thornton is staying in Enid. Chet has a deputy watching him."

She nodded, unable to think about Rocky Thornton and not really caring. Matt stood only a few feet away and his caress had ignited fires in her again. "I'll dress," she said, turning and hurrying toward the door.

"Vivian. Don't go."

Her heart stopped and she held her breath.

"Stay here until Baker gives up and Thornton goes back to Denver."

She let out her breath. What had she expected from Matt? Why would he suddenly open up and ask her to stay forever? If he had been thinking about forever, he would have asked her in the night.

"I'll think about it, Matt," she said, hurrying away from him. When was she going to go? And was she going back to his bed every night until she packed and left?

She showered, dressed and found Matt lingering on the porch over a cup of coffee. He stood the moment she came out and pulled out a chair for her.

"My brother called."

"I didn't hear the phone, but then I was in the shower."

"It's all set. They'll be here Saturday around noon."

She had to laugh. "Did you tell them that's the weekend I had planned to go?"

Something flickered in Matt's eyes, and he studied her while she wondered what was running through his mind. "No, I didn't tell Jared that." He leaned across the table and took her hand. "I'm glad you're staying," he said, his dark eyes boring into her. He stood. "As much as I'd like to stay right here with you, I have work to do. Pete will be driving Lita here."

"Pete's bringing her?"

"He doesn't think she should drive any longer, so yes, he is. He sleeps on her sofa."

"You and Pete are nice guys."

"Yep, we're adorable," he said with a grin as he came around the table, pulled her into his arms and kissed her.

When he released her, she opened her eyes to find him watching her intently. "I'll miss you. I'll call you."

She nodded and watched him stride away, her emotions swirling. He acts like a man in love, she thought. She needed to sort through her feelings and make some decisions and talk to him tonight.

It was late that night when they sat in the dark on the porch and the girls both slept.

"Come here, Vivian," Matt said, taking her hand, his voice becoming husky. "Come sit on my lap."

"Let's talk first."

He stood and took both her hands, pulling her to her feet and then picking her up. He sat down with her on his lap. "Women talk too much sometimes."

"Well, maybe if women talked half as much and men talked twice as much we'd all be happy," she snapped.

He chuckled as he ran his hand along her thigh. She caught his wrist and held his hand still. "Matt, listen to me."

"Sure, darlin'," he whispered, and leaned forward to kiss her throat.

For a minute sensations took all her attention. The sparks danced into flames between them and desire kindled in her. Erotic thoughts spilled in her mind and she closed her eyes, yielding to him.

His hands were everywhere while he kissed her, his mouth and his tongue ending rational thought. Her hands trailed over him, pulling away his shirt.

"Matt, we're outside—"

"It's dark. No one is within miles of us. The girls are inside asleep and you can hear them if they wake," he whispered, pulling off her T-shirt and tossing it aside. He unfastened her bra and it fell in a heap on the porch.

"I wanted to discuss—"

He cupped her breast to take her nipple in his mouth, his tongue stroking her until she wanted him and all her resolutions burned away.

With shaking hands she unbuttoned his jeans. Cradling

her in his arms, Matt leaned over her to kiss her while his hands tugged down her cutoffs. When they fell away, he pushed away the lace panties and then his hands were on her bare body, an exquisite torment that made her writhe and twist against him.

She slid off his lap, going down, her tongue trailing over him as she knelt between his knees and took his shaft in her hand to kiss him. He gasped and wound his fingers in her hair.

"Do you like that, Matt?" she whispered. "Do you?"

"Yes," he answered, the word little more than a growl.

"Then tell me," she said, letting her tongue trail slowly up over him. "Tell me!" she insisted, suddenly wanting other words from him.

He groaned and opened his eyes and their dark depths were stormy. He reached down under her arms to pull her up roughly. "I'll tell you, Vivian," he whispered, spreading her legs and pulling her over him to straddle him. "I want you. I want inside you now. I want your softness, your warmth. There, there—"

He broke off as she slid over him and he pulled her hips down, impaling her and then moving as she moved. Both were lost then and she clung to his shoulders, aware of his hands, yet more aware of his filling her, driving her wild and both of them moving in a frenzy.

Release exploded in her and she cried out, clinging to him, lost in sensation and only dimly hearing his hoarse cry.

Gradually, she became conscious of the world around her, of lying in his arms, draped over him, her head on his shoulder while he stroked her back and murmured endearments to her.

"I wasn't going to do that until we talked."

"But you did and it was grand," he said with male smugness.

He stood, groaning as he lifted her in his arms. He carried her to a bathroom and stood her in the shower and they washed and caressed and loved again.

Later, in his bed, she sat up, pulling up the sheet and looking down at him. He lay with the sheet over him to his waist and his arms folded behind his head. "You got your way," she said.

"Did I really? You sound as if I tied you down and had my way with you."

"It wasn't like that," she said in exasperation, knowing he was going to twist things around and tease her.

"I seem to remember some enthusiasm on your part and your getting your way a little there, too."

"Yes, I did. I like to love you—"

"Oh, darlin'," he said, reaching for her.

She pushed him back down on the bed, her fingers splayed on his chest. "Now, you listen to me, Matt Whitewolf—"

"Yes, ma'am."

"I've been trying to talk to you since hours ago."

"Could've fooled me. I thought you were trying to do something else. All those kisses—"

"Matt!"

He grinned and put his hands behind his head. "I promise. I'll listen and I'll stop talking. It would be nice if you'd take that sheet off, though."

"No, I'm not giving up the sheet," she said, holding it closer in front of her as she sat cross-legged beside him. "Then I'll forget what I'm going to say and you'll be kissing me again."

"That would be bad?"

"Are you going to listen?"

"Promise," he said, and closed his mouth.

She wanted to shake him and she wanted to kiss him.

She knew he was teasing her, but she wondered, too, if he was trying to avoid what was inevitable.

"Matt, last night and tonight are special. So very special, but we're rushing headlong into something and I need to sort out my feelings."

"I didn't feel like we were rushing headlong at all," he said solemnly, trailing his fingers over her knee. Even though she was covered with the sheet, she could feel the strokes of his hand and that slight touch was distracting, making her tingle.

"I can't move into your bedroom and then next week go blithely on to Houston." She looked away because it was too difficult to look into his piercing dark eyes and pour out her feelings. "Several more nights and I'll be so in love—" She turned around to face him again. "I don't want to leave here with bigger hurts and worries than I had when I came."

Her heart drummed as he sat in silence and stared at her and she could feel walls and barriers coming between them.

"I know you have your life the way you want it, but I have to think about how much hurt I want to stand."

"I suppose you're right, Vivian. I figured I'd worry about tomorrow when it comes."

"Well, I think I'll have a lot bigger hurt if I'm in your bed every night this week."

Another silence fell. Why couldn't he open up and tell her his feelings? Yet she knew that on occasion he had and he might again, and until he did, she would just have to wait and hope.

"So we just act like last night and the past hour never happened?" he said gruffly.

"That's impossible." She hurt and she wanted to slide over into his arms, kiss him and forget tomorrow. But tomorrow would come with all its problems and pain, so she might as well face it.

"I need to know what you feel for me," she said bluntly.

"Hell, Vivian, you should know after last night and the past hour," he said. "I know we don't have a future together. You have your business and your girls and your life. I've always known that, but we've got this time together and it's special. Come here," he said gruffly, sitting up to take her into his arms and kiss her.

She wanted to push away and tell him to listen, but then his kisses stopped her and the realization that he might have just said all he wanted to say also stopped her. Maybe he didn't feel what she did. If he did feel the same in his heart, he would have to come to face it in his own way. He would have to open his heart to her and tell her, express love or commitment or tell her goodbye. Otherwise, there was no choice left for her but to go out of his life.

Julia began to cry and Vivian stepped out of bed and wrapped the sheet around her, her gaze sweeping over him before she left to get the baby. With her door closed in her room, she sat and rocked Julia and thought about the conversation she'd just had with Matt.

She knew Matt had spent a lifetime with his feelings bottled up inside, and his reticence couldn't change overnight. And she shouldn't tell him she was in love with him because if he didn't deeply love her, it would just make him miserable.

She thought about the words she wanted to hear from him. She needed to think beyond them. If he said he wanted her to stay, that he was in love—would she want to give up the future she had envisioned for herself and the girls?

She couldn't imagine going to Houston to live. She couldn't stay on his farm, but she didn't have to go across Texas. She had selected Houston as a nice city to bring up the girls, a place big enough for her business to grow, a good climate. Now she didn't want to get that far away from Matt.

Until Matt wanted a commitment, she would have to pack and go, but she couldn't imagine going out of his life completely. What about one of Oklahoma's cities, which would be so much closer to his farm and where she could still be with him often?

Rocking slowly, she considered the possibilities. Oklahoma seemed better. Houston had begun to loom as far away, a final break with Matt. If she moved to Oklahoma City or Tulsa, she wouldn't be so out of reach. She would be near enough that their proximity could give their relationship a chance to develop and Matt a chance to learn to trust her with his feelings.

She knew the amount of money Baker had offered her had shocked Matt and he hadn't thought of her business being large until then. The differences between them seemed so large to Matt, and had loomed gigantic to her until last week. Could she give up a city life, her demanding business? Life on the farm was different from any way of living she had ever known. Did she really want that? She had to decide because if she didn't, she should pack and go as soon as possible.

She would get over him, she told herself, but the words were hollow. She suspected the love she had for Matt was deep and lasting and was a forever deal.

Maybe he didn't feel that strongly. If he didn't, she was wasting her time thinking about settling somewhere close so she could see him. Was she going to be like some of those women she had met in Atwater and Dakani? They wanted to know all about his house and the relationship Vivian had with him. When he was present, they hung on his every word. Was she just going to be another trophy to him? One of those women he spent time with and promptly forgot, and it was meaningless to him?

Vivian didn't know the answer to her questions. Maybe she was misreading him as much as they had. She remembered Kitty's words when she had slid out of the booth and leaned over to whisper, "Don't let him break your heart, hon. He can do it."

Was it already too late for that bit of advice?

Matt sat alone on the porch, sipping a cold beer, and thinking about Vivian. He heard an owl's lonesome hoot somewhere off in the distance and there was a hollow echo of emptiness in his heart.

I need to know what you feel for me.

Vivian's words rang in his ears. She was like life and breath to him. But how could he say that to her? He couldn't hold her here. He wasn't a marrying man; he had never seen a strong, loving family function together. He couldn't take her out of her world of success and money and big cities and hold her on an isolated farm. From the first he had known that he wouldn't have her here long. He would have to let her go and it amazed him that she had stayed this long.

Last night what they had found together had been extraordinary. He was lucky to have that night and the hours with her tonight. From the moment he started dreaming and fantasizing about making love to her, he had known that he would have to let her go afterward.

Glancing at his watch, he wondered if she would come back to join him or if she would just go on to bed with the girls. Even though it was late, he hoped she would come back out. He looked at the pile of her clothes he had gathered up for her. They had been scattered around his chair where he had dropped them after peeling them off her. Just thinking about that made him want to get up and go to her room and get her out of bed.

When an hour passed and she hadn't returned, he decided she wasn't coming and disappointment filled him. He sat lost in memories of the night before, wanting her.

He thought about Baker's offer and once again wondered what wealth she had left behind and what size business she had. Living on the farm must be so insignificant next to what her life was like. Sometimes around her, he thought she was as unattainable as a star. Yet in some ways, she was part of his heart and she would be forever.

He was beginning to feel that last night and tonight he had been an incredibly lucky man. Last night particularly had been a once-in-a-lifetime night, and it wasn't going to happen again. She was getting ready to go and letting him know every time they talked.

He should tell his brothers—hell, he had tried to tell them that the lady wasn't a permanent fixture in his life. It would be good to see them again, anyway, and they might be looking for an excuse for all of them to get together.

He stood and stretched and moved around restlessly, feeling caged, wanting to charge down the hall and pick her up and stop all her protests with kisses.

He stepped off the porch, knowing he had to get away from the house, jog, do something to get her out of his thoughts for a few minutes.

Monday morning they ate breakfast together and Matt kissed her goodbye before he went to work. Vivian watched him stride to his pickup and drive off, and she decided she better drive to Oklahoma City one day soon and look for a place to live. When she told Matt, was he going to be glad she wasn't going as far as Houston? Or had she really been taken in, thinking his lovemaking meant more to him than it really did?

The man had spent most of his life on his own, making his own decisions, doing what he wanted to do. Why did she think he would even want to change? Because of a night of love? It seemed foolish, and she was beginning to wonder again about just going on to Houston.

This week was her six-week checkup. The time had come to pack and go.

At noon Matt called. "Pete just called me. Lita has a baby girl."

"That's wonderful!"

"Yeah, it is. Mama and baby are doing fine and Pete is like a new dad. I understand how he feels, though. We can go see her and the baby tonight if you want."

"I'd like that."

"I miss you. I gotta run."

Vivian was happy for Lita and then thought about tonight and going out with Matt again. Both girls would be along and the hospital wasn't an evening out on the town, but still, she was going out with him. She thought about what she could wear and hurried to look at her clothes.

That night Vivian dressed in jeans and a blue shirt and braided her hair. As she walked into the den, Matt was sprawled on the floor with Mary Catherine, building blocks. Vivian's pulse jumped when she looked at him. He wore a fresh white shirt that made his skin look darker than ever. His shirt was tucked into his tight jeans and he wore his black boots. He looked sexy, handsome, too appealing.

"I'm ready," she said, knowing her voice had changed and was lower and breathless.

He turned to look up at her and his eyes narrowed. His gaze drifted down over her as he came to his feet.

"You look pretty," he said, touching her collar, unable to resist reaching out to her.

"Thank you."

"I'm glad I took you out last Saturday because now we've lost a sitter."

"I'm glad you did, too, for other reasons," she said in a sultry voice, and saw the change in his expression as desire flared in his eyes.

She waved her hand. "See, you bring that out in me."

"I'll show you later tonight what you bring out in me," he drawled and her pulse skittered. "I'll lock up," he said.

Vivian took Mary Catherine's hand while Matt picked up the carrier. He followed them through the kitchen and reached around Vivian to open the door when the phone rang.

Matt set the carrier on the kitchen table and answered the phone. A deep voice spoke.

"I want to speak to Matt Whitewolf."

"This is he," Matt said.

"This is Baker Ashland. I'm sure you know who I am."

Chapter 15

Surprised that Baker would call him, Matt wanted to slam down the receiver, wanted even more to be able to reach through the receiver, get the guy and punch him.

"Can I make an appointment to meet with you in town tomorrow?"

Shocked to learn that Baker was somewhere in the vicinity, Matt watched Vivian. "Yes, I think so," he answered. Matt wanted to say no, but he knew it would be wiser to hear what Baker wanted.

"There's a restraining order against coming to your place since Vivian is there."

"Okay. Addie's Grill at eight o'clock."

"Fine. I'll be there."

Matt heard the click and was tempted not to tell Vivian anything. Why worry her? Yet on the other hand, he knew she would want to know. He replaced the receiver. "Shall we go?" he asked, catching a curious look from her. He wasn't going to tell her in front of Mary Catherine.

In town, when they entered the hospital room, Pete was holding the new baby and he beamed at them. "Here she is. Another beautiful little girl."

Matt could understand how he felt.

Lita was sitting up in bed, looking serene and pretty. "Her name is Patricia," Lita said. "I won't be at work for the next week, Matt."

"That's fine. With Vivian cooking, the freezer is still stockpiled with casseroles."

The black-haired baby was asleep, but they all got to hold her, including Mary Catherine.

They left, eating supper in town and driving home to arrive after dark. Matt helped Vivian put the girls down for the night and then he took her hand to lead her out to the porch.

They got cold drinks and sat in the dark. "What is it?" she asked. "You've been preoccupied all evening."

Since Baker's phone call he had debated whether to tell her and how to tell her. He took her hand. "You know the phone call I got earlier tonight?"

Vivian heard the solemn tone of his voice as he hitched his chair closer to hers. A chill ran down her spine because he was studying her in an earnest manner and she knew bad news was coming. Only one thing could be bad news that he would wait until now to tell her.

"It was Baker calling you, wasn't it?" she asked. "Why would he do that? What did he want with you? He shouldn't even know you."

"He doesn't know me, but he knows who I am, and if the P.I. has done his work, Baker will have a sheet of facts on me that will include everything pertinent, my credit rating and all."

Agitated, she stood and moved to the porch rail to stare into the night. "Even here, he can reach out and touch me."

Matt went to stand behind her with his hands on her shoulders. "He's contacted me. That's all. I can handle whatever he wants with me."

"It'll be some devious thing. He probably wants to know what you mean to me and how involved we are."

"Forget him. I knew you'd want to know he's here, but just put him out of your mind tonight. He isn't worth worrying over, Vivian, and he's not coming out here." Matt turned her to face him, framing her face with his hands. "I know one way to drive him out of your mind." He leaned down to kiss her.

He could tell when she finally let go of her thoughts of Baker. Matt wanted to drive them out of her mind just as he had the night they had come back from El Reno.

He pulled her down on his lap, but when he began to peel away her clothes, she held his hands and looked at him soberly.

"Matt, I talked to you about this. We're rushing like a charging locomotive into the night. Or I am. I need to think things through because I'll be leaving here soon."

Fighting the urge to overcome her protests, he stared at her and knew he had to do what she asked. He pulled her against his chest and wrapped his arms around her. "All right, Vivian. I'll try to do what you want. I may forget or be overcome with desire, but I'll try. Don't go. At least sit here in my arms."

She did as he asked and it was torment for him, and he suspected it was for her. He had to do what she wanted, but they were throwing away what little time they had left together.

When Julia's cries summoned her, Matt kissed her goodnight and then sat down alone, his thoughts jumping straight to Baker. What did the man want with him?

* * *

The next morning under a clear, blue sky Matt drove into Dakani, arriving at seven. After a stop at the jail to let Sheriff Gonzales know Baker was in town, he drove to the café.

As he sipped hot coffee, he watched a man drive up in front and step out of a black car and he knew it had to be Baker Ashland. Dressed in chinos, a button-down mono-grammed sport shirt, tasseled loafers and wearing a gold watch on his wrist, Baker was tall, blond and probably by women's standards, very handsome.

He strode inside, glanced around and headed toward Matt at once with enough certainty that Matt realized Baker knew what he looked like. Matt stood and waited.

"Matt Whitewolf?"

"You're Baker." Matt didn't offer his hand, nor did Baker. An instant antagonism filled him as he thought about Mary Catherine and how terrified she had been of him at first.

"Shall we sit?" Baker said, sliding into the booth.

Matt sat down, facing him. He motioned to Addie, but she was already on her way with another mug and a pot of coffee.

She set the mug in front of Baker and poured coffee. "What can I get you?"

"Nothing, thanks. The coffee is fine."

His hands were manicured and he wore a wedding ring that had diamonds in the band, a pinky ring with diamonds on the other hand. Matt wanted to tell him to take off the wedding ring. The lady had been divorced from him over a year now. Instead, Matt waited in silence.

Baker moved the mug to one side. "I'll make this short. Vivian's been at your place for over six weeks. That's a long time for a healthy woman who had a normal delivery, so there must be strong feelings between you two. I have to ask. Did you know her in Denver?"

"No, I didn't."

"You were in Denver at a livestock show a year ago."

"I was, but I didn't know Vivian."

Relief was obvious in the man's pale blue eyes.

"I'll get to the point. I want my wife back. I did foolish things and lost her and I'm trying to get her back. At least back to Denver where I can have a chance at reconciliation. I've made her a generous offer if she'll come back and give us a chance, but she refuses. I assume she's refusing because of you. If you didn't know her before six weeks ago, the feelings between the two of you can't be strong, so I'm here to make you an offer if you'll get out of her life."

Anger boiled in Matt, and beneath the table he doubled his fists in his lap. "Forget it," he snapped, starting to slide out of the booth.

"Wait a minute," Baker ordered harshly. "I'll pay off your mortgage, get you out of debt for the combine and cattle. You can use the money. You didn't even know her six weeks ago, so you can't really be in love. Get out of her life and let me have a chance at winning back my wife and children." He said it all fast and Matt paused, furious that Baker knew so much about his business and angry with the attempt to bribe him.

"Baker, she doesn't want to come back. I don't want your damned money. Not a dime."

Matt stood up and Baker came to his feet swiftly. They were only a few feet apart and Matt shook as he fought the impulse to take a swing at Baker. He saw Baker's fists were clenched, too.

"Is she in love with you?" Baker snapped.

"You'll have to ask the lady that question—through your lawyer or detective. You stay the hell off my place and away from her. You know what you can do with your money."

Blinded by anger, Matt strode out of the café. He

climbed into his pickup, slammed the door and backed out of the parking space, turning to head home.

He had to go home and tell Vivian what Baker wanted. It would upset her. Matt clenched his fists on the steering wheel.

Damn, he wanted to flatten the guy! He had to tell Vivian and the sooner he did, the sooner she could begin to adjust to this new intrusion.

He picked up the cellular phone to call the sheriff and report on Baker.

When he arrived home, he drove straight to the house and found Vivian in the yard with the girls. While Mary Catherine played in her new sandbox and Julia sat happily in her baby carrier, Matt put his arm across Vivian's shoulders and strolled away from Mary Catherine's hearing.

"I talked to him."

"And—"

"He offered to pay off my mortgage if I'd get out of your life so you'd go back to him."

"Oh, Matt." She rubbed her head. "You didn't hit him, did you?"

"Wanted to, but I didn't."

"Thank goodness for that. He's the one with the violent temper, but he never vents it at anyone his own size. Was he still wearing his wedding ring?"

"Yes," Matt answered grimly.

"He isn't giving up. I wonder what he'll do now."

"He can't come out here. Vivian, stay until he's gone. How long can he stand to stay in Dakani?"

She gave him a bitter smile and shook her head. "I can't imagine him staying there one night. He won't hang around long. For him to come to Oklahoma, he really wants me back in Denver."

Matt squeezed her shoulder. "You have my pager number, my cell phone number. Want me to leave you a gun?"

"Good heavens, no! Baker isn't dangerous—not in that way."

"If he's the egomaniac you said, he may go to some drastic lengths to get his way."

"It won't do him any good. I'm not going back. I'd never take Mary Catherine back where he could be with her often. Not that he wants her, anyway." She looked up the road and he knew she was thinking about Baker and what he would do next.

"Let me worry about him, okay? I saw Chet Gonzales before I went to the café and called him afterward. He said they would follow Baker as long as he's in this county."

"I know you need to get to work. You've already lost a lot of the morning."

"I do need to," he said. He bent down to kiss her lightly and then looked intently at her. "Okay?"

"I'm fine, just annoyed."

"Yep. See you at supper. If anything should happen, that he tries to contact you, get in touch with me right away and call Gonzales. You have his number."

"I will."

Vivian watched him stride away and ran her fingers over her forehead once again. How complicated life can be! She needed to sort out her feelings for Matt, needed to come to grips with his lack of commitment—she should talk to him about it again, but she didn't want to push him. Never, ever did she want to do that. Did he love her? Was it their different backgrounds that was holding him back? Was the barrier between them his feeling of inadequacy because of his country ways and dysfunctional family as a child? Or was it his habit of always keeping things bottled up in himself?

Whatever it was, she wanted to know. Yet maybe he just didn't love her. She had to face that reality because he had broken women's hearts before.

After seeing him with his brothers, maybe she would understand him better. Could he open himself up with them?

It was Wednesday—Saturday his brothers would be here and then Sunday or Monday she would go. If he wanted to keep her, Matt had to learn to open his heart. If he didn't, she had to go. But where? Was she going to stay in Oklahoma or go on to Texas? Texas would mean goodbye permanently.

She gazed over his farmland and thought about Baker. His offer would enrage Matt, and it was a wonder Matt hadn't slugged Baker. She gritted her teeth. Why couldn't Baker just get out of her life? Yet she knew—had known all along—just to save his own face, Baker would not give up.

Mary Catherine called to her and Vivian went back to sit on the edge of the sandbox to play with her daughter.

Matt spent the next two hours rounding up strays and trying to lose himself in concentrating on cows and calves. It was noon before work slacked off and he was repairing a fence and stopped to think about what had happened that morning.

Baker Ashland was a slimy reptile and Matt knew Vivian would be on edge for the next few days and nights.

He thought about the talk they'd had in the night with her sitting in bed beside him and telling him solemnly how she felt. *Several more nights and I'll be so in love—*

Her statement tore at his heart. It sounded as if she were already in love with him. He didn't want to hurt her. To hurt her would be the last thing he wanted to happen and he couldn't imagine that she was in love with him.

He hadn't heard any "I love you" from her. Not at all. That sentence was the closest she had come, but it hadn't been a declaration of love. There were so many differences between them and she was never meant for him. He had always known he would have to let her go someday. *I don't want to leave here with bigger hurts and worries than I had when I came.* Vivian had said.

Impossible. He was not the man for her and he had never had any illusions about that. He had heard from women all his life—his mother, lovers—that he was incapable of loving. Well, he was able to love, but he wanted someone who knew how to be a good father and a good husband for Vivian. He had been told too many times that he didn't have a heart. Matt knew he was just one of the luckiest men on earth to get the time he'd had with her. He couldn't stand to think about her going, so he shut it out of his mind.

It was ten o'clock that night before she had both girls asleep and came out to join him on the porch. She was restless, nervous and unlike herself, and Matt silently cursed Baker for disturbing her.

When she stood to go to bed, Matt came to his feet.

"Damn, Vivian. Baker might as well be here on the porch with us. He's ruined the evening."

"I'm sorry. I know I'm distracted—"

"There's a way to cure that," he said, moving closer. "I know you don't want us to keep on loving, but lady, our time together is vanishing and we're throwing it away. It's too important to do that."

"How important, Matt? That's part of what I'm trying to figure out."

"I'll show you how important," he said, taking her in his arms to kiss her. Her hands pushed lightly against his chest, but he stroked her back and kissed her as if this was the last kiss he would ever have. "It's damned important, Vivian," he whispered against her ear, flicking his tongue in her ear while he slid his hands beneath her T-shirt to unfasten her bra and cup her breasts in his hands.

"Matt," she said. When his name came out with a rush of breath and there was no protest, his pulse soared.

He tightened his arm around her, kissing her, pushing up the T-shirt to kiss her breast and then peeling away her shirt while he unfastened her cutoffs.

She trembled in his arms. "Oh, Matt, you say this is important and then you say you know I'll be going as if it doesn't matter to you."

"It matters," he said gruffly, looking down at her. "Damn, it matters, but I know I can't hold you here."

"What makes you think you can't?"

"Don't tease me, Vivian," he said gruffly, and kissed her before she could answer him. He unfastened her jeans and pushed them away.

She grabbed his wrist. "Let's go inside. I feel exposed out here since you said someone could sit out there with binoculars—"

Matt picked her up and carried her inside to his bedroom swiftly, kicking the door shut. A small lamp burned by the bed, shedding a dusky glow in the middle of the room.

"Matt, this is just what—"

He stood her on her feet and kissed her and stopped her words. Then his hands destroyed all protests until they were wildly loving in his bed.

Moving with him, she clung to him and almost cried out her feelings. Wanting to tell him she loved him, Vivian felt hot tears spring to her eyes. If he wasn't in love, he wasn't going to want to hear declarations from her, but she was in love. Deeply.

She tightened her arms around his back and held him, feeling him shudder with his release as hers came and rapture swept away everything else.

Later, she lay in his arms while he stroked her and played with her hair.

"It's Wednesday, Vivian. I have you here until when—next Wednesday?" His fingers trailed lazily down her arm.

She laughed, yet her pulse leaped because here was the chance she wanted to discuss her leaving with him. "You keep moving the day that I go farther and farther away."

Her pulse drummed—was she making a mistake, misjudging the depth of his feelings? Was she going to be rebuffed by him in the next few minutes?

Vivian couldn't stop remembering the warnings from women that Matt was a heartbreaker. She looked into his dark eyes as he gazed solemnly back at her and she took a deep breath, knowing in the next few minutes she would have some kind of answer from him.

Chapter 16

"Matt, I've been thinking about it. All I need is a big city. It doesn't have to be Houston."

His hand stilled and he turned on his side, propping up his head to stare at her. "Where can it be?"

"I've been thinking about Oklahoma City."

Matt's heart thudded. *She might not go to Texas!* Joy leaped in him, but instantly, he held it in check. "Oklahoma City isn't as big as Houston."

"No, but it's big enough. I think I can start my business there."

Matt pulled her into his embrace, burying his face in her hair to keep her from seeing his raw emotions. *She would stay longer!* The idea glowed in his mind like a splendid gift. She would be here beyond next week, beyond next month—close enough he could drive to the city and see her and she could come back to the farm. He would see Mary Catherine and Julia!

Beyond the prospect of seeing them, his mind couldn't

function. He knew better than to expect too much because he knew in his soul that he was not the man for her.

"I want you to stay in Oklahoma," he said against her neck.

"That's what I needed to know," she stated solemnly. He raised his head to kiss her and the discussion was over for the night.

That Saturday, Matt's brothers arrived. First Jared, Faith and Merry and then Wyatt, his wife, Alexa, and his little girls, Kelsey, Rachel and Robin.

Vivian thought his brothers were handsome; both Wyatt and Jared were more relaxed and easygoing than Matt. She watched them stand in the yard at the grill and watched their little girls, who were happily playing in the sandbox with Mary Catherine, while the wives put lunch on the table.

"So you're moving to Houston?" Faith asked. Pregnant, she seemed wildly in love with her husband. They both were barely able to stop touching each other when they were together.

"I think I'll move to Oklahoma City," Vivian said, looking out the window at Matt. "I need a large city for my business, but I think that will do." She glanced at Faith, who was staring at her with curiosity in her large green eyes. "There's nothing serious between your brother-in-law and me," she said, thinking the words sounded false to her ears because she was very serious.

"I hope there is and so do his brothers," Faith replied quietly. "Jared worries about Matt living such a lonely, isolated life."

"Wyatt worries about him, too," Alexa said, looking as intently at Vivian as Faith had. "He's pretty set in his ways."

Vivian had to laugh. "I suppose Matt is. And totally opposed to marriage."

Someone yelled outside and Faith hurried through the back door, and then the moment for quiet talk was gone.

The brothers and their families stayed until dusk, then all piled in their cars. Jared hugged Vivian as if he had known her for years.

"Rope that cowboy, darlin', and haul him down the aisle with you."

She had to laugh. "I don't believe we're ready for that, either one of us."

"Shucks. I was hoping my old bachelor brother would finally get a family. And you have a sweet one."

"Thank you. It was nice to meet you, Jared."

"Nice to meet you. Hope we see you again."

Wyatt was the last one to say goodbye and he gazed at her solemnly. "It was nice to meet you. Matt told me about your ex and that you may move to Oklahoma City. I'm a detective there, so just come in and see us when you get there and I'll help you if he tries to bother you."

"Thanks, Wyatt."

"'Night," he said, turning to his brother.

Matt draped his arm across Vivian's shoulder and held Mary Catherine against his chest with his other arm while they watched everyone drive away.

"What a nice family you have."

"Yeah, they are. I'm getting to know them better now than when I was a kid. I was older than they were and the years made a difference then."

They headed toward the house. "Mary Cat, I'll read you a story if you'll get your pajamas on," Matt said.

"Yeah!" she cried. When he set her down, she ran ahead to dash inside the house.

"See, it's all in knowing how to talk 'em into getting ready for bed."

"Sure. You're the expert on talking someone into bed," she drawled.

He looked at her, his dark eyes changing as his arm tightened around her shoulders. "We'll see how well I do tonight."

She shook her head. "Matt, I want to wait. We've rushed into this, and I won't live far away and these are not going to be the last nights we spend together. I need to know where we stand with you. I'm old-fashioned and I need commitment," she said, her breath catching while emotions tore at her. She wanted to know what he felt. Vivian knew she was deeply in love with him. Mary Catherine already loved him. Vivian hated to press him, but she needed more from him.

With one of those fierce looks, he studied her. Was he struggling for words—or was she misjudging how deep his feelings ran? Silence stretched between them while his chest heaved, and she knew he was fighting his own inner battles.

"We have to sort things out, Matt," she said quietly, and turned to go, her heart hammering because they seemed to be at loggerheads. Everything in her cried out to walk into his arms and forget trying to get the right words from him. Yet she had to think of the future and her girls, too.

Friday Lita brought a friend, Janie Grayson, to help with the housework, so Vivian drove to Oklahoma City to look at apartments, leaving the girls at the farm with Lita and Janie.

The next days passed quickly and by Friday, as Matt drove across his field in his pickup, he could barely think about what he was doing because his mind was on Vivian. He had talked several times with Sheriff Gonzales, and from what they could learn, Baker had flown back to Denver the night he had been in Dakani and no one had seen him or the P.I. since. Matt couldn't dwell on Baker. It was Vivian who took up all of his thoughts.

She was drawing away from him. He saw the boxes that now were packed and closed, the suitcases she had packed. Several times this week she had driven to Oklahoma City to look for an apartment, and then when she returned at suppertime, she was busy all evening with the girls. As soon as she put them to bed, she tried to catch up on her work.

He knew he was losing her and he had always known this time was inevitable. He'd had more nights with her in his bed than he had ever dreamed he would, magical nights that he would always hold in his heart as the closest he would ever come to love. He had the hours with Julia and Mary Catherine that would be the closest he ever expected to come to a family of his own. Any time it hurt to think about them leaving, he pulled memories around him like a cloak against the cold winds of loss.

He had to let her go on with her life. It just hurt unbearably to watch her get ready to do so. He was as bad as Pete, getting tears in his eyes when he kissed Mary Cat good-night, tears he tried to hide from both Mary Cat and Vivian, but he couldn't stop them.

He loved all three females. He was deeply in love with Vivian, but it had never occurred to him how much he would come to love Julia and Mary Catherine.

Wednesday of the next week, when Matt sat down to supper, Vivian gazed at him solemnly. "I found an apartment for us today."

The words were like a knife plunging into his heart, yet he merely nodded. "I suppose that's good, although you know there's no rush."

Something flashed in her blue eyes, but he didn't know what. She bent over her supper and was quiet.

"When will you move?"

"That's the thing—it's vacant and I can get possession right away, so I think I can be packed and we can move Saturday."

The reality of their going made Matt feel all hollow inside. It hurt badly and he knew it was a pain that wasn't going away.

Friday afternoon Vivian unplugged her computer. Mary Catherine was in the yard with Lita, Julia and Patricia, the two babies in the shade in their carriers. By tonight when Matt got home, she would have everything packed and he was going to finish loading his pickup.

She paused, thinking about moving to Oklahoma City. The reality that he was going to let her go tore at her. He was just going to let her drive out of his life tomorrow. She hoped it wasn't forever, but once she was gone—she didn't know what he would do.

Vivian's thoughts were interrupted when a child's cry pierced the air and chilled her because she recognized Mary Catherine's voice.

She looked out the window and her heart skipped a beat. With sunlight glinting on his blond hair, Baker was in the backyard.

Chapter 17

Terror gripped Vivian when she saw Baker with his fingers locked around Mary Catherine's arm. He was pulling her along through the gate toward his car and Vivian's fear changed to fury. Lita was screaming repeatedly and Mary Catherine's cries became louder.

Vivian raced through the house. With icy fingers she grabbed the back door and burst outside, running past Lita and the babies.

"Call 911! Call Matt!" she ordered Lita. Vivian sprinted toward Baker and screamed, "Let her go, Baker!"

He looked up, and Mary Catherine jerked free, dashing away from him to Vivian as Vivian burst through the gate. Mary Catherine threw her arms around her mother's legs while she sobbed.

Vivian picked her up to hug her, trying to calm the hysterical child. "Shh, baby, it's all right. Go in the house," she said quietly, setting her down. "I'll be there in a minute, and Lita will be with you."

"Mommy!"

"Go on, sweetie. I'll be there in a minute."

Mary Catherine ran, and Vivian walked toward Baker, who stood facing her. "You know you're not supposed to be here," she said, shaking with fury.

"I know I desperately need to talk to you. Vivian, give me a chance. Listen to me. Are you going to just throw everything away? The girls' futures, your career, security— everything I can give all of you. You're tossing your future and theirs aside for some hick farmer."

"You're not supposed to come near me. You're breaking the law. What were you doing to Mary Catherine? Not anything that would make me want to come back to you."

He flinched, and she realized that accusation had hit its mark. Rage made her tremble violently. "What were you doing, Baker, pulling her along like that?"

"I was going to take her to Denver and then you'd have to come hear me out. If you'd come back, you'd see what you're throwing away."

"You were taking Mary Catherine?" she said, aghast and wondering if his mind had snapped in his blind drive to satisfy his ego. "That's kidnapping."

"I didn't kidnap her. I didn't even get out of the yard with her."

"Get out of here," she ordered through clenched teeth.

"Just listen to me for a minute. If you come back to Denver, I won't bother you. Just return and work with me. You've humiliated me, Vivian, in front of my colleagues."

"Baker, look what you did to me and to Mary Catherine! All I did was walk out and get a divorce."

"Come home."

"Home! I have no home there. I won't ever go back. Can't you understand that? Learn to accept no, Baker. No. No. Never. I'm never coming back," she pronounced slowly and emphatically. "And you're breaking the law," she added in disgust.

"Are you in love with Whitewolf? What can he possibly give you? Nothing! You won't be happy here. The little farm wife! I know what you like, and it's not life down on the farm with the farmer in the dell. He's a hick, Vivian. Uneducated, a clod—"

"Stop it!" she ordered, shaking with rage. "Get out of here. I'm never coming back, Baker. How you thought I would—"

He stepped forward and grabbed her arm as she raised it to protect herself. She saw a movement out of the corner of her eye.

Matt was there, and Baker was on the ground so swiftly, she barely knew what happened.

"Go on, Vivian," Matt ordered. "Get out of here."

Furious with Baker and worried what the two men would do to each other, Vivian turned to go to the house to make certain the sheriff was coming.

Baker got up, his fists clenched. "You hayseed. She's my wife and my family and I want her back."

"You bastard. You don't love her," Matt said. "How much do you know about what she likes and what she wants? How much do you think about her instead of about yourself?" His voice was tight, quiet and deadly, every word clipped and precise. "What have you done to help her or make her happy or win her love? What of yourself have you given her? When a man loves a woman, this is not how he treats her!"

Stunned, Vivian halted, immobilized by Matt's words and the emotion in his voice. She stared at Matt as the words poured out of him. He was shaking, trying to control his temper, but when she heard him tell Baker what a man does when he loves a woman, she was riveted.

"You think of her first, Baker. You give it all up, whatever you want, if it makes her happy. You don't take from her—you give to her.''

Warmth flooded Vivian and, momentarily, all the anguish of the past few minutes was gone. Matt's words rang in her ears and drummed in her heart. He was pouring out his love whether he realized it or not. And he was telling Baker exactly what he—Matt—had done for her. She realized that he was letting her go out of some misguided sense that he would be holding her back if he asked her to stay.

''You give to her because she is your world and you're nothing without her.''

''I've offered her a quarter of a million. What can you offer her, you hick!'' Baker snapped. ''You think a clod like you can hold Vivian?''

In the distance, a siren blared while Baker swung his fist. Matt dodged and got in another punch that flattened Baker again.

''You don't hurt the woman you love. You do everything in your power to keep from hurting her!'' Matt snapped, standing over Baker. ''Get up, you coward. What kind of man frightens a small child?''

''Here come the police,'' Vivian said quietly, thankful the authorities would stop the fight.

Baker heard the sirens and he stood, backing away from Matt and looking at Vivian. ''You witch!''

Matt hit him again, sending him reeling. He came lunging back and his fist shot out, striking Matt's jaw. Matt staggered back, gained his footing and started after Baker again, but Vivian grabbed his arm.

The sheriff's car roared up the road, dust spinning up behind it. It braked, rocking as the sheriff and a deputy spilled out. Chet Gonzales had his gun drawn, and Baker threw up his hands.

Chet held the gun on him while the deputy cuffed him

and led him to the police car. Chet came over to Matt. "Looks like he got in a punch."

Vivian looked up to see Matt had blood running from his mouth. He was breathing hard and she saw he was as furious as she. "You must have broken every speed record known," he said to the sheriff.

"Nope. My deputy spotted Baker and radioed and I joined him. Then we got the 911 call from Lita, which was sent through to us, but we were already on our way."

"He was going to take Mary Catherine," Vivian said.

"Take her with him? Kidnap her? Is she all right?" Matt asked sharply.

"Yes. Except she was frightened badly. She's in the house with Lita."

As Baker was led to the police car, he looked back once at Vivian. She turned her back to him.

Matt pulled out a bandanna and dabbed at the blood on his face.

"We'll take him in and book him and see how high we can get the judge to set bail. Maybe his lawyer won't find Dakani tonight," Chet said.

"Thanks for getting here."

"He goes to jail. If he gets out—and he'll probably have the money and influence to get out before he should—just call me if he bothers you again," Chet said, looking at Vivian.

"Thank you. I'll go see about Mary Catherine."

A pickup came speeding up from across Matt's land and stopped and Pete jumped out. He ran up to them. "Lita called me."

"She's inside. They've arrested Baker, Pete."

"Hi, Chet," Pete said, offering his hand. As he shook he looked beyond Chet at the police car. "I hope you throw away the key," he said, and turned to rush to the house.

"I'll call you, Matt, and let you know what happens."

"Thanks. Thanks again for getting here so promptly."

"Thank you," Vivian repeated, and turned to hurry to the house to see about Mary Catherine.

She was barely aware of Matt striding along beside her. She rushed inside to hear both babies wailing. Lita was trying to pat both of them and Mary Catherine was quietly sitting at the table with red eyes and tears streaming down her face. The instant the little girl saw her mother, she climbed down and dashed to her.

Vivian picked her up and held her tightly. Matt went to get Julia, and the moment he did, Lita picked up Patricia.

Matt left the kitchen, taking Julia to the den to walk her up and down and talk quietly to her, figuring one less crying baby in the room would help soothe the others as well as Julia.

In seconds Julia quieted and settled against his shoulder, clinging to him. He patted her and tried to stop thinking about Vivian and Mary Catherine. Both of them were white as snow and shaken. He knew Vivian was furious and Mary Catherine was terrified.

His jaw and his knuckles were sore, but that was nothing. What hurt were Baker's words—*hayseed, hick, uneducated, a clod.* As he'd run from his pickup, he'd heard all of Baker's accusations, his declarations that Vivian couldn't ever be happy on a farm. Matt knew it was the truth, but it hurt. He was all country and he wasn't educated like Baker probably was. Maybe he was a clod by some people's standards, but he didn't frighten little children. Yet he knew Baker was right—he was not the man for Vivian.

He looked at the baby in his arms and his anger and hurt diminished. Her big eyes watched him, and he was glad she didn't have any notion what had happened this afternoon. Hopefully, she would never know.

The kitchen had grown quiet, and he decided to go see what was happening. Vivian and Mary Catherine were nowhere to be seen and Pete's truck was driving away. Lita and Patricia were gone, so Matt assumed they had left with Pete.

He carried Julia to the bedroom looking in the open door.

"Come in," Vivian said. She sat in the rocker with Mary Catherine in her lap. Mary Catherine held her teddy bear and her blanket and had her thumb in her mouth, and she reminded him of exactly how she had looked and acted that first afternoon.

"I thought I'd put Julia down. She's one second away from sleep." He placed her in her tiny bed and he turned to go to Vivian and Mary Catherine. Leaning down, he brushed a kiss on Mary Catherine's forehead. She reached up to slip her arm around his neck and give him a hug.

Looking into Vivian's wide, blue eyes, he hugged them both. "I'll be in the kitchen," he said quietly to Vivian.

After Mary Catherine fell asleep, Vivian showered, trying to wash away dust, memories, shock. Everything but one memory. Matt's words to Baker on when a man loves a woman. How the words had tumbled out of him! Words that said so much more than just lecturing Baker.

What have you done to help her or make her happy or win her love? When a man loves a woman, this is not how he treats her!

Matt loved her. He could never have said those words if he didn't! In spite of the terror and anger she had felt all afternoon since hearing Mary Catherine's first cry, jubilation danced in her. She laughed under the shower, joy spilling over. Matt Whitewolf was in love with her. If he wasn't, he couldn't have made that speech.

His fury had made him open his heart and let his feelings pour out. If that had happened once, it would happen again. Now that he had faced up to his feelings and put them into words, how long would it take before he came to her with them?

"Matt loves me!" she said aloud, knowing the words would be washed away by the noise of the shower. "He loves me."

All the ugliness of the afternoon dimmed and faded while the one good thing glowed brightly as she clung to it, examining it over and over like a precious gemstone that was a new gift.

Now she knew she had made the right choice in moving to Oklahoma City, close enough they would date. Matt would open up his heart again. He had today; it shouldn't be so difficult the next time.

Couldn't he see, if he made declarations like that, that he was in love? Why did he fight it so?

Was it old feelings of inadequacy? Or his fear that she needed a city life? *You think of her first, Baker. You give it all up, whatever you want, if it makes her happy.*

Was that what he was doing? Holding back from declaring his love to do what he thought would make her happy?

She turned off the water and toweled off and a dark cloud came. She remembered Baker's harsh words—*clod, hick, hayseed.* Baker had said some of those cruel words to Matt's face, but had he heard the other names Baker had called him? She paused, trying to remember how soon Matt had appeared.

It didn't matter. Baker had flung enough names at him to hurt him. Only Matt wasn't a clod or a hick or a hayseed. He was generous and brave and intelligent—far more a man than Baker, who was cruel and selfish. She prayed Matt didn't give credence to anything Baker said.

That night they were quiet through supper. Afterward, Mary Catherine rode Molasses and then wanted Matt to read a bedtime story.

After the story he carried Mary Catherine to bed and tucked her in. "Good night, sweet dreams, sweet baby," he said softly, leaning down to kiss her cheek. She hugged his neck.

"I love you," she said quietly, and hot tears stung his eyes.

He straightened up, running his hand swiftly across his eyes, and turned to find Vivian watching him. She looked away and stood by the door as if waiting for him to go.

He crossed the room and at the door she looked up at him. "I told her I would lie down with her tonight when she goes to sleep." Her voice dropped to a whisper. "She's frightened."

He nodded, disappointed that Vivian wouldn't be out to sit on the porch because tomorrow she would be gone. Yet he understood and prayed that Mary Catherine didn't have bad dreams.

Saturday was moving day. Mary Catherine spent the morning crying because she didn't want to go, and Vivian was having a difficult time with her own emotions. Julia was fussy, and at first Vivian thought it was all the turmoil going on around her, but when she realized the baby had a fever, all thought of moving that day was canceled.

Matt was worried as they watched Julia's fever climb and he talked to Walt Bently several times.

At ten o'clock, Vivian found Matt in the kitchen. She carried Julia in her arms. "Matt, Walt Bently said to bring her in if her temperature went higher, and it has. I think I better take her to town."

Chapter 18

He stood and picked up his car keys, jamming them into his pocket. "I'll carry Mary Catherine."

"Don't wake her. I'll drive Julia to the hospital. Walt Bently said he would meet us there."

"I don't want you to drive by yourself."

"I can do that," she said, giving him a look. "I don't want to wake Mary Catherine. And she doesn't need to spend the night in the hospital waiting room."

"I'll get one of the men to drive you," Matt said, striding to the phone to call and ask for Royce Gunther.

Knowing it was useless to argue, Vivian went to get her purse.

It was almost two hours later when Matt heard from Vivian. "Matt, Julia has strep throat and they think we should stay here tonight so they can watch her. I sent Royce back. He said he would come get us tomorrow if they let us leave. You'll have to take care of Mary Catherine."

"Fine, Vivian. Do you want us to come to the hospital tonight?"

"No. Julia is sleeping now. I'll call you in the morning, and if Mary Catherine wants to talk to me, we're in room three twenty-nine."

He scribbled the room number. "Take care. I miss you," he said, and heard her break the connection. He didn't want to go to bed, afraid Mary Catherine would wake and call for her mommy and be frightened, so he got his magazine and went to their room. Turning on a small lamp, he sat with his feet propped on the bed, the magazine forgotten in his lap while he studied Mary Catherine.

For the first time, the enormity of Vivian's trust hit him. She had left Mary Catherine in his care. He was overwhelmed, his emotions undergoing an upheaval. He was always country around Vivian—too simple for her style of life. Had he sold himself short?

He thought how she had fit into living on the farm. One week had stretched into another, and never once had she seemed bored or restless or eager to go. Far from it.

He moved restlessly, standing and going down the hall. Vivian had changed from moving to Houston to Oklahoma City to be nearer to him; she had trusted Mary Catherine to him. Vivian and her girls had become *family* to him.

He walked outside and stood in the quiet yard, looking up at the night sky. Millions of stars twinkled against the blackness. Clear and beautiful, a silvery moon bathed the land in its rays. Peaceful and beautiful, sometimes the land got into a person and became part of them. Vivian and her girls had fit in here as if they had grown up on a farm.

His pulse jumped. Vivian was an independent, intelligent woman. Let her make the choice. He had been making it for her, assuming she wouldn't want this life. But if she loved him just half as much as he loved her—

Excitement gripped him. It was time he took the risk and told Vivian he loved her.

"Vivian, come home." He prayed Julia's fever would

come down and they would come home soon. He wanted them home, wanted Vivian in his arms. He wanted to tell her that he loved her, and ask her to marry him.

Sunday he fed and dressed Mary Catherine while Royce picked up Vivian and Julia. Julia was on antibiotics, and Vivian wanted to keep her away from Mary Catherine as much as possible until she was better.

Matt met them in the yard, and as soon as Mary Catherine had hugged and talked to her mommy, he took her with him in his pickup, promising Vivian he would keep her with him during the day so she wouldn't be exposed to germs.

He did the same Monday, and by Tuesday, Mary Catherine was trailing after him like a shadow. By that time, Julia was improving, but still not well.

It was a week later when the household returned to normal and Vivian seemed rested. Saturday night, falling into their old habits, she sat on the porch with Matt. She wore jeans and a T-shirt, the same as Matt. A cool breeze played over the porch and she turned to him.

"Matt, for one reason or another, I've been here all summer. Every time I get ready to go, something happens. Julia's birth, my car, my six-week checkup, your brothers coming, the hunt for an apartment, Julia's illness. Labor Day is coming up, and here I am."

He stood and leaned down to pick her up, moving her to his lap. "I'm glad," he said in a husky voice, and Vivian's pulse jumped. She was tingly, too aware of him, wanting him badly. She sat facing him, running her fingers along his jaw.

"I've wanted to talk to you, but because of Julia being sick, I had to wait."

"What is it?" she asked, looking at his solemn expression. Matt stroked her nape and she relished the streaks of fire his touch elicited.

"When you left Mary Catherine with me, I realized how much you trusted me," Matt said.

"Of course I trusted you," she said, and desire flashed hotly in her. She leaned forward to kiss him and he returned her kiss for a moment, then he pushed her back and framed her face with his hands. "I love you, Vivian. Will you marry me?"

The words dazzled her and there was a second when she couldn't get her breath, and then she flung her arms around his neck. "Yes! Oh my, yes! I thought you'd never ask, Matt Whitewolf!"

He wrapped his arms tightly around her and kissed her hard, his heart pounding with joy and excitement. He raised his head and held her face in his large hands while his dark eyes probed and searched. "Are you sure? Life on a farm? Here with me?"

"I am absolutely sure," she said.

"Aah, Vivian. I'll do everything I can to make you happy," he said, feeling as if he would burst with joy. "My girls, you, Mary Cat and Julia. I can't believe my blessings."

"You better believe it, cowboy. We came to stay."

He leaned down to kiss her and words were lost.

Vivian clung to him, her heart pounding with joy. Her cowboy—her home, her heart. This time it would be right.

Epilogue

The last Saturday in September, Vivian and Matt exchanged vows and then returned to the farm for a reception. Matt's grandparents, his brothers and their families, the men who worked for him, plus friends in two counties were present. Lita and Pete, home from their honeymoon, were staying in the house and keeping the girls while Matt and Vivian left on a week-long honeymoon.

In a tailored blue dress, Vivian milled around the house and porch, talking to guests, barely knowing what she was saying because of her excitement. Matt looked incredibly handsome in a dark tux and new black boots. He had his hair fastened with a strip of rawhide behind his head while hers was looped and pinned on top of her head.

Mary Catherine was dressed in a frilly pink dress and she looked happy with her new cousins.

Jared came over to give Vivian a kiss on the cheek. "Well, you did it, Vivian. Come here, Matt," he said, calling to his brother. "Here's a toast," he said, raising his glass and his voice, his words carrying over the noise of the crowd. "I propose a toast to the beautiful woman who finally lassoed brother Matt, hog-tied him and got him to the altar."

The women laughed and glasses clinked while the men whistled and cheered. As Vivian looked into Matt's dark gaze, her pulse jumped and she wanted to be alone with him.

She sipped the bubbly champagne and smiled at Wyatt, who had moved beside her and Matt.

"Matt, what's the latest news about Baker?" Wyatt asked. "The guy has the money to hire the best lawyers and he has no prior record, so he could walk on those charges," he said, looking back and forth between Vivian and Matt.

Relieved to finally be free of Baker, Vivian met Matt's gaze while she answered Wyatt. "Baker wanted me back to save face. The charges against him have been made public and his reputation is shredded. He couldn't convince anyone now that I would come back to him. He's out of our lives forever," she said, unable to tear her gaze from Matt's.

"Good news," Wyatt said. "And I think I'll leave you two alone."

"Sure," Matt said without taking his gaze from Vivian. "Let's say our goodbyes."

"I've told everyone goodbye except Mary Catherine and Julia. Let's find them."

She hugged them in Matt's former bedroom, which was now a playroom. Toys were scattered on the floor and Lita sat in a chair watching all the children.

"Come tell me goodbye," Vivian said, hugging Mary Catherine. "I'll call you tonight. I love you."

"I love you," Mary Catherine said, kissing her.

Matt picked Mary Catherine up to kiss her and she hugged him, kissing his cheek and telling him the same.

They kissed Julia goodbye, said their goodbyes to everyone else and dashed through a barrage of balloons that were set free as they ran to his pickup.

Matt raced away from the farm and reached over to hug Vivian.

"Watch it. I've already smashed into one of your trees and I don't want to do it again."

He slowed, stopping and turning to pull her to him. "Vivian, I'm the luckiest guy on earth," he whispered. "You've rescued me from my solitary life."

"Maybe we rescued each other." Her heart pounded and she clung to him, knowing she couldn't have a more wonderful husband or a better father for her girls. "My Galahad in blue jeans..."

* * * * *

Silhouette Stars

Born this Month

Jerry Hall, Tom Cruise, Tom Stoppard,
Nancy Reagan, Ringo Starr, Barbara Cartland,
Harrison Ford, Linda Ronstadt.

Star of the Month

Cancer

An excellent year ahead in which progress can
be made in all areas of your life. There may be a
period of change in the autumn but don't be
fearful as the outcome will be better than you
could hope and you will see the necessity for
change. A lucky break in the second half of the
year could have you splashing out.

SILH/HR/0007a

Leo

You could find yourself pushing too hard to achieve what you want especially in your personal life. So try a little tact and diplomacy and the results could be better than you dreamed.

Virgo

Travel and romance are both well aspected and if linked you could look forward to an extra special month. Late in the month a friend needs a helping hand but be sure of their motives before offering too much.

 Libra

Energy levels are high and there is little you can't achieve. Holidays are well aspected especially those in groups. Career moves at the end of the month get you excited about the future.

Scorpio

Your ability to communicate constructively may help to bring about an improvement in your financial situation. This, in turn, will help you to build towards the future with renewed vigour.

 Sagittarius

Romance is in the air and you will feel in demand both with partners and friends, making this a social, easy going month with very little to trouble you, so enjoy!

Capricorn

A social month in which you may have to make unexpected journeys. Work opportunities will bring an added financial boost and you will realise your talents are being fully appreciated.

Aquarius

Your love life receives a boost and should become more meaningful than of late. As the month ends you may find your energy levels are getting low so take a break and pamper yourself back to full strength.

Pisces

You have a decisive quality to you this month giving you the courage to make the changes you have long desired to make. Be bold and you'll be amazed by what you can achieve.

 Aries

The lack of financial resource has become an area of conflict in your personal life. You need to sit down together and make an effective budget plan. By working in harmony your relationship will improve dramatically.

Taurus

As your confidence returns you will feel more positive and able to tackle life with enthusiasm. A lucky break mid-month gives you cause for a celebration.

  Gemini

Travel is never far from your thoughts especially the more adventurous kind and this month should see you planning another experience. A friend may want to join you but be sure they are as bold as you before you commit.

Look out for more
Silhouette Stars next month

2 FREE

books and a surprise gift!

We would like to take this opportunity to thank you for reading this Silhouette® book by offering you the chance to take TWO more specially selected titles from the Sensation™ series absolutely FREE! We're also making this offer to introduce you to the benefits of the Reader Service™—

★ FREE home delivery
★ FREE gifts and competitions
★ FREE monthly Newsletter
★ Exclusive Reader Service discounts
★ Books available before they're in the shops

Accepting these FREE books and gift places you under no obligation to buy, you may cancel at any time, even after receiving your free shipment. Simply complete your details below and return the entire page to the address below. *You don't even need a stamp!*

YES! Please send me 2 free Sensation books and a surprise gift. I understand that unless you hear from me, I will receive 4 superb new titles every month for just £2.70 each, postage and packing free. I am under no obligation to purchase any books and may cancel my subscription at any time. The free books and gift will be mine to keep in any case.

S0ZEA

Ms/Mrs/Miss/Mr ....Initials.................................
BLOCK CAPITALS PLEASE

Surname ....

Address ....

....

....Postcode...............................

Send this whole page to:
UK: FREEPOST CN81, Croydon, CR9 3WZ
EIRE: PO Box 4546, Kilcock, County Kildare (stamp required)

Offer valid in UK and Eire only and not available to current Reader Service subscribers to this series. We reserve the right to refuse an application and applicants must be aged 18 years or over. Only one application per household. Terms and prices subject to change without notice. Offer expires 31st January 2001. As a result of this application, you may receive further offers from Harlequin Mills & Boon and other carefully selected companies. If you would prefer not to share in this opportunity please write to The Data Manager at the address above.

Silhouette® is a registered trademark used under license.
Sensation™ is being used as a trademark.